Dear Reader,

Arabesque is proud to publish the **At Your Service** series, a fictional account of four courageous and committed heroes serving in the Air Force, Army, Navy, and Marines. We know that you will come to admire and fall in love with these proud African-American military officers: Major Zurich Kingdom in ***Top-Secret Rendezvous***, Colonel Neal Allen in ***Courage Under Fire***, Captain Haughton Storm in ***The Glory of Love***, and Colonel Nelson Wainwright in ***Flying High.***

The **At Your Service** romance series is the story of their lives and the women they love . . . filled with patriotism, camaraderie, romance, passion, and intrigue! Each novel will draw you in and not let you go, as you come to appreciate the honor of each hero, as well as the commitment of the people they care about. The series is a fictional account meant to capture the essence of those serving our country, and as such we have taken creative license with the cover photography and the stories we know you will enjoy.

BET Books began planning this unique series honoring African Americans serving in the military in the Spring of 2002, not knowing that events would unfold in the war with Iraq in "Operation Enduring Freedom."

Now, more than ever, we hope that you enjoy this series yourself, or buy the books as gifts for someone special. We welcome your comments and feedback, and invite you to send us an e-mail to **BET Books@BET.com.**

Best regards,

Linda Gill
Vice President and Publisher

OTHER TITLES BY CANDICE POARCH

Lighthouse Magic

Bargain of the Heart

*The Last Dance**

*Shattered Illusions***

Tender Escape

*Intimate Secrets**

The Essence of Love

*With This Kiss**

*White Lightning**

Published by BET/Arabesque books

*indicates book is part of the Nottoway Series

**indicates book is part of the Coree Island Series

COURAGE UNDER FIRE

Neal caught her hands, leaned toward her and, with a gentle tug, pulled her toward him until their lips touched.

He expected her to jerk away from him. When she didn't, he swiped his tongue over her lips. Her sweet essence mingled with a touch of perfume and the sweetness of the kiss was almost painful.

She opened her mouth to him and for the first time in his life, he kissed the lips that had tempted him as a horny fourteen-year-old, standing on the cusp of tomorrow without a clue on how to deal with the girl who snubbed him. Even now she enticed the full-grown man. The distance between them seemed as palpable as it had years before.

With a pressing need to touch her, he captured her warm face in his hands, tasted her, felt her soft skin, knowing this was all they would ever share. A knot rose in his throat. The realization was heart-rending.

Slowly, he slid his hands down her arms. Holding both her hands in his, he carried them to his mouth and gently kissed her knuckles.

They had come so close once again, only to have the future snatched away. When she opened one hand to caress his cheek, his gaze jerked to hers. All that he felt was reflected in her pretty brown eyes.

COURAGE UNDER FIRE

Candice Poarch

ARABESQUE
BET BOOKS™

BET Publications, LLC
http://www.bet.com
http://www.arabesquebooks.com

Courage Under Fire is a work of fiction, and is not intended to provide an exact representation of military life, or any known persons. The author has taken creative license in development of the characters and plot of the story, although military bases and conflicts referenced may be actual. The cover photography is meant to evoke each branch of service, and may not be an exact representation of military uniform. BET Books/Arabesque develops contemporary works of romance fiction for entertainment purposes only.

ARABESQUE BOOKS are published by

BET Publications, LLC
c/o BET BOOKS
One BET Plaza
1900 W Place NE
Washington, D.C. 20018-1211

All Kensington Titles, Imprints, and Distributed Lines are available at special quantity discounts for bulk purchases for sales promotions, premiums, fund-raising, and educational or institutional use. Special book excerpts or customized printings can also be created to fit specific needs. For details, write or phone the office of the Kensington special sales manager: Kensington Publishing Corp., 850 Third Avenue, New York, NY 10022, attn: Special Sales Department, Phone: 1-800-221-2647.

First Printing: July 2003
10 9 8 7 6 5 4 3 2 1

Printed in the United States of America

Prologue

Arlene Taft sat through her husband's funeral with strained emotions. Ronald Taft wore his dress uniform. Although his wife couldn't see his shoes, she knew they were spit-shined black.

He was wearing his favorite Army uniform. He wore them with a sense of pride and honor for his country and for the fact that he—a black man who came from little—had progressed so far. He loved the Army and even more, he loved his status as an officer.

Arlene remembered when Ronald took her to her first formal military function. Since it was his ball she'd elected to wear a blue gown instead of her dress uniform.

Just a smattering of African-Americans had been in attendance.

"We'll go far in the military," he'd said to Arlene. They were both stationed in the Washington, D.C. area. Although it was unusual to get assigned to the same location for years, he'd lucked out with his posting at the Pentagon. Since she was a nurse, staying in one location wasn't unusual for her. She'd been at Walter Reed Army Medical Center for years.

As the years passed Ronald's postings required more and more travel—so much, in fact, that it was easy for him to take a vacation with a mistress without his wife's knowledge.

What was she to feel except betrayal, disillusionment, and a deep burning anger that she couldn't appease?

Her mother-in-law sniffled and moaned her grief beside her. She held onto the woman's hand, perhaps too tightly at times but Nancy Taft didn't complain. She was swallowed up in her own grief and she didn't even notice. The nurse had already revived her once with smelling salts. Ronald had been Mrs. Taft's only child—a truly beloved son. And somewhat spoiled. But she didn't blame Mrs. Taft for being a loving and giving woman. She'd accepted Arlene into the fold as if she were her own child. Nancy was a rarity. She seldom spoke a disparaging word against anyone.

Arlene's father was present with his new wife, a woman who was merely a few months older than Arlene. She was so unlike Arlene's mother that Arlene wondered what he saw in her except for the obvious appeal of a younger woman. Arlene's mother had died three years ago and Arlene supposed this was his way of moving on. He certainly dressed younger. His wife stood out in her lavish black attire. The skirt was higher and tighter than Arlene thought appropriate, but who was she to judge? She only wished she could see more of her father. Their relationship hadn't been the same since her mother's death.

The preacher's words droned on. They could have been disjointed ramblings because Arlene didn't hear any of it. She didn't know why she was grieving.

Her husband died on a boating trip with his lover—a lover Arlene must have subconsciously known had been out there. Did she have blinders on? The reality that he spent so little time with her should have been one clear indication. Randy Army officers rarely went without physical pleasures. She'd only deluded herself into thinking that her man was made of sterner stuff.

Arlene shook with his betrayal. She wondered if his Army buddies who laughed and joked in front of her knew of his exploits behind her back. Had their wives who called themselves her friends also been privy to the information? The military community was small. People knew each other's business, and they told. Yet no one had seen the necessity of informing her.

Somehow Arlene got through the funeral. She barely startled at the gun salute, and she made polite conversation at the reception held after the gravesite service. Her father and his wife left.

Arlene stayed on for a few days to console her mother-in-law. Then she flew back to Washington, D.C., telling Mrs. Taft that she would stay in touch and that she would send her mementos of her son.

It was Friday night when she unpacked her suitcase in the row house she'd lived in for years. The message machine was beeping. Ignoring it, she stood under the shower a long time, then went to the closet to pull on a robe, even though the outside August temperature hovered in the nineties.

Ronald's suits and clothes hung in the closet beside hers. Whatever happened next seemed to be outside of her.

She came back to her senses when she heard the doorbell ring. Shelly Bailey, her girlfriend since kindergarten, stood on the cement steps, a suitcase beside her.

Arlene glanced in the room. It was a disaster. Every piece of Ronald's clothing was flung about the room. A stack of black garbage bags was hidden under more clothes on the cocktail table.

Shelly glanced at Arlene's ravished features. Then she glanced around the living room, a worried expression on her face.

She tugged Arlene into her arms and held her tightly. "Girlfriend, I'm here. We're going to work through this together."

One

Some days were better than others. Arlene wanted to pull the covers up to her neck and spend the next few hours in her warm bed.

At nine, she made an effort to rise, but never made it up. She dozed again, off and on for two hours. A siren blared from afar, but that wasn't so unusual in the city.

The clock closed in on eleven when she finally considered actually getting up. She didn't feel too guilty. After all she'd worked the eleven-to-seven shift at the hospital the evening before.

Arlene contemplated calling in sick—perhaps spend the rest of what was left of the day in bed. Half of it was gone anyway. This was totally out of line for her. She'd never called in sick when she wasn't. But many things had changed in the last month and she didn't feel quite herself.

Suddenly the phone rang, a loud and unwanted sound in the quietness of her bedroom. Lazily, she reached out a hand, plucked up the receiver and barked out a groggy hello.

"Lieutenant Colonel Taft, we need you here stat?" the hospital scheduler told her.

Now! Was that woman crazy? Arlene wanted to avoid the day altogether, but she wouldn't dare say so out loud. A soldier was on call twenty-four-seven. If they needed her, she'd have to go.

"Due to the disaster, we need more nurses, especially specialists," the woman said.

"What disaster?" Arlene asked.

"Haven't you seen the news?"

"No. What happened?" Sitting up in bed, she reached for the remote. It was too far away. Now that she thought about it, she had heard more sirens than usual, but it hadn't pierced the fog that had settled on her.

"The Pentagon has been bombed. And both towers of the World Trade Center are gone. And that's just the beginning."

"Gone? *Impossible.*"

"Just turn on the TV. Every station is broadcasting. We need you here. Now."

"I'll be there as soon as I dress." Arlene fumbled the receiver back onto the hook and scrambled for the TV remote to press the power button. Every channel focused on the tragedy. It didn't take long for her to get the gist of the earth-shattering disaster. A deep sense of dread and sorrow flowed through her for the suffering the victims were experiencing. How could someone dare do this in America? She saw it in the news when it happened in Europe and Israel. *But here?* The U.S. seemed isolated from all that, but global involvement had brought the entire world closer—for the good as well as the bad.

With a quick prayer, she rushed out of bed so fast her head swam. Tugging off her nightgown and thrusting it aside, she headed to the shower. After taking the fastest shower in history, she listened to the news as she quickly donned her uniform. Her new hairdo of short red curls only took a moment to rake a comb through. Turning off the TV, she paused only long enough to grab a bagel and cream cheese to eat in the car as she drove the short distance to the hospital. Depending on the number of injured, finding time for a break once she arrived could be next to impossible.

At the hospital she was quickly directed to the trauma section. It was a beehive of activity.

"Lieutenant Colonel Neal Allen is one of your patients," she was told. "He has multiple fractures, scorched lungs and throat, and internal injuries. Right now, we're trying to keep him breathing on his own to clear his lungs and increase his chances of survival."

Arlene recorded his vital signs on his chart. He was still heavily sedated from surgery.

Neal Allen. That name was indelibly etched in her mind. Could this be the Neal Allen who had lived next door to her in middle school? Arlene shook her head at the foolish thought. It couldn't be. Of all the people for her to run into.

The Neal Allen she'd known back in Texas had been the bane of her existence. She would never forget the time he'd taken her red and white panties off the clothesline, attached them to a piece of cardboard, scribbled her name in huge bold letters across the front, and hung them on his father's flagpole. Her panties had flown for hours where the man had so proudly flown his American flag. All because she wouldn't walk to the movies with him. She'd already accepted a date with someone else, but even if she hadn't, she wouldn't have gone out with Neal. *What was that other boy's name?* she wondered. Perhaps she hadn't been diplomatic with her refusal but she didn't deserve that.

As Arlene looked at her patient, she realized he was that Neal Allen. Determined to find something to dislike about him, she noted how his physical appearance had changed a lot in the last twenty-one years from the gangly youth he'd been.

It was immediately evident that he worked out regularly. His relaxed state failed to mask his underlying strength. His chest and shoulder muscles were amazing. She felt the steel beneath soft skin when she attached the blood pressure cuff. His dark lashes covering his closed eyes were much too attractive. His hair was cut short, yet it still managed to look striking. As Arlene gazed down on him, she wondered if his character had changed as much.

She shook the memories away and got back to the business of keeping Lieutenant Colonel Neal Allen alive.

* * *

The next day when Arlene reported to duty, Neal was looking better. She wondered if he remembered her.

"How are we feeling today, Lieutenant Colonel Allen?" Arlene asked him as she slipped the pressure cuff on his arm.

"Good to be alive," he whispered in a raspy voice she could barely hear. It was tinged with the smoke damage from burning chemicals in the fire.

"Oh, you'll be feeling better in no time." After making a notation on his blood pressure, she slid the thermometer into his ear, then recorded his temperature. It was only slightly elevated.

"How did the others . . . ?"

"You saved quite a few people. They've been calling about you."

"But . . ."

"Don't try to talk. Save your throat." She smiled. Whatever their past, he was her patient and she was determined to give him the best care. "You're a hero."

"No . . . so much destruction. So many people injured . . ." he whispered.

"And many generous people who are out there offering help. You did your part, now let us help you."

"It wasn't enough."

Arlene patted his hand, wanting to ease his distress. "You gave all you could. No one can ask for more."

He closed his eyes.

Arlene didn't know if her words had any effect. She only hoped they eased his pain.

She kept peeking at him as she attended to his injuries. His concern for the others touched her more than she wanted. Could he have changed so drastically from that obnoxious kid she knew so long ago?

"Well, Little Miss Leave-Me-Alone."

Arlene stopped in her tracks, her hackles rising. She

forced herself to present a calm front. "We must be feeling better."

"Thought I'd forgotten you, didn't you?"

Arlene could only hope.

"Were you trying to hide your identity?" His voice rose barely above a whisper. She strained to hear him, but she heard nevertheless. His cute brown eyes were dancing with merriment for the first time. Even at her expense she was glad for it.

She'd hoped he'd forgotten about her past, darn it. After all she couldn't look the same and her last name had changed. Back then, he loved to tease her. "I don't have anything to hide. My life is an open book. I see you haven't changed from that obnoxious kid who lived next door to me."

"In some ways—in many, many ways—I hope I have. Changed, that is."

"Hmmmm." He had changed all right. Even with numerous injuries, she hadn't missed the striking proportions of his body. As his nurse, she'd seen all of him, and to her chagrin, she liked what she saw.

"We'll just work on getting you healed right now, okay?"

His smile faded. "How are the others who were brought in?"

"I don't know. I'm sorry. They were taken to hospitals all around the area." She pulled the sheet up to his chest. "I want you to rest your voice. Your throat is still raw. It must be painful for you to talk."

He clasped her hand in his, imprisoning it with a grip that belied his condition. "I need to know."

"I know you do. Believe me, we're all doing our best for the injured. Trust me."

"Can I trust you?" The seriousness of his tone surprised Arlene.

"Why wouldn't you?"

His stare was intense, as if his eyes spoke words he

wouldn't say aloud. Then suddenly he glanced away from her to the picture beside his bed.

She regarded the photo a nurse had found in his pocket. A pretty young girl with two thick pigtails. Arlene had brought a frame for it and put it on his bedside table, hoping the photo would give him pleasure. From her conversations with his mother, who called often, she garnered that the child was his niece, a cutie named April.

"Your mother and your niece have called several times. They're very concerned about you."

"What did you tell them?"

"That you're better, and that we're taking excellent care of you. As soon as your voice heals, we'll let you talk with them. But right now, I want you to rest your vocal cords."

He glanced at the clock. "It's time for you to leave?"

"Yes," Arlene said. "My shift is over."

"Can't you stay a little while?"

"Why?"

"I don't know. To talk about home. To read to me. Something—anything. I can't sleep."

She repressed the urge to stroke his forehead. "They'll give you something to help you sleep," Arlene said softly. "You need your rest."

"I don't want any more medication."

Arlene knew very well that she had nothing rushing her home. Her husband was dead—had seldom been around when he was alive. Since his death, things hadn't changed that much actually. Except for the expectation of his arrival. When she looked back on her marriage she saw that it hadn't been that great. She'd been complacent. And that was sad.

Arlene had nothing to go home to.

"All right. I'll read to you. What kind of books do you like?"

"Anything will do." Neal just wanted to listen to her voice. Her soothing voice intrigued him, not the story. He was disgusted with himself for wanting her near. Most of his waking hours were spent watching the disaster on TV.

His unit would be one of the groups dispatched to Afghanistan. He was disappointed that he wouldn't be among them.

Now he was punishing himself by listening to Arlene's voice, even though he knew she'd been responsible for his sister's and, thereby April's, unhappiness and pain.

But Ronald Taft *had* been Arlene's husband. He'd already been married and Bridget had no rights to him.

Arlene smiled—a smile he remembered so well when she was up to mischief. "Would one of my romance novels work?"

He smiled, and the image was amazing.

"How about a mystery?" Arlene amended, knowing the skewed notion men had of romance novels. "I'll find one that will keep your heart pumping for hours. Or I might get you something soothing enough to help you sleep. What's your preference?" She found herself stroking his hand even though she'd cautioned herself not to.

"Excitement, please."

There was that smile again—the one he'd used just after he'd teased her in middle school. Back then, Arlene hated that smile, but now she found it sexy. She chuckled. "I'll be back soon," she said, and went to meet with the nurse who would replace her.

"Arlene, we're transferring a call. This kid insists on speaking to you and only you."

For a change Neal was sleeping peacefully. Arlene's hand hovered over the phone so that she could catch it before the ring wakened him.

"Nurse Taft?" a young voice asked in a firm tone—too firm if her tone was an indication of her youth.

"This is Lieutenant Colonel Taft," Arlene responded.

"Good. I'm calling about Uncle Neal. I'm worried about him. When can he come home? I miss him. I *need* him." The little girl sounded as if she were near tears.

"Are you April?"

Silence answered Arlene. Then a hesitant, trembling voice said, "Yes."

"Your uncle is much better, April. He's responding well to the medication. But he needs time for his body to heal. It might take a little while."

Arlene heard sniffles on the end of the line and her heart cracked.

"Is your grandmother there, or your mother?"

"My mommy's dead. Uncle Neal is supposed to take care of me now."

"I'm so sorry, honey." Arlene's heart went out to the motherless little girl. She remembered Bridget well and was saddened to hear the young woman was dead. Neal seemed to be the child's security blanket.

"Grandma's worried about Uncle Neal. She wants to come there but Grandpa's too sick. Grandpa wants to come, too. But he can't."

"It won't be easy catching a plane right now, anyway. Maybe it's best they stay home. Anytime you're worried about him, just call me, all right?"

"Will you tell me the truth?"

Arlene closed her eyes, moved by the hope in the child's voice. "Always."

"Uncle Neal's really doing better?" she asked with a skepticism too old for one so young.

"Yes, he's much better. I promise." That much wasn't a lie. Arlene wouldn't lie to her.

"He's really not going to die? Grandma said he wouldn't but I thought she was just trying to make me feel better."

"No, he's improving every day. I wouldn't lie about that."

"Thank you."

"You're very welcome, dear. Did you get your grandparent's permission to call?"

"Uncle Neal gave me lots of phonecards so I can call him anytime I want to."

"And you know how to use them?"

"Sure," she said with a confidence that belied her age. "He showed me how to use them. And I've been reading for years. I can read directions."

Arlene smiled. "You're a big girl, aren't you?"

"Yeah. I can do lots of things."

When Arlene hung up the phone, she caught Neal's steady gaze as he watched her. He was always watching her in that strange way. Why? What was he looking for? "I didn't know you were awake," Arlene said finally. "I'm sorry I woke you."

"It's okay," he whispered. But a deep sadness seemed to steal over him. She understood some of what he felt, only her grief was different. Her sorrow was tinged with adultery, mistrust and hurt. The loss of a beloved sister was so much worse.

"I'm so sorry about your sister," Arlene told him.

He nodded and turned away from her. Nothing could be said to ease the sorrow of a loved one. And she didn't even try to appease what she couldn't anyway.

She thought of Bridget again. She'd been five years younger than Arlene. They knew each other, but their ages were too far apart for them to run in the same circles. But Bridget had looked up to Arlene. And Arlene sometimes babysat for Mrs. Allen. Bridget had been as full of energy as her precocious brother had been, but not quite as mischievous. Their mother was practically useless when it came to handling two such active kids. Sometimes it seemed she didn't even try.

Arlene glanced at the photo on Neal's bedside table. "April is very pretty. She resembles you."

"You think so?"

"Yes. Although she also reminds me of Bridget at that age. She definitely has your nose and your smile."

His smile was not filled with humor.

"Are you comfortable?" Arlene asked, straightening his covers.

He nodded.

With nothing more to offer, Arlene touched his hand and left the room.

Considering the meticulous care she gave him and the gentle comfort she offered his family, it was difficult to believe that Arlene was the vindictive woman who wouldn't give her husband a divorce, even after she'd already agreed to do so, simply because she discovered another woman was pregnant with his child. According to Ronald, his relationship with his wife had been over years ago. He'd finally decided to end it and she'd agreed. Then, when she discovered Bridget was pregnant with his child, she refused to give him the divorce, threatening to ruin his career if he tried to get one.

Ronald and Neal were both career Army men. The threat of adultery could damage a black man's career in a heartbeat. White officers could sometimes get away with unsavory behavior. Even with the barrage of publicity, only a few cases actually amounted to anything. The press usually died down after a fashion. Besides, officers protected each other. Yesterday, as well as today, black men lived by a different, more cautious code.

Another worry nagged at Neal relentlessly. He was responsible for raising his niece. Would he heal well enough to return to his post so he could properly care for her? He wasn't ready to retire. But if his body betrayed him, he would have no other recourse. He wanted to expose her to the world. There was so much for her to learn—so much to see.

April had lost her mother and father only a month ago. And now her guardian was in the hospital. His parents were too infirm to care for a rambunctious eight-year-old. And April had always been full of energy. Every week since his sister's death, his mother called, telling him about some mischief April had gotten herself into. He'd lecture the child, but her deeds weren't that serious, and Neal didn't put that much energy into the lectures. She'd lived through enough traumas. He wouldn't make her life any more unbearable than it already was. He needed to be with her.

Neal had paid for a live-in nanny to care for her until he could take the responsibility for her.

She was already on her third nanny so far. The second one had been frightened away when April put her hamster in the woman's bed. The woman awoke in the middle of the night when the hamster crawled up her leg.

Neal had hoped to get April in a few weeks. Now there was no telling when he would be able to return to the real world and care for her.

He could imagine the frightening thoughts running through her head, especially with his accident so close to her parent's death.

It was Saturday. Neal had been in the hospital for two weeks now. It was Arlene's day off and she debated going in to visit him. He expected to see her every day. They had fallen into a routine of sorts, although sometimes his mind seemed to wander. Some deep, dark secret from the past, perhaps. Arlene got the feeling he didn't like her for some reason. But she certainly couldn't be part of whatever troubled him.

When she arrived, the phone in his room rang. By now it was second nature for her to reach for it.

"It's time to send Uncle Neal home," April said when Arlene answered it.

"He's healing very nicely," Arlene told her. "But he isn't quite ready to return home."

"But I need him *now.*" Every situation was urgent as far as April was concerned.

"He misses you, too, sweetheart."

"My nanny is a witch." A long, labored breath followed that pronouncement.

Arlene smothered a laugh.

"How so?" Arlene couldn't help but ask.

"She doesn't understand me."

"Maybe if you explained your problem to her . . ."

"She doesn't understand, though. She's too old. I need help!"

"Honey . . ."

"Can you believe she got mad because my guinea pig got out of the cage and went into her room?"

"It just happened to get out?"

Silence greeted her. Arlene surmised that the rodent had plenty of help.

"I may have *accidentally* left the door open when I took her out to play with me. Maybe I didn't latch the door good enough. But it was an *accident*. Everybody makes mistakes. Why can't I make them?"

"I see," Arlene said. Evidently Nanny didn't like little animals scurrying around the house.

"And my hamster won't stay in the cage. Nanny keeps calling it a mouse and threatening to kill it. Can you believe she'd kill my hamster? I told grandpa on her too. He told her not to kill my animals. She's a mean old lady."

"Let me get this straight. The hamster gets out of the cage on its own. You didn't give it any help?"

"No. Never."

I just bet it did, Arlene thought.

"Is it my fault he keeps getting out? I do everything I can to get that thing to stay in, but every morning when I wake up it's gone. And it stays away until it gets hungry. Then he comes back looking scrawny and starved."

"So after the hamster got out of the room on its own, it found its way to your nanny's room, too?"

"What can I do about *that*?" April asked affronted. "He got out on his own. It's the hamster's fault. Why doesn't she blame him?"

"She can't exactly talk to the hamster."

"I talk to him all the time. But does he listen when I tell him to stay in a cage? Nanny's mean. He's got to be careful around her and I told him that, too. But Grandma says that's a man for you. They never listen."

Arlene couldn't contain her laughter.

"And then there's my dog."

Did the child have a zoo in that house? Arlene wondered. "A dog?"

"Nothing worth getting mad about. It just chewed on her raggedy old house shoe. And then it peed on the carpet in her room. But that was her fault. She shouldn't have scared it. If I was a baby, I would have peed too if that old hag had frightened me. It's just a puppy."

Arlene peeked at Neal to make sure he was still sleeping. "I take it she doesn't frighten you."

"Not really. I hate her!"

"Have you spoken to your grandparents about this?"

"They don't understand because the mean witch always gets to them first before I even get a chance to tell them *my* side." The sigh that came over the phone was long and defeated. "Now I'm stuck in my room until I learn to behave. I'm going to spend the rest of my life cooped up in this room. Can I come to Uncle Neal? Please? Please? I'll take care of him. I won't bother him. I promise to be good."

Arlene's heart clenched. April desperately needed her uncle. "Sweetheart, you *are* good." She was just an eight-year-old acting her age.

Early Monday afternoon, General Ashborn presented Neal with the promotion orders to colonel and pair of eagles. He also received a special commendation for his rescue efforts.

Arlene borrowed a disposable camera from one of the nurses and snapped pictures.

"Congratulations, Colonel," Arlene told him once the general left.

"Thank you," he said.

"This is absolutely wonderful."

He studied the commendation as if it held the secrets to the universe. "So many people were hurt far worse than I was. So many lives lost. I don't feel I deserve this."

"That doesn't mean we can't recognize our heroes. You deserve your commendation, Neal. You have something to be proud of."

Neal's phone rang again, and Arlene picked it up as if it were her own.

"My hamster's dead!" April wailed over the phone.

"What happened?" Arlene asked, ready to go to battle with the mean old nanny who had the nerve to kill a child's animal.

"My dog bit it."

"Your dog?" Arlene pressed a hand against her chest to still her quickened heartbeat.

"It got out of the cage again. It wouldn't listen to me. And Pickles ate it. It was bloody and dead on my carpet this morning. I didn't even hear him last night."

"Oh, I'm so sorry, honey."

"I want Uncle Neal. Please can I come?"

"Honey, your uncle is improving daily, but it will take some time before he's ready to come home. You can't stay in a hospital."

"I'll be good, and I'll be quiet, too. I promise."

Arlene's heart ached for the little girl. "Who will keep your animals if you leave?"

"I'm mad at Pickles. She ate my hamster."

"It's not quite Pickles' fault, honey. Her natural survival instinct encourages her to eat animals. Dogs are made that way."

"It's mean."

"It seems like it. But those instincts keep them alive when they don't have someone special like you to take care of them."

"I feed her. I even give her food from my plate sometimes, even when Nanny gets mad."

"I'm sure you take very good care of her. And you must continue to do so until Uncle Neal is well. Okay?"

A few sniffles came over the wire before a weak, "Okay."

"Good."

"I buried him in a shoe box in the back yard. Grandpa said a prayer over his grave."

"That's good."

"I made a cross out of some sticks and planted a flower by his grave. My mama's flowers were prettier. You think he'll like the flowers?"

"I'm sure he loved them."

"I miss my hamster, and I miss my mom."

"I know you do, sweetheart." Arlene struggled to hold back tears.

A couple of sniffles preceded, "My friend Keneta has a boyfriend. I'm never going to date a boy."

Arlene smiled and swiped the wetness away from her eyes. "You might feel differently when you enter high school."

"They're so hardheaded. Grandma said that's why my hamster's dead. Because boys are hardheaded. They're the devil's spawn, she said. They always do what you tell them not to. I don't want any hardheaded boys. It hurts too much. I'm not getting any more boy animals."

"Oh, sweetheart. They aren't all bad." Thinking back on Neal when he was a boy, April wasn't too far off the mark, Arlene thought.

"Grandma says they are. Nanny agreed, but I don't believe anything she says. She wanted to dump my hamster in the trash. Can you believe that? She wanted to treat him like he was trash."

This woman was toast if Arlene ever had anything to say about it.

"Grandpa wouldn't let her. He made her keep him so we could bury him."

Arlene closed her eyes briefly. So much grief for one so

young. First she buried her mom. Now her pet. Arlene's own pain seemed miniscule in comparison.

"What's the devil's spawn? Nanny called me that and I'm not a boy."

"You're not the devil's spawn. Put your nanny on the phone."

"She'll be mad at me."

"Right now."

A few seconds passed before an older woman answered the phone. "Hello?"

"Mrs. Carter, I'm Colonel Allen's nurse. He has asked me to speak to you about April."

"She's a handful, I tell you that."

"All little eight-year-olds are handfuls," Arlene said.

"Mine weren't."

Did the woman think she raised angels? They were probably just good around her. "You do understand that she's just lost her mother and her uncle who is now her guardian is gravely injured. He would appreciate it if you can keep things calm for her and give her a little consideration."

"He wants me to spoil the child?"

"Consideration means not calling her bad names that might label her for life. Children are very sensitive about that. She also loves her animals. If you could be a little generous toward them, he would be grateful." Arlene chose her words carefully. After all, Neal couldn't search out a new nanny in his condition. Still, the nanny had to show some kindness toward the child. No child deserved to be labeled the devil's spawn. Of all the nerve!

When Arlene hung up, she wondered if she'd overstepped her authority. She glanced at Neal. He was watching her, his emotions unreadable. Even sick, she couldn't always read him. He hated taking pain medication. He was so good at hiding emotions that she couldn't always tell when he was in pain. What else was he covering up?

"I hope you don't mind," she said.

He shook his head.

Neal seemed always to be thinking, always considering some matter. Arlene wondered what was going through his mind. Sometimes she felt he was measuring her, and wondered why. She wondered if she came up lacking.

Near the end of Arlene's shift, while she recorded Neal's vital signs on a chart, a gorgeous, honey-brown hued woman wearing an Army uniform entered Neal's room.

"Hello, Neal. I was told you were improving," the woman said as she walked to the bed.

He nodded.

"Just ring the bell if you need anything," Arlene said to Neal, and prepared to leave.

"Hello, I'm Natasha. Neal's wife."

Wife. A ring hadn't been among his possessions and he never mentioned a wife.

"Nice to meet you," Arlene said and left the room.

Neal's wife *would* be what men considered a knockout. Why hadn't Natasha visited him before? Or called him? Perhaps she was stationed elsewhere and had trouble getting to D.C. April called every day. Surely his wife could have called him once.

For some indescribable reason, a shaft of disappointment swirled through Arlene. *You weren't falling for your patient, Arlene. So what's going on?* She took a deep breath and continued the last of her duties of the day. Neal was thirty-six—certainly old enough to have married at least once.

Neal watched Arlene leave the room, surely thinking he'd lied to her.

"Why are you here, Natasha?"

Natasha approached his bed. "I know this is bad timing, but the sooner we get this divorce moving, the better. If you sign the papers now, the divorce will come through in six months. I got the papers a couple weeks ago, but I wanted to give you some time."

"How generous," he whispered. His voice was a little stronger than it had been, but not much.

"Give me the papers."

Natasha took the manila envelope out of her huge purse and retrieved the papers.

"The lawyer tagged the places where you should sign," she said.

Neal activated the remote for the bed so he could sit up.

"I'll help you with that."

"I have it," he shot back. If he could handle a divorce, he could damn well handle a remote. He scanned the papers, making sure he wasn't signing away everything he'd ever saved. A five-year marriage that only halfway worked for the first three years wasn't worth everything he'd ever worked for.

Now Neal was grateful Natasha had insisted on a prenuptial agreement, fearing if things didn't work out, he'd end up with the little her father had left her. He knew very well his assets amounted to more than hers. He wanted to keep it that way.

Neal signed the papers and handed them to her.

"How is April?" she asked, as if she really cared.

"She's fine."

"Good." Natasha checked the clock. "Well, I have an appointment. I hope everything turns out well for you."

"You, too," Neal told her, knowing very well that she was rushing off to be with her new boyfriend.

Now uncomfortable with him, she quickly left. A part of Neal's life was nearing a close. He shouldn't feel anything, should be grateful to see the last of her. Still they were married for five years, and parting wasn't easy.

He glanced at the clock and wondered if Arlene would stop by once again before she left. He was falling for her just as he had as a lovesick thirteen-year-old. Every time she came in the room, his system went into overdrive. He had to work at keeping his emotions contained. She was forever leaning over him or touching him in her warm manner. And her touches sent his heart thumping. He watched the clock—continued to wait for her to return.

She didn't and he was even more disappointed than he'd been with the ending of his marriage.

Arlene had the next two days off, and for the first time since Neal arrived, she didn't go by the hospital to visit him. They were the longest two days of Neal's life.

She returned on Thursday. When she came into his room, she was very businesslike. She did the chores she usually did and was about to leave the room when he grabbed her arm.

"What's going on?" he whispered.

"Nothing. Did you have a good weekend?"

"I expected to see you."

"Wasn't your wife with you?"

Neal sighed. He needed to clear the air. "We're separated. She brought the divorce papers by for me to sign."

With an unbelieving glint, Arlene's eyes widened. "She brought you papers while you're in the hospital?"

Neal shrugged. "They needed to be signed. My marriage has been over for years. We're just getting it done legally."

"I'm sorry, Neal."

"I'm not."

"Are you okay?"

Neal nodded.

Arlene squeezed his hand and went about her rounds, wondering at the cruelty of people, or was it just that they didn't care anymore as long as their needs were taken care of? She hoped she was never uncaring.

April called practically every day since Arlene's conversation with the nanny. Somehow the energetic child brought Arlene out of her own grief.

"Are your bags all packed?" Neal asked.

"They are. Most of my things have been shipped to Korea," Arlene said. Korea was her next tour of duty. She was scheduled for a short stay there.

"Aren't you going to miss this place?"

Arlene nodded. "I'm definitely going to miss the D.C. area. The beautiful old homes. The rhythm of the city. The museums and activities on the Mall. The theaters. Cherry blossoms in the spring. The restaurants. But it's time for me to see other parts of the world." The things she mentioned were only a few of the activities Arlene would miss, but the day after she returned to work after burying Ronald, she'd asked for a change in location. She realized she'd grown stagnant. She was pleased the change had come through quickly.

Neal was leaving the hospital today. He was taking a flight to Dallas to finish his recuperation near his family. April needed to see that he was still alive and recuperating. Arlene had halfway fallen in love with the child over the last few weeks. She would miss their lively conversations. If she'd had a child, she would have wished for one like April.

She would also miss Neal. Darn it. Tears clogged her throat. How had she fallen for him so quickly? She didn't fall in love with him or anything stupid like that. It was just . . . in their month and a half together, they had formed a bond of sorts.

As Neal prepared to leave the hospital, he realized he had mixed feelings about Arlene. He'd grown to respect her skills and even fell in love with her a little over the last several weeks. It was difficult reconciling the vindictive woman Bridget had said Ronald had painted her, with the tender, caring woman who dealt so well with April, his parents and friends who had called frequently about his condition.

Perhaps Ronald had been wrong. It was possible that Arlene refused to give him the divorce he craved because she was in love with him. After all, he had been her husband. She had first dibs on him. Bridget, God his baby sister Bridget, who Neal had loved so much, had found her happiness on the dregs of another woman's lost dreams.

It hurt to think about his sister. The two of them had always been protective of each other. It seemed his connection to family stability had been broken with her death. Family was special to him. Sometimes he thought the only thing keeping his life in perspective was April, simply because she needed him.

For the last month she'd called almost daily, wanting him home with her. The doctors wanted him to stay in D.C. another week or so before he went to Texas, but he couldn't. He was going home.

Arlene drove him to Dulles International Airport. The trip on Rt. 66 West was almost bumper-to-bumper traffic. Normally he would have flown from Washington National, but their full flight schedule hadn't resumed yet. From Dulles, he wouldn't have to change planes.

From the passenger seat he assessed her. He was accustomed to seeing Arlene in her nurse's uniform. She was beautiful today in dark blue slacks and a matching V-neck top with a gold necklace. She looked elegant and fetching.

"Thank you, Arlene, for all you've done for me and my family."

"You're very welcome," she said.

Words couldn't express his gratitude. He'd received many letters of good wishes from the families whose loved ones he'd saved, and his friends from Buckley Academy had called him often—even sent flowers and cards. But Arlene had been his steady champion. And he couldn't think of the words that would express how indebted he felt.

They finally arrived at the airport. Arlene let him off at the terminal and requested a wheelchair. He went through check-in while she parked the car. The lines were long due to increased security. Although he could stand for short periods, and as much as he hated it, he was glad she'd insisted on the wheelchair.

Being an athletic man his entire life and even more so to become an Airborne Ranger, he found it humbling being pushed through the airport to his gate while Arlene walked beside him carrying his cane. He shouldn't complain. After all that had occurred, he was grateful to be alive, and well enough to even take the flight.

"Can I get you anything?" Arlene asked him. "A sandwich, maybe?"

"Nothing. Thanks. Just sit and relax."

She sat in a chair by his wheelchair. He took in the beautiful elegance and warmth of her face, the tenderness in her eyes, and wondered if he would ever see her again—hoped that another twenty-one years wouldn't pass before their paths crossed again.

He started to ask her for her phone number—ask if he could visit her once he healed, but decided against it. April was his responsibility now. And he couldn't ask Arlene to be a part of her husband's baby's life, have her pain thrown in her face on a daily basis.

The fact that he had gotten custody of April had been the final breaking point of his marriage. Natasha made it clear that she didn't want a kid of her own, much less take care of somebody else's. He certainly couldn't expect Arlene to care for her husband's child.

This would be their final good-bye.

Preflight boarding for his flight was announced and Arlene started to stand. Neal caught her hands, leaned toward her and, with a gentle tug, pulled her toward him until their lips touched.

He expected her to jerk away from him. When she didn't, he swiped his tongue over her lips. Her sweet essence mingled with a touch of perfume and the sweetness of the kiss was almost painful.

She opened her mouth to him and for the first time in his life, he kissed the lips that had tempted him as a horny fourteen-year-old, standing on the cusp of tomorrow without a clue on how to deal with the girl who snubbed him.

Even now she enticed the full-grown man. The emotional distance between them seemed as palpable as it had years before.

With a pressing need to touch her, he captured her warm face in his hands, tasted her, felt her soft skin, knowing this was all they would ever share. A knot rose in his throat. The realization was heartrending.

"Thank you," he whispered while gazing into her eyes. There he saw the need that held him in its own grip. Slowly, he slid his hands down her arms. Holding both her hands in his, he carried them to his mouth and gently kissed her knuckles, closing his eyes against the strength of his need.

They had come so close once again, only to have the future snatched away. When she opened one hand to caress his cheek, his gaze jerked to hers. All that he felt was reflected in her pretty brown eyes. There was so much he wanted to say yet he felt compelled to remain silent. With hundreds of words left unspoken between them, the attendant wheeled him back.

He'd been given a commendation for courage, but he felt far from courageous when he caught one last glimpse of Arlene looking after him. The attendant whirled the wheelchair toward the terminal. He didn't dare glance back with longing for what he could never have. Dear Lord, fate would have it that he could only move forward—toward April.

Two

Eighteen Months Later

Nearly two years had passed since Arlene put Neal on the plane to Texas. He'd sent her a thank you letter and a basket of beautiful flowers that arrived just before she left for Korea, but they hadn't communicated since. Yet, she'd thought of him often. Just the other day she thought she saw him walking across the park. The man she'd glimpsed had walked with a brisk, sure gait. She realized that Neal would be back to form by now, but the image of the man she'd seen was not the image of Neal she remembered.

"Arlene, I can't tell you how glad I am that we've finally made it to the same base. How often has that happened?" Shelly Bailey asked, bringing Arlene back to the present.

Weeks ago, Arlene moved to her new assignment at a base located several miles from Frankfurt, Germany. Some of their military bases were not huge operations as in the States but several small areas called Kasernes, structured more like Ft. Myer, and not like the large Ft. Belvoir, which lay south of Washington, D.C. Arlene worked at the Regional Medical Center that served all the bases in the area, even the Air Force.

"Not often enough. I've had a tough day. I need this break. And I'm glad you're here to spend it with me."

Military personnel learned quickly how to make new friends at new locations. But a tour was even better when a true friend lived nearby. One with which they could share fears, the past and secrets.

Arlene and Shelly were whiling the Friday evening away in one of Germany's infamous pubs. They'd eaten hors d'oeuvres and now they were relaxing over beer. Shelly loved German beer.

Arlene sipped her brew. She wasn't a beer drinker. She preferred wine, but she let Shelly talk her into trying the German brew. It was better than most brands she'd tried, but she wouldn't order it again.

Arlene glanced at her watch. They might even order dinner later, better yet, picking something up on the way home held more appeal.

"We need to take this show to my place," Arlene said. "If we crash out, then all we have to do is fall out. No worries about getting home."

"Girlfriend, you've turned over a new leaf in the last couple of years."

"It's called freedom. I don't have to cook unless I want to. Don't have to answer to anybody."

"Except Uncle Sam."

"There is that."

"Let's stop by the commissary and pick up some wine or more beer."

"I'm with you."

Arlene dug into her purse and pulled out her jumble of keys. Then they made their way to her new, small model burgundy Mercedes that wasn't sold in the U.S.

Frankfurt was one of the more modern German cities, yet it still held ancient castles and old cobbled squares. With a mixture of the old and the new, a few skyscrapers—mostly bank headquarters—dotted the skyline.

Shelly continued to chatter on the short drive to the commissary. Once there, they trolled for a parking space before going inside to select more snacks to go with their drinks. After much more discussion than Arlene thought was necessary, they were still not sure what they wanted, so they chose several more.

"Arlene Taft. Arlene? Is that you?" a voice rang out.

Arlene turned in the direction of an unfamiliar male voice—to see Neal who was with a girl trying to nudge him down an aisle.

"Neal?" she asked.

"Wait a minute, April," he said, turning the girl to face Arlene. "I want to introduce you to someone." His gaze was riveted on her face, then moved slowly over her body. Warm heat spread all over Arlene.

The child stopped tugging and walked quietly beside him. Arlene's heartbeat accelerated. She didn't understand her reaction to seeing Neal.

"This is Arlene Taft. Remember she took care of me while I was in the hospital?"

"I remember you. You're the nice lady who talked to my nanny." Arlene was unprepared when April threw herself into her arms and hugged her tightly. Arlene stepped back before she caught herself, fearing both of them were going to land on their backsides. She laughed and closed her arms around the small, energetic figure.

"Thank you, thank you, thank you for sending Uncle Neal back to me."

"I didn't do it."

"Yes, you did," she said, then glanced up at Arlene. "She's pretty, Uncle Neal."

Neal laughed. Arlene blushed. "I agree with you there. She is, indeed," he replied.

"Can you have dinner with us?" April asked, rubbing her stomach as if she hadn't eaten in days. "I'm starved, and Uncle Neal promised to take me to a restaurant off the base after he buys me some jeans at the Exchange."

"I don't think . . ." Arlene started, shaking her head.

"Can you?" Neal asked. "We don't want to put you on the spot, but we'd love to have you."

"I don't see why not," Shelly cut in.

Arlene blushed, embarrassed that she'd completely forgotten her best friend was standing near. She tugged Shelly closer. "Colonel Neal Allen, meet my best friend, Lieutenant Colonel Shelly Bailey."

Neal extended a hand. "It's a pleasure to meet you, Shelly."

"Same here. Just give me your keys, Arlene, and I'll take myself home. Just pick your car up tomorrow."

"But we had plans . . ."

"Don't leave, Shelly. You're both invited," Neal said. "Please join us."

Shelly held up her six-pack. "I have my own plans for the evening."

With mixed feelings, Arlene dug into her purse for the keys. Shelly took them from her before Arlene changed her mind. She knew Arlene too well.

"See you later," Shelly said and started walking down the aisle.

"Shelly . . ." Arlene called out.

With a smile, Shelly waved the beer and continued down the aisle.

Arlene gazed the jeans and shirt she wore. "I'm not dressed for dinner."

The once over Neal gave her made her feel as if a hand stroked her body. "You're fine," he murmured. His voice had lowered to a husky timbre. It was too easy to get lost in the way he looked at her.

"They've got new designer jeans at the PX. We have time to stop there before we go," April reminded them.

"Another time," Neal shot back.

"But they'll sell out."

April's voice broke the spell Neal was weaving over Arlene. Arlene cleared her throat. "I'm sure we have time, don't we?" she said.

"Later," Neal said. "They've got enough jeans to supply the entire base and several Kasernes." Neal led them out of the commissary, prompting Arlene by placing a hand in the small of her back. His touch seemed to singe her skin through her blouse. He whispered to Arlene, "I was dying to get out of shopping. April loves to shop and shop and shop. Then she has to try everything on. Worse than a week on a mission."

"Typical male attitude," Arlene told him.

Neal held up his hands. "I'm guilty."

While Arlene tried to contain her reaction to Neal's closeness, April skipped a few paces ahead of them and stopped at a navy BMW. She should have known he'd have a sports car complete with manual transmission. Neal activated the electronic key and April opened the door and hopped into the back seat. In Germany, children under twelve were required to use special booster seats and sit in the back. Arlene sank into the smooth leather of the passenger seat and Neal quickly maneuvered them out of the crowded parking lot.

Arlene rarely went to the commissary when she didn't have to literally fight for a parking space. Someone was waiting as they pulled off.

Arlene studied Neal. He looked so different from the seriously injured man she'd cared for. The burns in his throat had healed. His voice was strong and purposeful. He moved with a sure gait, not with halting, healing steps.

And he looked fabulous. God, did he look fantastic. His buff body—the muscles rippling beneath his shirt—were a treat for a woman who hadn't had any prospects of sex in the last two years.

Remembering their parting kiss that had been too intimate to be friendly, Arlene looked toward the darkened streets.

"When did you arrive?" Neal asked softly. He slid a Toni Braxton CD into the player. The music was slow and intimate. April wore earphones to her CD player and snapped her fingers to her own beat.

"A few weeks ago. And you?"

"Nine months. April and I arrived in August. I'm surprised we haven't crossed paths before."

"Not surprising really. This place is huge. How do you like Germany, April?" Arlene asked, trying to break the intimate feeling that enveloped the car.

"I like it. I don't have nannies anymore except when Uncle Neal goes away on trips. I hate when he leaves," she said. "I have a German friend though. I can speak the language better than Uncle Neal."

"Good for you. Maybe you can translate for me."

"I'm the one," she said. "Uncle Neal and I speak German when we're alone. He says it's a good way for us to learn the language."

"Practice makes perfect," Arlene said.

"Yeah. That's what he says." She snapped her fingers a couple more times. "I've got a soccer game tomorrow. Can you come?"

"What time is the game?" Arlene had never been to a soccer game. Baseball, basketball and football often, but never soccer.

"I don't know. Uncle Neal knows."

"It's at one."

"Where is it?" she asked.

Neal quickly told her.

"I'm the best player on the team," April said.

"We're modest, aren't we?" Neal quipped.

"Well, I am."

In half an hour they arrived at the restaurant. Arlene ordered wiener schnitzel.

"Are you married, Ms. Taft?" April asked pointedly, looking at her bare ring finger.

"No, I'm not," Arlene responded. She definitely saw traits of Neal in the child.

"Uncle Neal isn't married either. You're just alike."

"April," Neal rumbled in a warning tone.

"I was just going to say Uncle Neal doesn't have a wife. You don't have a husband. That's all."

The food froze in Arlene's mouth. Out of the mouths of babes.

"Eat your food," Neal said.

April shrugged and ate another forkful. But she watched Arlene closely, as if checking her out and making sure she'd make a suitable candidate for her uncle.

Arlene could have told her that she had no designs on her uncle right now. She wasn't the best when it came to choosing men. Her husband was a perfect example.

April waved at someone across the room. "Uncle Neal, Carole is over there with her parents. Can I go and say hi?"

"May I?"

"Well?"

Neal sighed. He'd use the object lesson later. "Yes."

"She's a bundle of energy," Arlene said as the little girl excused herself and left the table. It was obvious Neal did his best with teaching manners.

"You can say that again," he responded while watching his niece maneuver around the tables until she reached the Jacksons.

Once April arrived, he directed his attention back to Arlene.

"Where were you stationed before?" Neal asked Arlene. The atmosphere grew thicker and more intimate without April's constant chatter. Arlene almost wished her back.

"Korea. And you?"

"I've been in the States. It took longer than I thought to recover. But I'm finally where I need to be."

Wasn't he, though? "I'm glad."

"Why didn't you write me?" His voice softened to a low timbre.

"I don't know. It didn't seem appropriate. Tell me, how are April's animals?"

"They're doing better than I am. She gave most of them to friends before we left. My parents kept the dog."

April returned with Carole. "Uncle Neal, Mrs. Jackson says I can stay the night if it's all right with you. Can I?"

"May you."

April didn't play dumb this time. "May I?"

"It's inappropriate to spring this on the Jacksons at the last minute. We've talked about this before."

"My mom doesn't mind. Really," Carole said. Both girls were rocking back and forth in their enthusiasm with pleading frowns on their faces.

"You have a game tomorrow."

"I can come home and change before the game."

Both girls were practically prancing in their eagerness to spend the night together. Neal glanced in the Jacksons' direction. Mrs. Jackson smiled and waved. Neal waved back, then focused on the girls.

"All right," Neal said. "But be on your best behavior and don't stay up late."

"I'll be good and we'll go to bed early. Promise."

Yeah. He really believed that.

April released Carole and hugged Neal. Then she shocked Arlene and hugged her too.

"Thanks for saving Uncle Neal. I hope we can have dinner again. Don't forget my game tomorrow."

"April, that's rude," Neal admonished.

April used the innocent expression she'd perfected that wasn't innocent at all. "She can always say no if she doesn't want to see me play."

"You're putting Arlene on the spot and I won't have that." Neal gave her his no nonsense stare. "Apologize."

April shrugged. "Sorry. You don't have to come, if you don't want to."

"That's not an apolo—"

"I'll try," Arlene said, wanting to end the argument. "Enjoy the evening with your friend."

"You don't deserve such a treat," Neal told April, his eyes narrowed.

"Thanks for coming," April said, as if Arlene's attendance were a foregone conclusion. With the assurance that she'd gotten her way, the two girls darted away, but not before Arlene heard, "Do you think he's going to kiss her?"

In the hospital, Neal couldn't do very much about the relationship April and Arlene had forged. But now he reconsidered allowing his niece to become more involved with Arlene. Arlene hadn't once mentioned their connection, and it bothered Neal that she avoided talking about Bridget and Ronald. Wouldn't it be better to discuss the ugly past so they could put it behind them? She was hurt, he was sure and she had to deal with it in her own way. Because of that, he decided to follow her lead.

Still, from the time he saw her that evening, he knew the awareness that had escalated during his hospital stay hadn't diminished one bit. He was as affected by her now as he'd been two years ago.

He could never forget that his first responsibility was for April. April's father had been Arlene's husband, and that fact would fester. Maybe they could form a tenuous relationship for a while, but it wouldn't last and he couldn't have April hurt yet again.

The little girl had experienced so much pain in the last couple of years. She was finally adjusting and living the life of a normal ten-year-old. She made the honor roll. She had many friends. She was happy and outgoing. He wanted to keep it that way.

He knew he'd been sending Arlene the wrong signals, but because of April, as much as Neal wanted to explore the kiss he started at the airport, he didn't. Besides, how would it look if he tried to jump her the moment he met her again?

The prolonged anticipation was almost unbearable. How was he going to get through this without taking her into his arms? He looked her over seductively and forced himself to open the door, and he got out the car before he did something foolish.

"Thanks for dinner," Arlene said, as he met up with her beside the car.

"Thanks for joining us." He felt as eager, as erratic, and as unfulfilled as a summer storm. Her enticing scent teased him.

They walked in step up the sidewalk. "April is a wonderful little girl. You've done a magnificent job of raising her," Arlene said, digging into her purse for her keys.

Icy fear clutched Neal's heart, abating some of the heat that had built to boiling temperatures. Yes, she seemed fine but . . . "I worry about her."

"Why? She's outgoing. She certainly isn't shy about voicing her opinions."

Neal chuckled. "That's for sure. April has never been shy. Still, repercussions don't always surface immediately. It's years sometimes before the full ramifications of traumas are brought to life."

"I think you're worrying about nothing. If April was unhappy or troubled, I believe she'd tell you."

"Maybe."

Arlene opened the door to her duplex. "Would you like to come in?"

Neal dug his hands into his pants pocket to keep from touching her while he fought the overwhelming need to have her. "Thank you, but no. It's been a long day."

He stood close to her and her perfume beaconed him to claim her. She lifted her face to encourage him to kiss her soft lips and plant stringing kisses on her neck. He wanted to touch her nipples, which had hardened beneath her thin blouse. He wanted to pull her close to him and press her soft curves against his hard body, but he didn't do any of those things. He fought to keep his hands in his pockets and touch her lips briefly before he left with a hard-on like he hadn't had since he was a teenager.

Disappointed at his brief response, Arlene said good night and went inside, watching Neal march to his car, wondering about the mixed signals. What was it that had suddenly turned him off? The look in his eyes indicated he wanted to kiss her longer. Everything had been fine until they reached her house. Did he think she wanted more than he was willing to give? Did he have a significant other on the base?

No, the way April talked she would surely have mentioned the fact. So that left her. She turned Neal off.

In the distance she heard her answering machine beeping. Shelly, no doubt.

Arlene dropped her purse on the table and peeled off her blazer. Before she could push the play button, the phone rang. She answered it to Shelly's inquisitive voice.

"I know the ten messages on my answering machine are from you. I just got in the house," Arlene said.

"Well, how did it go?"

"We had dinner. That's all." Not even a goodnight kiss, Arlene thought, disappointed, but wouldn't dare say. He'd done more at the airport. After all this time, surely he was dating someone.

"Did he ask you out again? Did you get any time away from the munchkin?"

"No and yes. She went home with a friend."

"And?"

"And nothing. We finished dinner and he took me home. As a matter of fact, I just walked into the house."

"How boring can you get?" A long sigh followed. "And I thought he had such promise. He was definitely good-looking. It's all going to waste. What on earth happened?"

"What did you expect? You wanted him to jump my bones the minute he laid eyes on me?"

"Well, you could do with some excitement. Let's face it, girlfriend. You lead a rather uneventful life."

"In other words, boring. Thanks a lot, friend. I really needed your knowledgeable viewpoint."

"There you go putting words in my mouth. I didn't say boring, did I?"

"You didn't have to. Good night, Shelly. I'll be over tomorrow morning for my car." Arlene placed the receiver gently on the hook. *Boring.* She thought her life was rather . . . well, fulfilled didn't exactly fit the bill. But it wasn't boring either. Between work, friends, and volunteer work, her life was rather full. It would be especially so this summer, since there were so many places she wanted to visit within a train ride of Germany. Most European countries were close enough for long weekend trips.

Shelly didn't know what she was talking about. Her life wasn't boring at all just because she didn't have a significant man in it. "Uneventful, my eye."

The next afternoon, Arlene found herself at the soccer game, with her bottled water and sitting among soccer parents in a comfortable green folding chair she purchased from the PX. April arrived with Neal.

"You came," April said, trotting over to Arlene and hugging her. Arlene was unaccustomed to so much affection, but she returned the girl's warm embrace.

Neal approached at a much slower pace than April's sprint. He set his chair beside Arlene's.

As April joined her teammates, Arlene heard her whisper to someone, "Arlene's my uncle's girlfriend."

Arlene was too embarrassed to look at Neal. She felt the heat seeping into her face, and she had the feeling that Neal was embarrassed himself.

"Out of the mouths of babes," he said and sat in the chair beside Arlene. He wore jeans with a blue polo shirt. His impressive physique stood out in stark relief. Arlene loved the breadth of muscles in his impressive shoulders and the fit of his muscled thighs beneath the jeans. With just the sight of him, her heart started tripping. There still seemed to be a powerful aura about him, even in casual clothing.

"I'm still getting accustomed to sudden fatherhood knocking against a willful ten-year-old."

"I learned before that she had a mind of her own. Must have been born that way. Still, she isn't as willful as you were at that age."

Neal chuckled. "I don't remember any of that. I thought I was a model child," he said tongue in cheek.

"You wish," Arlene said, remembering the opposite.

"My sister often complained about April's antics and I laughed. It's not quite as funny when the shoe's on the other foot."

"You'll get used to it."

"God forbid. I don't know if it's possible."

"Your mother managed."

"With the wool pulled over her eyes. She couldn't handle us and we weren't much help, poor woman."

Arlene wondered if he regretted causing her so much heartache. But he was never bad—never got into real trouble. He was just mischievous and willful.

"How are your mother and father?" Arlene asked.

"They're fine. Mama's still involved in charities and Dad makes speeches about his WWII experience as an African-American officer."

"You must be proud of him."

"I am. How is your dad?"

"I guess he's fine. Since Mom died, things haven't been the same." Arlene waved a hand. "You don't want to hear about my baggage."

"Yes, I would. Why the distance between you?"

"It's like he wants to forget the past. He and Mom had a great marriage, or at least I thought it was good. But soon after she died, he remarried."

"That often happens when the marriage was good. He wanted to recapture the happiness he had with your mother before he gave himself a chance to heal."

"I keep telling myself that. But it shouldn't mean he has to forget the other people in his life. He has new friends. He sold the house and moved to a new city. His new wife is my age, for goodness sake."

Neal captured her hand in his. "Maybe you have to keep trying. Eventually he'll come around."

"I try to keep the lines of communication open."

Other parents and teammates began to arrive. So did the coach.

The team started warm-up sprints and exercises. Neal introduced Arlene to nearby parents while they waited for the game to begin, then he introduced her to Carole's parents, Colonel Henry Jackson. "This is his wife, Mona."

"Lieutenant Colonel Arlene Taft. You're the Arlene April couldn't stop talking about last night. I feel as though I already know you," Mona, a short, compact figure the color of nutmeg said.

"I can imagine," Neal lamented, shaking his head.

Mona chuckled. "She was quite impressed with you because you took such wonderful care of her beloved uncle while he was in the hospital."

"Believe me, she has thanked me effusively," Arlene told her.

"Did she give you the family history while she was at it?" Neal asked.

"She may have left out a few details. Not much. It's a pleasure to meet you, Arlene," Mona said and extended a hand. The other held her folded seat.

Arlene shook the woman's hand. "It's nice to meet you," Arlene said as Mona parked her chair beside Arlene on the side away from Neal. Henry engaged Neal in conversation. Neal towered at least five inches over the ebony-hued man.

"We've known Neal for many years," Mona said. "Henry is career military. They met about ten years ago and have kept in contact every since. I'm glad Neal has met a wonderful person like you. You're good for April, too. The girl rather adores you."

"Perhaps that's because she doesn't know me. We've only met once."

"But you've spoken on the phone numerous times. It's hard to fool children. They know when you're real or trying to fool them. You've made quite an impression. She likes the way you put her nanny in her place."

"Oh, my goodness. I can't believe she told you about that. I didn't put the woman in her place."

"According to April, you were her champion and that meant a lot to her."

A little weary, Arlene shook her head. Children grew attached quickly and she would not want April hurt because she expected more from Neal and her than she could possibly deliver. April didn't need to be part of her life's drama.

The referees and players took their positions on the field and conversation ceased. But Arlene's mind was working. She didn't know if it had been a good idea coming to April's game. The child might put more into Arlene's presence than was warranted.

Neal leaned closer to her, the slight whiff of his aftershave reaching her. "Have you played soccer?"

"A time or two. I don't know the game very well."

"The parents play a scrimmage game against the players in a couple of weeks. Think you're up for it?"

"Hmmm," was Arlene's only reply.

"It's more fun than anything else. Most parents take out the Ben Gay after."

"I see." From the looks of him, Neal wasn't one of the parents needing the Ben Gay.

But her attention was focused on April, who played forward. They were fifteen minutes into the game and neither team had scored. The ball was kicked to April and she dodged opponents, aiming the ball for the goal. An opponent tripped her. Parents complained and while April picked herself up, the ball sailed to the opposite end of the field. Minutes passed before the ball was kicked to April again. This time she dodged opponents, then kicked the ball hard and it flew over the goalkeeper's head into the net.

Parents stood in a roaring cheer as the players whooped and went to the center of the field.

A soccer game with April and Neal implied more than the casual "thank you" relationship she'd envisioned. She was included in their regular family routine.

The kiss she and Neal had shared at the airport hovered on the edge of Arlene's mind and the fact that he left her at the door the night before with only a brief kiss. What was his game? Was he thinking of that long-ago kiss? Did he mention the game because he was working his way into her life on more than a casual basis? Was he taking things slowly—feeling his way? Or was she putting more into this than the situation warranted?

You don't have to think everything through to the Nth degree Arlene, she admonished herself as she settled in to enjoy the rest of the game.

Three

First thing Monday morning, Arlene was called into the adjutant's office. Only an elite group of nurses had been selected to work when the Sheikh of a small Middle Eastern state arrived for lung cancer surgery. Evidently the man had smoked like a chimney since age fourteen.

Since working with Neal, Arlene had been assigned to patients with breathing difficulties on a regular basis. But Middle-Eastern men lived under a different code. She couldn't exactly browbeat him without causing an international incident. And that was exactly what she did to whip her patients into shape.

"Excuse me, Colonel. Are you sure you want me? My methods aren't exactly by the book," Arlene said.

"They want the best and you have the clearance."

Arlene shut up. You didn't refuse an assignment of this magnitude. This was the Army. Once given a duty, you did it—without questions, whether you wanted to or not.

Right now the Sheikh was in surgery, she was told. Some of his wives and sons waited nearby. Recovery would be tedious. He had many enemies, and armed guards were already at his room door as well as posted outside of surgery. Since Arlene was scheduled to tend to him alone, she had very little to do until he was in recovery.

She hated assignments like this. VIP patients were often difficult to handle and complained about everything.

* * *

Byron Jones came to the office door and saluted. His cinnamon-hued face was pulled tight with apprehension. His hat was clenched in one hand.

Thinking about Arlene and some approach to getting in her bed, Neal saluted and motioned the younger man to a chair. He'd let the perfect opportunity slip by Friday night when April spent the night at the Jacksons'. Not that he would do so the first time he'd seen her in nearly two years. True, he'd wanted to. But at least he could have started things rolling with more than a tiny kiss. At least he could have held her in his arms.

Saturday, with April's eager eyes cataloging his every move, he could only kiss Arlene lightly on the lips. When he walked to the car, April's smile nearly ranked with the sun's brilliance. He needed a sitter.

"Sir, you called for me?"

"Yes, I did," Neal said, pulling out the papers and a box containing a medal. "This is a commendation for the exemplary work you do."

The younger man's eyes lit up to rankle with the sun. His whole body relaxed. "Thank you, sir."

"Thank *you*. You deserve it." Byron was an extremely hard worker and had no idea of his own value. It was obvious no one had expounded on his intelligence or encouraged him to seek higher education.

Often in the military, just like in civilian life, there were plenty of slackers. Neal's father had always drilled into him that if he wanted to get somewhere he'd have to work twice as hard to get it. Too many men believed they could work themselves to death for nothing, and thereby never tried.

Even without anyone to encourage Byron, he was different. Neal had noticed that soon after he arrived in Frankfurt and Byron was assigned to his unit.

"Have you thought about furthering your education in communications?" Neal asked.

"Not really, sir. I'm leaving the Army next year, at the end of my tour."

"I see. I'm sorry to hear that. You have plans in place for civilian life?"

"Just to return home. Get a job. I should be able to get something in this line of work."

Neal chose his words carefully. He wanted to lead the young man into other options without turning him off.

"Have you considered a career in the Army?"

"Not really. My neighbor thought it would be good for discipline."

Neal knew that many weren't given a choice. It was the military or jail. Was Sergeant Jones one of them?

"Are you aware that many universities offer courses here? Did you know you can complete your college degree, at least part of it courtesy of Uncle Sam?"

"Yeah," Bryon said, "but I never thought about taking advantage of it."

"There are advantages to getting a degree. Better pay and opportunities if you choose civilian life. An officer if you choose to continue in the military. A degree can offer a better living for you and your family."

Sergeant Jones chuckled as if he didn't believe this could happen for him.

"You don't believe it's possible?"

"No disrespect Colonel, but college isn't for everyone, you know?"

"I'm aware of that. But you're capable. I hate to see talent go to waste. Besides, I think I'm a good judge of your capabilities. Your only limitation is your willingness to take the step."

"I'll think about it, sir. May I go?"

Neal leaned back in his chair. "Before you do, tell me how are things with you and Tina?"

"Better. I looked into those counseling sessions you want me to take."

"Those sessions are a priority."

"Yes, sir."

"You're dismissed, Sergeant. You'll get these at the ceremony in a few days."

Neal watched the young man leave the room. It was unfortunate that the prospects of a college education hadn't been drilled into him as a young man. College and the willingness to work hard could make a big difference between success and failure.

In the States, Neal visited junior and senior high schools to talk to students about the opportunities the military afforded. The military paid for the education of those who entered through the ROTC program, and gave them a monthly stipend. They attended boot camp during the summer. When they completed their education, they entered the military as officers. This assured them higher salaries. And Neal felt that as long as a person had to work anyway, they might as well try to climb as high as possible.

Neal realized that everyone wasn't a type-A personality. Everyone didn't want the rigors that went with top management. But that didn't mean they couldn't aim for a higher salary than they would achieve without becoming an officer or without a higher education. There was plenty of room in the middle road. Sergeant Jones did his job better than some of the officers above him. Why shouldn't he reap the benefits of his talents?

Neal checked the time. It was past noon.

Most of a Ranger's time was spent in training. Mornings were spent on physical training—a three to five mile run. After a short break they went to a training area, where their session lasted until lunchtime. After lunch they spent the afternoon cleaning weapons and making sure radios and other equipment were in top condition.

Since it was lunchtime, he thought about going to the hospital and scoping out the cafeteria to see if Arlene was on her lunch break.

* * *

Arlene picked up the phone, put it down, and picked it up again. Her conversation with Neal kept replaying in her mind. Although Shelly was her best friend and felt like family, her only close family was her father.

Arlene punched in the numbers to her father's office. He was at work this time of day.

"May I speak to Joe Epps please?" she asked when the receptionist answered.

"Who's calling please?"

"Arlene Taft, his daughter." Arlene hoped he wasn't playing the role of young player and didn't want it known that he had a daughter in her thirties.

Seconds later, he came on the line.

"Arlene? How are you?" Apprehension was in his voice.

"I'm fine. We hadn't talked in a long time . . . and I just wondered how things were."

"I'm good."

"How is Monica?"

There was a short pause before he said, "She's okay."

The silence stretched. Distance separated them and Arlene didn't know how to close the gap.

"I've missed you, Dad."

He blew a long, shaky breath. "I've missed you, too, baby girl. I don't know how this happened. Your . . . Casey would be mighty upset the way things turned out."

Casey was Arlene's mother. "I know. She believed in family."

"The most important thing, she'd say."

Tears escaped Arlene's eyes. God, how she missed her mother! Arlene sniffed. Straightened her shoulders. "She was right."

"Yes." Joe cleared his throat. "In your letter, you said you were going to Germany. You sound a long way away."

"I'm near Frankfurt."

"How do you like it there? You never liked staying too far from home. Always liked to plant your roots and stay put."

"I love it. I needed a change."

"I want to see you. When are you coming to the States?"

"Probably the end of the summer. But you could always visit me here. Monica might like the vacation. I have a spare bedroom. I'll even give you my car for transportation."

"We'll see," he said. "Monica doesn't like to travel much."

Arlene didn't want to suggest he come alone. She didn't want to interfere in his marriage. For some reason Monica didn't like her and Arlene didn't want to be a bone of contention between them. But she needed her father. He shouldn't drop out of her life.

"How are you handling everything?" He cleared his throat. "With Ronald gone."

"I've adjusted," she said.

"It's not easy getting over a loved one."

"No. It isn't." Their situations were totally different. She never told him about Ronald's philandering. He only talked to her once after the funeral.

"Maybe we can get together this summer," Arlene said before hanging up. She didn't understand why Monica felt threatened by her. Why would her father marry such a woman?

Arlene realized she hadn't given her father her phone number. He could find her if he wanted to. He could easily get her number through base locator.

The phone call reminded her of Neal. He'd prompted her to take the first step. She thought of Neal's relationship with April. Arlene had been that close to her father once. She wondered if they would ever find their way back.

Neal almost made it through the entire week without calling Arlene. By Friday he couldn't stand the distance any longer. He picked up the phone and dialed. When she answered on the second ring she sounded winded.

"Arlene, April and I would like to invite you to dinner with us."

"I had planned to cook."

"Will it keep?" he asked.

"Why don't the two of you join me at my place?" Arlene amended.

His heart jolted and his pulse pounded at the sound of her sweet voice. The week had crawled by. He hadn't wanted to seem too eager.

"What time?" he asked, not about to turn down a home-cooked meal or give Arlene a chance to renege.

"Six okay?" she asked.

"Just enough time to pick up April after soccer practice. See you at six. What can we bring?"

"Yourselves."

Instead of the relaxing bath in the old claw foot tub, Arlene had anticipated all day, she grabbed her purse and keys and headed to the commissary. Complaints and demands from the Sheikh had absolutely drained her, and she'd thought all day of luxuriating in the water, a dash of bubble bath scenting the brimming tub. Perhaps April and Neal would be a welcome balm, although she should have taken Neal up on his offer for dinner out. After the week she had, she didn't feel like cooking, but she didn't want to go out either.

She smiled when she thought of April. Arlene wished she could bottle her energy and take a spoonful like a tonic.

Neal had a totally different effect on her. Arlene's heart thumped at just the sound of his voice. The kiss they'd explored two years ago still nagged her in the middle of the night. And now that she'd seen him again, her emotions had gotten worse. She didn't understand it.

Neal had been a rotten kid. He'd pluck her hat off her head and toss it into the air just to rile her. He'd picked on her mercilessly. Her mother had been overprotective. Arlene had been an only child, and her mother had insisted on walking her to the bus stop every morning even when she was twelve and thirteen. The street was full of kids and all the other parents didn't worry. And practically every morning Neal would tease her on the bus. There were many fights with her mom before she finally just watched from the window.

Certainly Neal had changed as he matured, and she wondered about his personality before the accident and his sister's death. Perhaps the accident had changed him. Perhaps responsibility for a child had changed him. The Army probably most of all. Still, she shouldn't get caught up in a relationship with him. A great soldier didn't necessarily make a good husband. Husband? How did she get there? Neal reminded her of a player. With him, she could envision herself hurt just as she had been with her husband.

What she needed was a nice stable man. One who didn't like a lot of excitement. In other words, boring. After the whirlwind relationship with her husband, she could use someone boring. As long as he was beside her every night instead of across the world with one of his girlfriends.

Sometimes, Arlene wondered who the woman had been. At the time, she'd been too hurt to even inquire. Did it really matter? By the time she arrived in Colorado to identify her husband's corpse, the woman's body had been retrieved by her family and shipped home, wherever that was.

For weeks, Colonel Mayes had tried to get her on a date. She'd spoken to him just the other day and he'd asked to take her out. She'd tell him she would go out with him tomorrow. There was no sense in letting Neal think that he had exclusive rights with her.

She could handle a friendship with Neal. She couldn't handle a relationship.

At the commissary, Arlene chose pork loin, something quick to prepare. At a deli down the street she purchased apple strudel for desert. Perhaps she'd have time for her bath after all.

As soon as Arlene shoved the loin garnished with apples into the oven, she called Colonel Mayes and accepted his dinner invitation for the following night.

She knew she'd made the correct decision. Arlene remembered Neal's mother. A shy, retiring woman. Neal and his father had absolutely traumatized the woman, which was one of the reasons Bridget had spent so much time with Arlene. With trembling hands, Mrs. Allen had popped pills to soothe her nerves. The bottle soon replaced the pills, and before it was all over, she was taking both.

The kids more or less raised themselves because Neal's father, the General, was away half of the time. When he was home, he'd always barked at his wife for letting the children run wild. And the woman would get even more nervous. Sometimes Arlene wanted to knock that man off his feet because poor Mrs. Taft just wasn't cut out for rambunctious kids or an overbearing husband. Not everyone was. And truth be told, Neal hadn't been the easiest teen to raise.

He certainly hadn't been the best teenage neighbor. He egged her house, flicked her ear if he was in touching distance, even pulled her bra off the clothesline one day and hung it on the mailbox right when everybody was getting off the school bus. When she saw it, she could have died on the spot. She could have killed Neal. She snatched the bra off the mailbox and balled it in her hand, wanting to smash his face with her fist.

Now, Neal seemed to arrange his life around April. Arlene had to give him credit for that much. He seemed a much better parent than either of his parents had been. But Arlene didn't really know him. A week didn't make her an authority on him or April. And his stay in the hospital was an aberration. One could never use someone's reaction when they were ill.

Calling Colonel Mayes had been a good decision. Arlene wasn't ready to settle down yet. She only dated casually. Nothing serious.

By the time Neal and April arrived, Arlene was in a much better frame of mind. She'd soaked in the tub for a short half hour, but it had been enough to revive her. The food was ready and hot.

And Neal looked like a million bucks in his jeans and shirt. April wore jeans with her cute yellow shirt as she burst into the door with cheer and energy.

"Oh, candles!" April said. "Your table is so pretty. I'm so starved."

"April, that's rude."

"I didn't think I had to be on my best behavior. Coach Williams worked us to death and you wouldn't let me eat even a snack before we came here."

"You have to be on your best behavior *everywhere*."

"Sorry."

"Well, you're in luck. Food is ready," Arlene said, tweaking the girl's nose. "After you wash up in the bathroom right there," Arlene said, turning her in the proper direction, "you can help me get the food on the table."

"Oh, great," she perked up after her uncle's chastisement, and ran off.

"You're spoiling her," Neal said.

"I'm not the parent," Arlene told him. But his retribution for her sassy remark was to gather her in his arms for a kiss. He cupped her chin in his hand and rubbed his thumb over her skin.

"I needed an appetizer," he whispered. "I've wanted to kiss you since I first saw you in the commissary."

"Well, what took you so long?" Arlene asked.

"I was crazy," he said. Her short hair exposed the graceful column of her neck. He stroked her there, her soft skin warm against his fingers setting him on fire. He lowered his head and pressed his lips to hers, tasting the sweetness that had only teased him before. He felt her hands on his forearms fingering the hard muscle, and he slipped his arms around her back, pressing her to him.

"Hmmmm."

When the water stopped, they moved apart. April bounded back into the room.

Arlene took a moment to recover from the mind-blowing kiss—a kiss that held even more promise than the one they had shared at the airport. *And it was delicious,* Arlene thought, in a daze as she caught her breath.

She wasn't happy with April's intrusion as the two of them escaped to the kitchen. Arlene dished up the food and they carried it to the table. She lit the candles and turned the lights out. The candles cast a romantic illumination in the room. The feeling of intimacy heightened even with April's chatter as a buffer.

"Arlene, have you thought about getting married?" April asked.

Arlene almost choked on her meat.

"April!" Neal said.

"I just wanted to know," she said in that innocent voice. Arlene learned that April was about as innocent as Neal had been at that age.

"No, I haven't thought about getting married again."

"Again? You were married once?"

"Yes."

"What happened to your husband?"

"That's enough April," Neal said, placing his fork on the table, his lips pinched.

"He died," Arlene said.

"Oh, I'm sorry."

"It happened a while ago."

"My mom and dad died, too."

"I'm sorry. You must miss them," Arlene said.

"A lot."

"My mother died years ago. I miss her too, but the pain

dulls and leaves only the good memories after a while. But you never forget her and you always love her."

"That's true. I'll never forget my mother. I have a picture of her on my dresser. I guess I'm lucky. And I have Uncle Neal. That's why I'm so glad you saved him for me."

"You're lucky to have your uncle. But I didn't save him. The doctors did their part and so did your uncle."

"Did you have an uncle like Uncle Neal?"

"I was married when my mother died. My husband helped me through the pain. And my mother-in-law. She was always kind to me."

"Oh. Maybe Uncle Neal can help you now."

Neal gave up chastising April. It didn't do any good anyway. He was a hero in his niece's eyes. He seemed embarrassed by her adoration, but also saddened that he'd lost his sister and April her mother.

Arlene wondered why April didn't mention her father. Perhaps she was a product of a broken home. It was so sad that so many marriages fell apart these days. Military marriages were even worse than civilian ones. Whether civilian or military, the children suffered most.

But the fact that April had hinted at Arlene and Neal as a couple since they met the week before was disturbing. Didn't Neal date other women? Did April try to fix Neal up with every woman he dated?

"I don't know why April has this fixation with you," Neal said.

"She's nice. And I like her."

"I like you, too," Arlene said, and April smiled.

Oh, no, Arlene thought. What was she going to do about April?

Although Arlene was concerned for April's fixation on her, the evening wasn't uncomfortable.

"This guy at school keeps pestering me," she said at one point.

"Who is he?" Neal asked, ready to take the boy to task.

"I can handle him, Uncle Neal. I was talking to Arlene. Anyway, he wants to date me."

"You're too young to date," Neal said with a finality that seemed to shake April.

Arlene frowned at Neal. "Do you like him?" she asked April.

She peeked at her uncle before she said, "I don't know. I'm still thinking about it. He puts these secret letters in my coat pocket, but I know it's him."

"Is he cute?"

"April," Neal warned.

"This conversation is between the women, Neal," Arlene said pointedly.

Neal clamped his mouth shut.

"He's to die for."

"But you don't like him."

"I'm still trying to decide. What do you think?"

"You have to trust your feelings."

April shrugged with a defeated sigh. "But all my friends have boyfriends."

"You have to decide if you are considering him because you don't want to feel left out or because you really like him."

"Hmmmm," she said, sounding older than her years. "I think it's because I don't want to be left out. But he is nice. I don't want to hurt his feelings."

"Why can't you be friends?"

She shrugged again. "I guess we can be friends."

Arlene watched Neal breathe a sigh of relief.

After the meal, everyone pitched in to clean up. Then they played Scrabble and Monopoly before Arlene served dessert. Neal didn't give one quarter, and he won half the games. That wasn't fair. They all raved over the strudel and ice cream.

"You have a game in the morning, young lady. It's past your bedtime."

"My game isn't until one."

"It's at eight and you need your sleep."

"Are you coming to my game, Arlene?"

"What did we talk about before we came? You can't continue to put Arlene on the spot."

"But . . ."

"No buts," he said with a tone and look April didn't defy.

April looked so forlorn that Arlene relented. "I'll try, okay?"

Light danced in April's eyes. "Okay," she said and hurled herself into Arlene's arms.

Arlene was lost with this girl.

Four

Arlene didn't have the heart to miss April's game since the girl seemed to look forward to it so much. But she didn't wait around afterward because the coach detained the girls for a meeting. Arlene said good-bye to Neal and left to prepare for that evening's date.

So why was she feeling guilty, as if she were cutting out on April and Neal? *And what do we do when we feel out-of-sorts? We go shopping.*

Arlene spent a couple of hours searching for the perfect dress for her date. She selected a teal dress with a perfect V. It also emphasized her hips without fitting too snugly.

She made her way back to her home and took a relaxing soak. Halfway through dressing, Shelly arrived.

"Girl, you're going to give George a heart attack in that dress. He's not used to that much excitement," she said.

"Don't worry. Colonel Mayes is used to women who dress much more flamboyantly."

Shelly gave her a long look. "Are you sure you aren't confusing him with Neal?"

Arlene pursed her lips. "I'm sure."

"Do you want to tell me why you find it impossible to say no to April and why you're going out with the most un-Arlene-like man on the base tonight?" Shelly asked, stretched out on Arlene's chair while Arlene applied makeup.

"What's wrong with Colonel Mayes?"

"You can't even call the man by his first name for

starters. It's almost like he's your teacher or supervisor instead of a date."

"George, okay? Do you like that better?" Arlene asked.

"I don't have to like him."

"I'm glad you remembered that."

"Hum. I can just imagine a kiss. Very dignified, very British-like. Now, a kiss from Neal would rock your safe little world. And that's exactly what you need."

Exasperated, Arlene snapped. "It's just a date, Shelly. I'm not marrying him."

"All right. Let's analyze this."

"Let's not."

"Arlene, you're easygoing. George is easygoing. Contrary to popular opinion, two easygoing people don't necessarily make a perfect match. One of you should have some spirit."

"Thanks for telling me I'm boring. I didn't need a reminder. You already told me once."

"Don't go there." Shelly blew out a long breath. "Now I've hurt your feelings. I never said you were boring. You're my best friend because you're the voice of logic when I'm outrageous. You've never done a spur-of-the-moment thing in your life."

"That's not true."

"On a picnic you pack everything, down to the napkins, plastic forks and cups. While I, on the other hand, would stop by the deli and pick everything up. Even then I'd forget something. My date and I might have to drink from the wine bottle while you'll have perfect crystal glasses."

"And your point is?"

"You plan every last thing to the last detail months in advance. Colonel Mayes is the same way."

"How do you know?" Arlene asked.

Shelly studied her fingernails. "It's just something I heard."

"Which makes Mayes and me a good combination." Arlene raked the comb through her hair. "I do things on the fly all the time. It's part of my job description."

"I'm not talking about work. You're a nurturer. You think things through to the last detail. You're warm. You're giving. A nurse is the perfect profession for you. Mayes is a nice man. But you and Mayes as a couple . . . I just can't picture it."

"Humph." Peeved at her friend's assessment, Arlene donned her earrings and jabbed herself in the process. "You're not quite the stereotype either," she said rubbing the hurting spot. "You're an accountant. They're supposed to be bookish. You're the exact opposite."

"We're not discussing me. Now Neal is a different story. Girl, he watches you like a hawk pinning a juicy rabbit in his sights. Did you know you even light up when he's around? Just talking about him makes you lightheaded."

"You're taking nonsense, Shelly. You only saw us together once. Once doesn't make you an authority." Arlene didn't want to admit the feelings she had for that man.

"In this case, once is enough."

And then the doorbell rang, saving her from having to respond.

"I'll get it," Shelly said. Like a shot, she came off the chair and ran down the hall.

Arlene studied herself in the mirror. Did Neal think she was boring? *Stop it, Arlene. If you listen to Shelly, you'll loose your mind. Before you know it, you'd be just as crazy as your best friend.*

By the time Arlene made it to the living room, Shelly and George were on the couch deep into conversation. The Colonel stood when Arlene entered the room and handed her a bunch of beautiful and fragrant roses.

"You look lovely, Arlene." It wasn't as easy reading him as it was reading Neal. When his eyes respectfully remained on her face, Arlene didn't feel heat spread all over. *Stop comparing,* she admonished herself. Why go out with George if she was going to think about Neal the whole time? Arlene took a deep breath, vowing to forget Neal for one evening and stepped forward.

"Thank you. For the roses, too. They're fabulous." Arlene smelled the blossoms, searched out a vase, and filled it with water. She set the vase on the fireplace mantle and pinned one rose in her hair.

Mayes wore a suit and tie. Arlene was glad she'd taken care with dressing for the occasion.

"Well, have a wonderful time, you two," Shelly said from her position on the couch.

"It was a pleasure meeting you," the Colonel said, extending a hand to Shelly. The shake lingered longer than Arlene thought appropriate, but Shelly extracted her hand and rubbed them together in a nervous gesture.

Shelly was rarely nervous about anything. What was with her?

"I'll call you, Arlene," she said and left. And then Colonel Mayes and Arlene were on their way to the restaurant.

He played a Temptations CD, and she settled back to enjoy the smooth and pleasant ride in his luxury Mercedes. The ride was smoother than her smaller car. George was a very competent driver. He didn't drive like a wannabe racecar driver. She got that feeling sometimes when she rode with Neal.

"I wanted to take you out since the first time I saw you jogging a month ago. I'm glad you agreed."

"So am I," Arlene said. But deep down she knew they weren't connecting. "Where are you from?"

"D.C. actually."

"I've been in D.C. for the last fifteen years."

"I only go back to visit family. I miss the beat of Chocolate City, though."

"So do I. Especially the Eastern Market, the Wharf. The people."

Arlene relaxed as they compared their experiences. Still, it didn't take long for Arlene to realize she and Mayes weren't connecting in a romantic way, Arlene thought as they continued to make small talk. Not the way Arlene and Neal did.

The date wasn't unpleasant. It was comfortable even. Just that the atmosphere wasn't electrically charged. The air wasn't sizzling with emotions.

About a minute after Colonel Mayes left Arlene's house, she was already pulling off her earrings and sliding her feet out of her heels when she heard the doorbell ring. Wondering if Mayes had forgotten something, she opened the door—to Neal.

"Neal?" she asked. She curled her hands around the earring. The sharp point pierced her hand.

"May I come in?" The serious expression on his face made her pause.

"It's . . . late."

"This won't take long." She stepped back as he passed her on his way in.

"Where is April?"

"She's spending the night with the Jacksons again," Neal said.

Well, he was in now. "Have a seat," she said, motioning toward the couch. She felt very uncomfortable. Did he know she'd gone on a date with another man? And why did she feel guilty as if she'd done something wrong?

Arlene sat in the chair across from him, wondering what had brought him over.

"I know we haven't made promises or anything, but I thought we had the beginnings of something special."

"I . . ."

"Look, I was taking things slowly because I wanted to make sure that we were on the same wavelength. That I wasn't rushing you."

"Neal, you can't be sure of what you feel for me. What if your feelings spring from my caring for you in D.C.? We met under unusual circumstances."

"I've thought about that, too, Arlene. And I know what I feel for you hasn't got a thing to do with your profession. I've had other nurses. I didn't fall for them." He scrubbed a hand over his face. "I'm not saying I love you or expect you to love me at this point. Just that I have strong feelings and I want to at least explore what we can be for each other. I don't want to run away from my feelings."

Neal fell silent and the silence stretched between them.

"The way you're running away from yours."

Arlene's back straightened. "Who says I'm running from anything?"

"Wasn't your date with Mayes just that? Running away because you were afraid of what we can have together? Running away before you even gave us a chance?"

"How do you know I went out with him?"

"I have ways . . ."

"Don't start checking up on me or we're through." Arlene fell silent, but for only a few seconds. Then she waved a hand. "Maybe something's here. I don't know. We have a past, too, Neal. Let's not forget that."

"You can't blame me for what I did as a kid."

"I don't. It's just . . . I don't know you anymore."

"Well, get to know me. That's what dating is all about, isn't it?"

"I don't know if I'm ready for you. My husband . . ."

". . . died nearly two years ago. Is it April? Do you have a problem with her?"

"Of course not. How could you think that?"

"Not all women could accept her. And I have to admit I should have gotten a sitter so you and I could spend more time alone."

Arlene studied her hand. "I don't have a problem with April."

He looked relieved. "I'm glad." He stood and approached her, grasped her hands and pulled her out of the seat.

A delicious shudder shook her body. Why didn't she

feel this way with Mayes? Neal's nearness was overwhelming. She felt a ripple of excitement.

"The reason I came tonight was this," he said, drawing her closer and brushing a gentle kiss across her lips. "I was disappointed that you were out with another man." His hand moved gently down the length of her back. Instinctively, her body arched toward him.

"We haven't made any commitments," Arlene whispered in an unfamiliar voice, as if she were trying to convince herself as well as Neal. The mere touch of his hands sent a warming shiver through her.

"Consider this a commitment," he said as he lowered his head and his lips pressed against hers once again, and Arlene's breath caught with the sweetness of Neal's kiss. His arms gathered her close to the hard body she'd often admired. He had regained the strength he'd lost from his stay in the hospital. He began to slip his hands up her arms ever so slowly. Her breasts tingled against his chest.

Her hands caressed the hard contours of his shoulders and back. And his hands glided down her back to her hips, tucking her curves neatly into his own contours. She moaned softly against his lips.

She had lost her mind. Only moments ago she'd completed one date and here she stood with another man, savoring the sweet kisses he strung over her face and mouth.

His hand caressed her breasts. She arched into the touch of his long fingers.

"I've wanted you for nearly two years, Arlene." His eyes brimmed with tenderness and passion.

"I've wanted you, too."

"In the hospital you always smelled sweet. Even though I was in pain, your gentle touch aroused me. I wondered if you knew."

"No, I didn't," she whispered.

"At the airport, I wanted to do more than kiss you . . . even though I couldn't do more at that point."

"Stop . . ."

"I need you, Arlene. I couldn't get you out of my mind. I still can't—as much as I've wanted to."

"Why did you want to?"

"They always say you can't go back, but I only want to go forward."

He was mesmerizing her with his words, and she wanted him as much as the air she breathed. Arlene hadn't made love, hadn't kissed a man beyond a friendly peck since her husband's death, except for Neal. Was she ready for what his kisses promised? For what her body ached for?

"Neal . . ."

Their foreheads touched.

"Not ready yet?"

She closed her eyes against her need, against the need she heard in his voice, felt against his body, saw in his eyes. "Not quite."

He inhaled a long breath. "I can live with that." He gathered her close and kissed her one last time, grounding her hips against his own with a hunger that belied his outward calm. The kiss left her breathless and wanting more. But she couldn't go to bed with him just because she was desperate to have him. She needed so much more.

He stepped back from her, leaned against the door.

Arlene felt stranded in the middle of the floor. She raked a hand through her hair.

"I'm taking April to Switzerland in a few weeks," Neal finally said. "I know I'm arranging yet another trip with her, but soon she'll leave. She's spending the summer with my parents. Then we'll have all the time you can spare together. Come with us, Arlene."

"Let . . . let me think about it."

"We'd both love to have you."

And if she were on a trip with him, she wouldn't be free to go on dates with Colonel Mayes. For a moment, he regarded her, his eyes dark and unfathomable.

"Are things serious between you and Mayes?"

"No," she responded too quickly and then glanced away from him.

"I'm serious about you."

Arlene jerked her head to look at him. "We hardly know each other," she repeated, still debating if planning outings with Neal was a safe decision at this point.

"You've known me more than twenty years."

"No. I've known you two months. What I saw back then, I didn't like."

"I hope you've changed your opinion."

"That remains to be seen."

He approached her. Lifted a hand and captured a curl. Soft hair curled around his finger. "Why haven't you had children, Arlene? You were married for years. You're the warm, nurturing type. The type of woman who would want them."

He was the second person that night to refer to her as nurturing. Arlene hated thinking of the wasted years she spent with her philandering husband. She crossed her arms beneath her breasts and turned her back to him. "My husband didn't want children. I didn't want to expose them to a home where they weren't wanted and loved by both parents. They would have picked up on the fact that Ronald didn't want them and that something would have torn them apart. It was better this way."

"You would have wanted them."

"Yes, I would have, but somehow I didn't think that was enough."

"Your love would have been enough," he said quietly. "Let me know your decision . . . about Switzerland."

She faced him once again. "I will."

Neal turned, opened the door and went out into the tepid night. Arlene heard the motor to the powerful sports car start and saw him leave the curb.

"You're mistaken, Neal. You still have the remnants of that wild boy in you." But did she really want him to change completely?

The pleasant feelings left over from their lovemaking still spiraled through Arlene's body as she made her way to the bedroom and prepared for bed. What on earth was she going to do about her feelings for Neal and April? Was she ready for what both entailed?

The fact that Neal had fallen for Arlene as far back as middle school was news to her, Neal thought. So she thought he picked on her just to be mean. Because of his actions, she'd always snubbed him and tried her best to make him feel unworthy of her time, mainly because he made *her* feel unworthy. Now she realized that that wasn't the impression he was trying to make with his peers. He couldn't have her, so he made sure she knew he was there. Made sure she didn't forget him.

Neal vowed he wouldn't let her get away. Not this time. Certainly not with that loser Mayes. The thought of Mayes cutting in on his woman had acid curling in Neal's stomach. He'd waited too long, wanted too much just to let her slip into another man's arms so easily.

When he'd gotten the call that Arlene had dinner at the restaurant with Mayes, he was floored. One of the guys in his unit was having dinner with his wife there. Had seen him around the base with Arlene and April. Neal thought Arlene and he had an understanding going on. Obviously the situation had been one-sided.

Not for long, Neal vowed.

The following weekend, April talked Arlene into participating in the scrimmage with the parents against the players. Arlene had more fun than she'd had in a very long time. She felt muscles tightening even before she left the field, and once she made it home, she took a long soak in the tub. Then she picked April up to spend the afternoon with her.

"I'm going to get a manicure and pedicure today, April. Would you like to have them done for you?" Arlene asked.

"I'll really be out-of-this-world happy. Carole goes with her mom all the time. But no one's ever taken me."

"Well, now you'll get to go with me."

They had their first disagreement when April wanted to try a vivid red on her nails.

"Does Neal let you wear those colors?" Arlene asked April. It was a special treat for April, but Arlene didn't want to push it.

"I've never worn red before, but that doesn't mean he won't let me."

Arlene was well aware of April's cunning nature. She'd wrapped Neal around her little finger. "Tell you what. This time, let's go with light pink. We'll ask Neal if he'll object to colors and next time you can try it."

April wasn't too keen with that scenario. "But this color is so pretty, Arlene. It'll look soooooo good on me."

"I know, honey. But I'm getting clear. It makes your nails really shiny." Arlene usually got hers painted some shade, but to prevent an argument she thought getting hers done in clear might be a better option.

"This is so much fun," April said, and then giggled as the woman tended to her toes and feet.

"Women need to pamper themselves sometimes, don't you agree?"

April nodded.

Later that afternoon during family time, they went swimming when Neal joined them in the pool. Arlene guessed it didn't make sense to get all wet after the salon visit, but it was all in the name of fun.

Arlene had seen Neal several times, but with most of his body exposed in the swim trunks, his buff body took her breath away. Muscles rippled as he swam in their direction. He had a magnificent body.

"Uncle Neal. I had the best day ever."

Neal's attention on April gave Arlene time to catch her breath.

April regaled Neal with the details of their salon visit. He complimented her toenails and fingernails, although he couldn't see much of a difference.

While April carried on about the salon visit, Neal realized how much she missed by not having a mother to do the women kinds of things with her. He was okay with sports and most school activities, but he readily admitted he was out of his element in nail salons.

"Carole and Monica are here. Can I swim with them, Uncle Neal? I have to show them my nails."

"Okay," he said and watched her climb out of the pool to join her friends.

He swam close to Arlene. "Have I told you how lovely you look in that bathing suit?" he said.

"This old thing?"

"It might be a one piece, but my imagination has been spinning all kinds of wicked things I'd like to do to you." His eyes slowly scanned her body.

Arlene blushed. The scars from his surgery had narrowed to faint lines, but they didn't detract from his attractive body.

"Thanks for keeping April today," he said, humor gone. "It meant so much to her."

"She's a joy."

"I can share some things with her. But not the special things she can only share with another woman."

Arlene touched his brow. "You worry a lot, but you're doing a fantastic job with her. Really you are. You haven't a thing to worry about."

He watched April play in the pool with her friends and only hoped he was.

"Neal?"

He focused on Arlene. "Yes?"

"I remember the last year I was in Dallas, you stopped

picking on me. We barely interacted at all. I've always wondered about the change."

Neal inhaled sharply. "I knew I'd lost you. That was my first year at Buckley Academy and I was starting to grow up, I guess. I couldn't pull those stupid pranks any more."

"Why didn't you tell me what you felt?"

"Would you have listened?" he shot back.

Arlene regarded him as she thought back to that time. She'd absolutely hated Neal. If he'd approached her, she would have thought he was playing another game. She would have wondered when the jack-in-the-box would spring again.

"No," she finally said.

"Didn't think so."

Arlene was taking a restroom break before she left work for home on Monday. While she washed her hands at the sink she noticed a faint bruise on one of the volunteer's cheeks. She looked too young to be wearing a wedding band on her ring finger.

Tina was printed on her nametag and she fingered her cheek as she gazed in the mirror.

"That's some bruise," Arlene said.

Tina started. "It's nothing. I mistakenly hit myself with my hairbrush," she said quickly and dropped her hand.

I just bet you did, Arlene thought. She wiped her hand on a paper towel and extended her hand. "Arlene Taft."

"Tina Jones. Nice to meet you."

"I don't see you around here often."

"I just volunteer a half day a week. My girlfriend baby-sits for me when I'm here."

"That's a nice arrangement."

"I like getting out and doing something other than changing diapers. I love my baby, though. I wouldn't take nothing for her."

"I bet she's precious."

"She is. Her name is Makayla."

Arlene dug into her purse for a card. Finding it, she wrote her home number on it and handed it to Tina. "If you ever need to talk to someone, call me. There is help for abused women."

Tina snatched her hand from the card. "I'm not one of those women. Nobody abuses me."

"I'm not saying you are. Just that if you need someone to talk to, I'm available."

Slowly, the young woman reached for the card, scanned it and tucked it into her pocket. "Thanks," she said and left the room.

Arlene's heart went out to Tina. She couldn't be long out of high school, barely old enough to have a baby. Arlene would bet her last dollar Tina's husband was abusing her. She hoped Tina would feel comfortable enough to talk to her before her husband seriously injured her.

April sat beside Arlene on the train ride to Switzerland. The ride took several hours, but the view along the way was breathtaking.

April had studied about the Alps in school that fall and she had become fixated on visiting the village where the mountains wrapped around them.

Neal wanted her to see all the surrounding countries, even parts of Africa, during their tour in Germany. Travel was one of the benefits he loved about his military career. He had the opportunity to see places he never would have as a civilian. The added benefit was exposing April to other cultures. She didn't have to choose the military for a career, but at least she would make her own opinions, gain exposure about the world she otherwise wouldn't possess.

"Can I get you ladies anything?" Neal asked from across the way. The train was packed with tourists. It was Memorial Day weekend and both he and Arlene had Monday off.

"We have plenty of drinks and food in my backpack if you're thirsty," Arlene said, reaching for the heavy bag she'd packed to the gills.

Neal hadn't thought about lugging food on the train, but he was glad that Arlene had thought of it.

"Maybe later," he said.

"I'm thirsty now," April said.

He stifled a groan. Extra trips to the bathroom. It didn't take him long to learn what excess drinking did to a child's bladder. At least there were bathrooms on trains, unlike car trips.

He looked across the aisle and studied Arlene. He couldn't help comparing her to his ex.

Neal's ex had been wild and exciting, just like him, he'd thought at the time. He discovered wild and exciting wasn't all it was cracked up to be. Their relationship hadn't worked. She was on an eternal high that even he couldn't keep up with. She wasn't made for children, but she was cut out for wild parties and excitement that never ended. She seemed never to mature; she seemed to maintain a twentysomething mentality forever.

He hadn't seen Natasha since she handed him the separation papers. And he wasn't curious about what she was up to. That was the sad part about their relationship. They had been married for five years and he just didn't care.

Marriage was an institution he took seriously. The next time around he wanted someone more stable, more grounded.

More like Arlene.

Arlene occupied the aisle seat and April the window. Arlene pointed something out to April and handed her a snack of cheese and crackers and a half apple from a sandwich bag.

When April got hungry he would have just gone to the dining car and purchased them a meal. Not Arlene. She thought of the details in advance.

Her thoughtfulness was one of the things that intrigued

him from the very beginning, Neal thought, as he settled more comfortably in his seat and nodded off.

The intimacy they shared a week ago had kept him tossing and turning in bed for hours at night. Yet again, they were on an outing with April. He felt he was taking advantage of Arlene by having April around all the time. He'd have to employ the sitter more when they returned to Germany, but Neal wanted the pair to forge a relationship. He wanted the problems to present themselves now instead of later.

Switzerland was one of Europe's richest, best-organized and most expensive countries. Two-thirds of the population spoke German, but very different from Germany. The Swiss interpretation had a singsong quality. Most Swiss also spoke English.

April was out-of-this-world excited when the train pulled into the station right on time. The station and streets were clean if teaming with people. There was only a touch of light left—enough to see the shadows of the sharp ragged peaks of the Swiss Alps.

In no time they were hailing a taxi to a quaint bed-and-breakfast where Neal had reserved the three bedrooms. Neal had reserved all the bedrooms for the weekend.

In the foyer, a warm, hearty-looking couple greeted them. The man was tall and lean. The woman was lean as well and looked very strong. A pot of tea was sitting on a table.

"As soon as you settle in, come downstairs and have tea with us," the proprietor said.

"I can't wait," April said. "Forget dinner."

Neal and the man carried the suitcases upstairs. He and Arlene made quick work of unpacking. Although they shared the one bathroom, a sink was in Arlene's room and she took a birdbath before she met the other two in the hallway. She kept her home clean, but the sparkling B&B put her cleaning skills to shame.

The proprietors offered rich chocolates and cheese, but Neal told them they were having dinner first. The woman offered to leave the fare out for them. Arlene and Neal thanked the couple and soon left.

Outside, full night had fallen. The lights illuminated the streets of tourists searching out restaurants.

"Have you been here before?" Neal asked.

"No," Arlene said. "This is my first European tour."

"How long have you been in the service?"

"Fifteen years."

"How on earth did you escape a German tour?"

"I spent most of my time in the D.C. area." She didn't tell him that after she discovered her husband's infidelity, she'd asked for a tour overseas. She wanted something new. Not the same memories of how she'd waited for years for her husband at that lonely spot in D.C. only to discover he was vacationing with another woman. But she wouldn't let Ronald's infidelity dampen her mood.

"And you? I take it this isn't your first tour."

"No. I've been here a couple of times. I stay in that B&B each time. They're wonderful people and it's ideally located."

Neal took them to a tiny restaurant off the beaten path where the food was delicious.

"Not even Carole has been here and she's been everywhere." April rolled her eyes in her expressive manner that had them all laughing. "She told me about the restaurants her dad took her to and it wasn't nearly as nice as this," April said.

"I'm glad you approve," Neal replied.

They browsed the shops before they made their way back to the B&B.

"Chocolates!" April moaned as if she were in heaven.

"Only one," Neal admonished.

"I can't eat just one chocolate, Uncle Neal. These are to die for."

"Well *you're* going to eat just one," Neal told her as he tried to make the impossible decision of selecting just one for himself.

"This is a vacation." April's hand hovered over the bowl. Since she could get only one, she had a difficult time picking it out.

Neal knew how delicious the Swiss chocolates were. They *were* on vacation, after all. "Okay," he relented. "All right. Maybe two."

"You're the greatest uncle in the world."

Neal chuckled. "Especially when you get your way."

April went about choosing hers, then sat on the couch and enjoyed her treat with Arlene and Neal.

Neal tried the cheese. The area was known for its many varieties.

April yawned.

"Okay, time for bed."

"Do I have to?" she asked.

"You've got a full weekend planned. You don't want to be too tired to enjoy it."

April made her way upstairs.

"I finally have you to myself," Neal said, tugging Arlene in his arms.

Arlene gave him an impish grin. "Now that you have me, what are you going to do with me?"

"That's a loaded question." He lowered his head toward hers. "Let's start with this," he whispered as his lips touched hers.

Saturday morning they prepared to ski.

"Are you a strong skier, Arlene?" Neal asked. "It's a good time to ask you, isn't it?"

"I'll stick to the bunny slopes. My skiing experience is two church trips four years apart."

"You'll learn in no time," April said. "Uncle Neal and I skied practically every weekend in Germany."

"You'll be ready for the more advanced slopes. I won't hold you back. I signed up for one of the classes."

"Let Uncle Neal teach you. He's good," April said.

"I'm sure he is. But if he's teaching me, he can't ski with you. Have fun."

"Be back soon," Neal said. He kissed Arlene, leaving her mouth burning with fire before he left with April. It was enough to start a heat wave in her body before the cold from the snow kicked in and the tutor began the class.

Arlene went through her training. She definitely would never be a world-class skier, but it was fun. And as long as she kept moving, the cold didn't take over.

A couple of hours later Neal and April returned with cold noses.

"It was great!" April told her.

"Go in and get some hot chocolate," Neal told April, handing her some money. When the girl left, Neal circled Arlene's waist from behind.

"Have a good lesson?" he asked.

"I did," she said and smiled. As his hand caressed her middle, she was carried away by her own response; she failed to notice the movement of his hand until she felt the shock of ice against her warm stomach. She squealed. "You rat!"

He dropped the snowball on the ground, then pulled off his glove and caressed the cold spot with his warm hand. She felt his uneven breathing on her cheek as he held her close.

"Better?" he whispered with amusement, his breath hot against her ear.

"Much," Arlene responded in a breathless sigh.

April came out carrying a carton holding the drinks. "I got chocolate for everyone."

At last, reluctantly, they parted a few inches. "Perfect," Neal said, reaching for the carton.

"Thank you, April. You're so thoughtful. I was freezing."

As Arlene sipped her drink, she enjoyed the moment with April and Neal, and she realized it was getting more difficult to resist his charms. She had never been able to resist April.

Arlene really liked April, but if she hadn't been there, those beds would have been burning up with passion. As they took scenic train routes, toured glaciers and medieval castles, Arlene could only think of what was inevitable between Neal and her.

Five

Since Arlene arrived at the base, time had flown by, Neal thought. Right now a lump clogged his throat. Arlene and Neal were at Frankfurt's airport waiting for April to board the plane to Texas. He thought of her as his baby now and he was reacting as any natural parent would.

Mrs. Jackson and Carole were visiting family there and promised to drop April off at Neal's parents' home. He ruffled her hair and she complained. He was going to miss the spirited sprite.

Unexpectedly, she threw her arms around Neal's waist. "I'm missing you already, Uncle Neal and I'm still here. I don't understand what's wrong with me."

Neal cleared his throat. He didn't realize parting would be this difficult. "I'm missing you, too, sweetheart. So I've got the same bug you have."

Tears hung in her eyes, trying not to spill over. Abruptly she left him and went to Arlene and hugged her, too. April was so affectionate, Neal thought for the thousandth time. She could be so easily hurt and he was so far away from her that he wouldn't be near if she need him.

"I love you, Arlene."

"Oh, honey." Arlene's expression revealed how startled she was by the declaration. It took a moment for her to get her bearings. The tears Neal couldn't shed streamed down Arlene's cheeks. "I think you are a very special little girl. I love you, too."

"Take care of Uncle Neal for me, okay? Please don't let him get hurt."

Arlene hazarded a brief glance at Neal and brushed a hand across her cheeks. "I'll do my best," she said, her throat hoarse.

And then with the sandwiches, books and goodies Arlene had packed for her safely tucked away in her backpack, April dashed away to stand in line with the Jacksons. Carole engaged her in conversation but April kept glancing back at Neal and Arlene as if they could either postpone the trip or join her. Finally, she waved and faced the terminal.

When April boarded the plane, Neal and Arlene stood like statues looking at the plane until it taxied down the runway and flew out of sight.

Neither of them had much to say as they made their way to the car. On the drive back to town, the air was thick with the loss of April's vivacious spirit.

"Well," Arlene said in the strained silence. "We have to say something."

Neal chuckled. "I've been waiting for the time when I could get you alone and . . ."

"I know. It's a catch twenty-two, isn't it?"

He nodded. "As much as I need time with you, I don't want her gone."

Arlene looked at him in horror. "You didn't send her way because of me, did you?"

He shook his head. "My parents and I agreed that she would spend summers with them. They miss Bridget. They need to spend time with April. Lord knows how they'll keep up with her. But she's older now and my dad's health is a little better than it was two years ago. She'll only be in Texas for a couple of months." But those two months would pass so slowly they were going to feel like years.

Arlene nodded. The arrangement sounded reasonable.

"I picked up steaks at the commissary yesterday. I put them in a marinade before we left. They should be perfect now," Arlene said. "I could grill them. Fix baked potato and salad to go with them. I know it's a simple, boring dish. Nothing exciting, but I'm not in an exciting mood just now." Boring came to Arlene's mind. Boring is what Shelly called her. Boring. Arlene hated that word. She should have planned something more exciting like Tex-Mex or a German dish.

"Sounds good. I'll help."

Arlene relaxed. Maybe everyone didn't crave rip-roaring excitement. Her husband had been exciting, especially to another woman. But Arlene didn't relax completely. She remembered Neal's wild nature. A person's underlying personality didn't change with age. Some of that energy must be hidden away in him somewhere or channeled elsewhere. And she couldn't help but wonder if one day he would tire of boring old Arlene.

But Arlene didn't know how to be other than who she was. Perhaps her unassuming nature had been the reason her ex had sought pleasure elsewhere. Lord knows, their lovemaking hadn't lit up the sky. It wasn't even close to the most exciting thing that ever happened to her. Even she had craved more. It was obvious he had as well and acted on it. She wondered if Ronald had raised the roof for this other woman.

This was getting depressing. Arlene wished she hadn't issued the invitation for dinner. She wouldn't be able to keep Neal any more than she'd been able to curb her dead husband's philandering nature. And going to bed would be an even bigger problem. After one experience with her, he'd head for more exciting pastures. It would be the end of their pleasurable time together.

Arlene glanced at Neal as he navigated toward her house. The optimism she'd felt earlier quickly dissipated.

Neal knew something was bothering Arlene. He'd watched her for a long time now, and he wasn't about to leave tonight with a chaste little kiss. They'd spent enough time together for her to get to know him as a man in place of the annoying kid from years back.

They'd eaten the delicious dinner, washed the dishes and tidied up the place, and had even taken a short walk to the park across the street and looked at the flowers.

But since April left, something had come over Arlene. And he was going to get to the bottom of it.

When he shut the door, Neal lifted a hand, and caressed Arlene's neck. "What is it?" he asked. "You've been preoccupied all afternoon."

She pasted a smile on her face, as if he didn't know better. "Nothing's wrong."

Exasperated, but also filled with a burning need to hold her, he dipped his head and kissed her. Although she kissed him back, he could tell her heart wasn't in it.

He lifted his lips from her and stroked her face. "I must be losing my touch."

"It's not you."

"Then what is it?"

"It's just that I don't want to set myself up for something I can't live up to."

Puzzled, Neal shook his head, but didn't let her go. "I'm not getting this."

Arlene sighed, stepped back from him, his arms falling slowly to his side. She went to the window. "Let's face it, Neal. I'm not the most exciting woman you've ever been with. I'm just steady, reliable old Arlene. You can always count on her. Even my name is boring."

Neal couldn't believe his ears. "You aren't boring, Arlene."

Arlene's chuckle held no humor. "I couldn't even keep my own husband excited enough to hold on to him. He had affairs behind my back. I know you, Neal, and you wouldn't be satisfied with me either. Here we're starting this relationship and you know as well as I do that in a few months you'll be gone."

"I can't believe the self-assured woman who browbeat me in the hospital has these doubts." Her husband had been an asshole. "You're a wonderful woman."

"I know. Wonderful and reliable. Like I said, boring Arlene."

He approached her, placed his hands on her shoulders. "Not to me, you're not. There's more to you than your work and your reliability. You're lovely. You're energetic. You're everything I want. And damn it, I've wanted to get you into bed for just about forever. Even plotted strategies for getting you there."

"Well, let me tell you, sex isn't so great with me either. My husband could tell you that."

"Just because he was inept hasn't a thing to do with you, Arlene. It takes two people to make a relationship work." Neal rubbed her shoulders and turned her into his arms. "You excite me more than I could ever tell you," he said and kissed her with an urgency he'd only dreamed of.

She was reluctant and stiff at first but then slowly warmed into his embrace. He caressed her face with his fingertips, kissed her neck. The heat of his gaze sent liquid fire straight through her.

"You've driven me crazy forever," Neal whispered against her cheek. "How could you think for a moment you were anything but exciting?" he said, as he smothered her lips with a series of slow, shivery kisses, urging her to believe his words.

Arlene didn't know if she believed him or not, but with his soul-shattering kisses, his hypnotizing voice, she forgot all her misgivings through her body. Neal caressed her body in a heated fashion. She was soon a quivering mass of sensations when he guided her down on the rug in front of the fireplace.

His hands slipped inside her plain white panties. She panicked. Why hadn't she worn something more exciting?

"Relax," he said.

His breathing accelerated and her heart quickened and

she forgot about the panties as he dragged them down her legs and opened her blouse.

"You're sweet all over," he said, slipping her bra strap down her arms and gazing at her breasts. His lips touched her nipple with tantalizing possessiveness. Her nipples hardened from his touch. He captured the second dark bud in his mouth. Arlene could barely stand the currents of desire flowing through her. She thought her body would melt into a puddle.

Wanting to get closer to him, she dragged his shirt over his head and felt the muscles she'd only dreamed of since they swam in the pool.

"Touch me, sweetheart. I love touching you. I love your touch."

Arlene unsnapped and unzipped his pants and lifted the boldness of him into her hand. The muscles of his stomach contracted on his deep groan. She felt her breasts crush against the hardness of his chest—skin to skin, they were as one.

"I'm on fire, baby," he said and leaned more into her. They kissed frantically.

As he kissed her, his fingers entered her, stroking back and forth, then he caressed her intimately, slow, gentle strokes that turned her world on an axis until she screamed from the force of her climax. Before the last shudder left her body, he started to enter her.

"Ah . . . protection . . ." Arlene barely had the presence of mind to remember.

"What . . . oh." Neal snatched some things from his pockets, change spilling on the floor. Then he located a prophylactic, tore open the package with his teeth. She glided it on him and then he entered Arlene. Their pleasure was pure and explosive. She couldn't seem to get enough of him as they rocked to a beat as old as time itself.

As they moved together, Arlene felt she was truly making love for the very first time. And she was shocked when the pleasure again built to a crescendo. For the first time, she experienced an orgasm during lovemaking. She thought for a moment her world had somersaulted. She clutched Neal tightly to her, his arms around her.

Afterwards, Neal grabbed pillows from the couch and held her in his arms, her head resting on his shoulder. He kissed her tenderly and pulled her close. She turned her head and kissed his neck. He smiled down at her. Arlene felt different somehow, that something cataclysmic had occurred and she didn't know where it would eventually carry her.

"Well, we've proven you're an exciting woman, Ms. Taft. Any more excitement and I would have exploded." They had made the trip to her bedroom. He stroked her hip. They were luxuriating in the aftermath of their second time at intimacy. Twice wasn't enough for Neal. He wanted to spend the night planted in her body. It was a matter of boldly executing the right approach.

On the living room carpet had been wonderful, but in the bedroom he could settle in for the night.

"Ronald wasn't worth your worry, Arlene. It was his deficiencies that were the problem, not you," Neal told her much later. "He should have left the other women alone to concentrate on pleasing you."

"You talk as if you knew him."

"I didn't."

"He died with a woman he was having an affair with. I don't even know her name. I didn't even know he had taken leave. I thought he was on an assignment."

"You what?" Neal stiffened with shock. Only his intense training in controlling his emotions held him in check. He thought she knew April was her husband's child.

"Stupid, huh? I should have known something was going on. He was always traveling on assignments. Since he traveled, we thought it best that I stay in Washington. At least once a month he came to the Pentagon. Instead of working he was screwing some other woman."

Neal stroked her arm to keep from responding.

She turned her head toward him and smiled up at him. "I don't want to talk about him anymore. I want a snack. You have worn me out."

As Arlene and Neal put a snack together, Neal knew he had to tell her the truth. But how, knowing that a battle as fierce as any battle the Army Airborne Rangers had fought would ensue?

But he was honor bound to tell her the truth. It was only fair. As an officer—especially as part of special ops—he was expected to be above normal men. Not everyone believed it, but he believed in honor and integrity and moral fortitude.

"I have some new tapes a friend sent me from home," Arlene said.

Turning out the kitchen light, she settled on the couch with Neal. She was a little reserved, a little unsure after their intimacy. But intimacy was far from Neal's mind right now.

"Would you like to see one?"

"Arlene, we need to talk," he said, dreading what was to come.

He sat on the sofa table and held both her hands in his. They were so close; he clasped her legs between his thighs.

"What is it?" she asked around a frown. "You don't want to see a movie?"

"It's not about the movie."

"You . . ."

"Arlene. I don't know how to tell you this, or how you'll take it, or how it will affect our relationship, but I thought you knew. I would never have gone to bed with you without telling you the truth first. But I can't regret what we shared together. And I want more with you. I care for you—a lot."

"You're alarming me."

"April is your husband's child. My sister—Bridget and Ronald were having an affair. Bridget died with Ronald in Colorado."

Arlene snatched her hands from his and hopped off the couch, shoving his leg out of her way. She didn't know where to go. She backed away from him as if he were something that slithered on his belly.

"You knew this all along?"

Neal's lips were stiff as he said, "Since their deaths, yes," knowing very well that he was losing the best thing that had ever happened to him.

"And you conveniently waited until *after* we went to bed to tell me?" Fury almost choked her.

"I didn't know you were unaware until our conversation a few minutes ago."

They stood as combatants across an invisible battle line as her curt voice lashed out at him.

"You could have mentioned it at any time. Like in the hospital. Or two months ago when we met again. Whether you thought I knew or not you could have broached the subject." She threw the words at him like stones and shook her head. "God, I was such a fool." The chuckle that emerged from her throat was dry and sarcastic. "For a second time. Your timing is damn convenient, Colonel."

"I'm not playing games with you. I'm trying to be as honest as I can."

"Pardon me if I don't believe you."

His voice was cold and measured when he responded. "Never question my integrity, Arlene. You can question a lot of things about me, but not that. We need to talk more about this. Details."

"Leave."

"Arlene . . ."

"Get out!" She marched to the door and opened it, stood beside it as unyielding as a statue.

Neal approached her. Stood in front of her for seconds. Arlene glared at him with all her unleashed fury.

"If it would make you feel better, hit me. You can't hit him. You can't hit Bridget. April is the innocent in all this—and you. I can't leave you like this."

"Get out."

He stood still, looking deep into her eyes. "This isn't the end of this conversation or us," he finally said and marched out the door.

Arlene slammed the door shut. She was so angry she shook. For some reason his betrayal seemed worse than Ronald's. Standing on rubbery legs, she made her way to the couch and fell into the cushions. She felt paralyzed with anger—with pain—especially with grief.

Her husband denied her the baby she'd wanted desperately. Refused to pursue an assignment that would keep him in one place at least for three-year periods—only to have a baby by another woman.

She wished he were standing before her so she could knock him into tomorrow.

Boring. The woman who had stirred Neal's blood more than any woman ever had thought she was boring. And what did he do? He took her to bed the moment April left town. After getting thrown out, Neal knew Arlene thought he was every bit the uncaring, uncouth boy of thirteen. And deceitful. About as bad as her husband had been.

He realized now that her husband had been playing both Arlene and his sister. Obviously the man had never asked her for a divorce. Arlene was handy for him at home, and his sister had been his excitement away from home. Just another man who could never be satisfied with one woman and screwed up any chance he might have had with her.

April lost more than anyone in this drama. She was left with neither parent.

Arlene was left thinking she was a boring woman who couldn't satisfy her husband—a man who didn't deserve satisfaction as far as Neal was concerned.

Two weeks had passed since Neal had gotten himself thrown out of Arlene's home. That rankled him. Nobody—but nobody threw him out. His team had just returned from an assignment in the Middle East. They had shipped out the day after his fight with Arlene.

Usually most of a Ranger's time was spent in training and preparation. Lately with happenings all over the globe, they went out on more missions than usual.

Neal was bone tired. He wanted three things: a bath, a stiff drink, and ten hours of uninterrupted sleep. And he wanted Arlene, but he couldn't have her.

The plane landed. First they unloaded the gear. He had called in his report on his way back.

He smiled and checked his watch. There was a fifth thing. He'd call April. She must have left about fifty messages by now. She also knew Arlene's number. He wondered if she had called her and what Arlene had said to the child. Arlene was mature enough not to say anything out of line, but still . . . Jesus. What a mess.

Neal finally headed home. He'd call April after he chilled out. He wasn't fit to be around anyone right now. He took his bottle of bourbon and a shot glass upstairs and set both on the nightstand. He pulled off his grungy clothing and left them in a pile on the floor. Then he stepped under the warm, welcoming shower spray. The water sluicing down on him felt like a stream from heaven.

Neal had just stepped out of the shower when he got a call from Byron.

"I'm in trouble, Colonel. Tina and I got into it again."

Neal inhaled a deep breath, looking at the bourbon on his table and the empty glass he had yet to fill.

"What happened? Did you hit her?"

"Not exactly."

"Then exactly what?" Neal snapped. He didn't need this tonight.

"I smacked her, okay? I didn't use my fist. She's really yanking my chain with her gambling. And she called some woman she's been talking to at the hospital where she does some volunteer work. They might arrest me."

"I'll be right over."

Pulling himself together, Neal dressed as quickly as possible and made the short trip to Byron's place.

"What is Arlene's car doing here?" he wondered as he parked behind her and watched her go into the house. He cut the motor and left the car, walking in no more than a few seconds after her.

Byron and Tina were paired off on opposite sides of the room. Arlene stood in the center of things.

"What are you doing here?" she asked Neal.

"I called him," Byron said. "If Tina can call in support, so can I."

"What's going on?" Neal asked.

"Things got a little out of hand," Tina said. "Byron started shouting and stuff and I got scared."

"She lost the damn money I gave her for bills on gambling. Look in the damn fridge. The baby doesn't have any milk. She shoulda been buying groceries, but she goes to the slot machines instead."

"I was trying to *make* some money," Tina said, holding an ice pack to her cheek.

"Let me see your face," Neal said.

"I've already looked. She's okay," Arlene said.

Neal went to Tina and looked for himself. Satisfied, he pressed the ice back to her face.

"I don't really need it any more," she said. "It's not like he punched me, or anything."

"He's got no business hitting you, period," Arlene said, throwing daggers at Byron.

"She had no business throwing away our money. And you have no business telling other people about our business," Byron said to Tina.

"Have you started counseling yet?" Neal asked Byron.

"My first session is tomorrow, sir."

"I still think you should call . . ." Arlene started.

"Don't miss it," Neal said.

"I said I'd go and I will."

"In the meantime, do you have enough money for food?" Neal asked.

"I got a little put by for a rainy day. I got it covered," Byron assured him.

"What am I going to do with you two?" Neal asked.

Tina's eyes darted to Neal. "I didn't mean to spend the money. If he'd let me work, I'd have my own to spend."

"Then who'd keep the baby? I can support my family," Byron said.

"You really need to leave the house until you get your temper under control," Arlene said.

"I don't want him to leave me," Tina said, fear in her voice.

"I'm not going anywhere. This is our home," Byron said, approaching Tina and pulling her into his arms.

"Byron, you're putting your career in danger by hitting on Tina. This can damage your record if the MP's are called. You've got to control yourself if you continue to stay here. Arlene, maybe you can show Tina something about money management."

"What? That isn't the point." She pointed an imperious finger at Byron. "His abuse . . ."

"We'll talk about it. I'll meet you at your house," Neal demanded.

"Neal, I totally disagree with how you're handling this. If he actually *does* go to counseling, they need to be separated until he has his anger under control," Arlene insisted. "He's like a keg of dynamite."

"I don't want him to leave," Tina said. "Don't make him leave," she said, a clear reminder of her youth and her attachment to Byron.

Neal grasped Arlene's elbow in his hand. "We'll discuss this at your place."

Arlene wavered, then said, "Call me if you need me, Tina. You have both my home and work numbers."

"I will. Thanks for coming."

"Thanks, Colonel," Byron said.

Neal and Arlene left. Once they were near their cars, Arlene rounded on Neal.

"Not now," he said.

Stiff as a board, Arlene opened her door. Neal went to his car. He gathered his thoughts as he followed her home over the darkened streets.

"We haven't done Tina any favors by leaving her in that house with Byron," Arlene said as soon as Neal stepped into the foyer.

"Do you think I could get a hello or how are you?"

"You're here for Tina's benefit, not because of you and me."

"Correction. We're here for Tina *and* Byron. They're a couple. They aren't mutually exclusive," Neal said.

"Well, Tina isn't popping Byron upside the head, is she? He needs to be out of that house."

"Tina doesn't want him to leave," Neal retorted. "That's why she usually calls me when she's frightened."

"Abused women often stay with the abuser out of fear and loss of self-esteem. Byron still needs to be out of that house. It's a dangerous environment for Tina. These things don't get better overnight, Neal. You know that. The situation usually worsens before it gets better."

"I know. But when I suggested a separation before, Tina went ballistic. She doesn't want to be away from him."

"She's too close to be objective. You are his commanding officer. Why haven't you taken appropriate action against him?"

"Arlene, neither of them have any family support. They love each other. All they have is each other. Without a doubt, he cannot continue to hit her, and given a chance, they will get through this. Byron has potential, he can go far in his career. This is not only his chance, but their chance as a family to create a promising future."

"*If* he decides to attend the sessions, that is," Arlene said.

"He will."

"How do you know that?"

"Because I am his commanding officer, and I will take mandated action against him. And because he really loves Tina and he doesn't want to risk losing her."

Arlene scoffed. "What does he have to worry about? Tina doesn't have enough self-confidence to leave him."

Neal raked his hands over his head. "They both have problems. It'll probably be a good idea to send Tina to the same counselor Byron is seeing. But in the meantime, I would appreciate it if you would be her mentor."

"I don't have a problem with mentoring her."

"And Arlene, make sure you aren't subconsciously passing your own bias against me onto Tina and Byron."

"My bias!"

"Your unwillingness to deal with your husband, April, me and you."

"Let's get one point clear. There is no you and me."

"Still not ready to deal with it?"

"Oh, I'm dealing with it."

"How?"

"Ronald's dead. Bridget's dead. I can't do a thing about their affair."

"But you have to deal with the betrayal mentally. We need to talk about it, Arlene."

"When you're half drunk?"

He advanced toward her. "Have you smelled liquor on my breath?"

"Give me a break. It's only nine, and your eyes are bloodshot."

"I just returned to base a couple of hours ago," he said. "For the last two weeks I've been working my ass off far from the safety of this base."

Arlene rubbed her forehead. "I forgot you were away. April called a couple of times concerned about you."

"She usually calls me every other day. If she can't reach me, she knows I'm away. What did you and April talk about?"

"Certainly not about her father. You don't have to worry that I'll say something inappropriate to her."

"I don't think you're stupid, Arlene."

She hesitated, torn by conflicting emotions. "She was concerned about you."

"You mind if I sit?"

"Be my guest. Can I get you something to drink?"

"Thank you."

"What would you like? Soda, tea?"

"Water would be nice." A shot of vodka even better, but Neal knew she didn't have any.

Arlene turned and walked into the kitchen for the drink. She got a glass and napkin. She was too jittery to drink or eat a thing.

When she reached the living room, Neal was fast asleep. When Rangers went on missions, they sometimes went days with little sleep. Neal looked as if he'd been run over by a truck. She went to the closet for an afghan and placed it over his shoulders. His hand whipped out and caught her arm. His eyes were open and instantly alert.

"Sorry," he said and let her go.

"You're too tired to go home. Go down the hall and sleep in my bed."

"Last time I was here, you only had one bed."

Arlene didn't have the heart to make him sleep on the sofa in his condition. "Take the bed, Neal." He needed real sleep on a comfortable mattress.

"I'm not putting you on the sofa."

She wouldn't argue with him. "Okay."

"You'll sleep with me?"

She nodded, knowing she wouldn't. As soon as he hit the bed, he'd be asleep and he'd never know.

"I'll be there after I clean the kitchen. Go ahead."

When Arlene went to her bedroom to change, Neal's clothes were thrown over a chair and he was in bed, the sheet around his waist. His strong torso gleamed in the subdued light. She experienced a gamut of perplexing emotions. A tingle started in the pit of her stomach. Her body ached for his touch. But every time she thought of April a flash of grief ripped through her.

Arlene was suddenly anxious to escape from Neal's disturbing presence. If she wasn't so angry with the entire mess they were in . . .

Arlene went to the bathroom and changed clothes. Then she grabbed a blanket and settled on the couch.

A suffocating sensation tightened her throat. Every time she thought the drama of her husband's betrayal was over, something came along to lance a fresh wound.

Six

Arlene was taking this silent treatment too far. Neal knew if he gave her too much time, she'd be stepping out with Mayes again. Whether she liked it or not, he was going to be in her face until she was reasonable.

That night, he pulled into a parking space behind her and hopped out the car.

"What are you doing here?"

"Just conversation."

Arlene kept her eyes averted. She wouldn't look at him and start thinking how much she missed the sex, or how good that hard body felt against hers. Even more, she missed going to sleep wrapped in his strong arms.

"It's late and I'm tired." Then she stopped. Maybe he wasn't here because of her. "Is Tina okay?"

"As far as I know. If she wasn't, she'd have called you, I'm sure."

"Then you don't need to be here, do you? Tina's the only thing we have to discuss. Unless you want to be reasonable and get Byron to leave."

"Try telling Tina that. Good luck, by the way. Oh, I forgot. You've already tried—unsuccessfully."

"Your attitude about this is unforgivable."

"I can't make her do what she doesn't want to do."

"You are Byron's commanding officer. You have plenty of control over him."

"It's going to take some time for him to change his destructive ways. We need to give him that time. Now I didn't come here to talk about them. I'm here about us."

"There *is* no us. Look, Neal, I'm tired. The Sheikh is being unreasonable. I'm tired of his wives being underfoot the whole eight hours I'm there, jockeying for position and secretly waiting for his death so that one of their sons can take his place. The last thing I'm going to talk about is us. I'm going to bed—alone."

Finally finding the keys in the nether regions of her purse, she opened the door and let herself in, closing it in Neal's face.

Arlene leaned back against the cold surface and stepped out of her shoes. She was blaming Neal for something he had no control over, she realized, now that she was alone. Actually she didn't blame him for Ronald's infidelity. He couldn't have controlled the fact that Ronald had an affair with his sister, but he'd known. All this time he'd known and elected to keep quiet. Guilty by omission.

Right now, she was going to concentrate on an area where she might be able to do some good before it was too late.

Tina.

Arlene wasn't quite sure which approach she should use with mentoring Tina. She didn't want to appear preachy. The young woman would hate that attitude and resent Arlene too, thinking she was looking down on her. Arlene had thought for days trying to come up with a solution for the dilemma. She'd never mentored anyone before.

Arlene finally thought the best approach was to let Tina observe how she handled expenses. Arlene didn't have the best money management system, but it worked for her and it was better than no system. And far better than playing the numbers. Arlene was working the second shift on Friday. She called Tina and asked her to spend the morning with her.

So at eight the next morning, Arlene made a quick trip

to the bakery for strudel. Baked products was one of the things she really loved about Germany.

She brought some cookies for the little girl, but Tina arrived alone.

"Where's the baby?" Arlene asked. She'd been looking forward to holding the little girl. Having no kids of her own, spending even a little time with children was a treat.

"My girlfriend's keeping her. We help each other out sometimes like when I do volunteer work."

"Oh, that's good."

Tina wore a revealing burgundy top with tight jeans. No wonder her husband wasn't about to leave her even if she spent him into bankruptcy. Men loved attractive, flashy women. Arlene envied Tina with that freedom. She never had the nerve to dress that way. At thirty-seven she wasn't about to start.

"I have strudel if you'd like a snack. There's coffee, tea, juice or soda."

"Maybe later, thanks." Tina dropped her purse and keys on the sofa.

"My office is in the spare bedroom. I thought I'd pay bills this morning. It's boring but has to be done."

Tina rolled her eyes toward the ceiling. "Tell me about it."

In the office, Arlene had all the bills and her checkbook lined up on the desk. She pulled up a chair for Tina and they set about paying them.

"I don't use checks. I use money orders," Tina said.

"Do you have an account at the credit union?"

"Byron does, but I don't."

"The difference between credit unions and banks is that banks charge fees if you don't carry a minimum balance. Often that balance is a thousand dollars. The credit union doesn't charge you the fee. So you can save the money you're paying for money orders each month."

"I've never had a bank account."

"It's good to have an account."

Arlene and Tina made out checks for each bill. Then they

recorded the checks and amounts spent in the check register and subtracted the amounts from the previous balance.

"With recording the expenses, I'll always know what I have in my account," Arlene said. "Whenever I go to the ATM and take money out, I always record that amount in here and the fee if there is one."

It was sad that children didn't learn this information before they left high school and home. Arlene thought of the thousands of youth who never got the training.

After they completed the bills, Arlene pulled out her statement from the previous month and she and Tina balanced the statement against her register. There were two items Arlene hadn't recorded. They were the amounts that were automatically taken out for her mutual funds.

"One of these funds is for my retirement. The other is for big expenses I might have like a large vacation or expensive purchases like furniture. If I need the extra money, it's available."

"I wish we could save that much."

"When I first started working, I could only afford to save twenty dollars a paycheck. I know it wasn't much, but I figured it was better than nothing. And small amounts add up. Each pay raise, I increased the amount I saved. Twenty changed to twenty-five. Even if it was no more than an extra five dollars. The little bit adds up. At twenty dollars a paycheck, I saved five hundred, twenty dollars that first year. It doesn't sound like much, but at the end of three years, it gave me more than fifteen hundred dollars."

"I wish I could work, even if it was part time. My girlfriend and I had talked about getting part time jobs. I'd keep her kids when she worked and she'd keep mine when I worked. Then our money wouldn't be eaten up with child care."

"That sounds like a wonderful idea. Why didn't you?"

Tina rubbed her hands together. "Tell that to Mr. Macho, my husband. Told me he wore the pants in our house. He could take care of his family. We got into a big fight over that. I was too scared to bring it up again."

"A lot has changed in the last few decades. Working isn't about who wears the pants. It usually takes two paychecks to make it. Everything is so expensive now."

"That's why I was playing the numbers. I thought it would bring in some extra cash."

"Oh, Tina. Gambling is the number one way African-Americans *lose* money. Only a very small number break even or get ahead even a little. If we saved the money we gambled, we'd end up nearly rich. Think about it. The money you've gambled. If you had saved it, wouldn't you have a lot more?"

Tina hopped out of the seat and paced the carpeted floor. "But it's hard making ends meet off of one paycheck. I had to come up with something." She splayed her arms wide at a loss of what to do. "I love my husband. He's good to me most of the time. And he took me away from the streets and all that bad stuff back home. You don't know how it was in our house. My mom would keep getting these boyfriends and they moved in with us. I was scared to come home from school because they might catch me alone. They were looking at me the way they had no business doing. If Byron hadn't married me, I would have been raped by now. I just know it. I know you think he's bad, but he's not. Byron's a good man. I don't want him thinking that I think less of him because we need more."

"Oh, Tina." Arlene didn't know what to tell her.

Tina crossed her arms beneath her breasts. "Last weekend, it was his birthday. I wanted to buy him a nice present. I didn't have enough money for it. So I gambled, hoping I could make the extra. It worked for my mama. She always made money when she gambled." Tina dropped her arms to her side. "But I lost everything. I couldn't buy him anything. Even though he says it's okay, I know he felt like I don't care enough about him when he does so much for his family."

"Did you tell him what you just told me?"

"He was so mad because I lost the money, I just couldn't tell him why."

"Gambling doesn't work."

"What else can I do? He won't let me work."

Arlene thought that if the two of them could sit down and calmly discuss their situation it would help. But obviously, her husband felt that his ability to pay the bills was linked to his manhood.

"Husbands and wives should work together to build their lives. You're not a bystander. You're in this marriage together. You are supposed to support each other. Your working a job outside the home doesn't make him less than a man."

"I know that, but he doesn't see that."

Maybe Neal could talk to him, Arlene thought. "Your husband is attending anger management sessions. Maybe he'll come to understand your motives through the discussions. Hopefully, you'll be able to talk to him about your feelings. Women need some means of independence. I've always worked. You should be able to help each other. You are equal partners in the marriage."

Arlene wasn't a preacher or a counselor. She didn't want to go too far. And she didn't want to imply that Tina should disrespect her husband. But they *were* partners. She wasn't his servant. She wanted Tina to understand that.

After the bills, Tina went with Arlene shopping. "Are you sure you have the time?" Arlene asked.

"Sure. Makayla's in good hands. I don't take chances with my baby."

While they shopped, Arlene saw a crystal chess set. Her father really enjoyed playing chess. His birthday was coming up soon. Before she knew it, she'd purchased the gift.

She stored the gift in the trunk of her car and Tina went with her to buy groceries for the week.

Arlene thought about Neal. She'd left the house early

the next morning before he wakened. By the time she returned, he'd left.

When Arlene returned home she picked up the phone and dialed her father's work number. She'd been thinking about him a lot lately. She was told that he was in a meeting and she didn't leave a message. She went to the post office and mailed the gift. Hopefully it would arrive by his birthday.

"Did you learn something about managing money from the Lieutenant Colonel?" Byron asked. He was sitting at the kitchen table waiting for dinner.

Tina stirred the chicken and dumplings she made from scratch, then put the spoon down. Byron always loved her dumplings.

"Yeah. I thought she'd be stuck up. You know how some people are when they have more than you do. They look down on other folks. If she was, I would have read her right quick. But she was real nice."

"The Colonel is real down to earth, too. Stands to reason he wouldn't date a sista who wasn't. Even though she strikes me as a bit uptight."

"She is. In a nice way though. Guess it's her nature. Not everybody's the same." Tina frowned at him. "Did you say they're dating?"

"Yeah. Started before his niece left. Come here," Byron said, pulling her to him. "I don't want to talk about them when I've got you so close to me."

Tina sat on his lap and linked her arms around his neck. "We won't have any more problems with being broke at the end of the month, will we sugar?"

"Hmmmm."

He rubbed her hips and kissed her deeply. "You know I love you baby, don't you?"

"I love you, too. But I don't hit you."

"You don't have to deal with the stress I have to put up with."

"Why are you under so much stress?"

"I want to give you more. I want to make a better life for you and the baby. You're my family."

"You give us enough. You aren't alone in the marriage, you know. I'm right here with you. I don't know what I would have done if you hadn't taken me from my mama's house. Don't you know how special you are to me?"

He smiled. "You need to tell a brother that now and then. With me you don't have to worry about a thing."

"It's just sometimes I feel like your child, not your wife."

He rubbed her hip and kissed her neck. "Baby, it would be indecent to even think about the things I love doing to you if that was true."

His touch was stirring her. It always did. He was the only lover she'd ever had and he never disappointed her. "I'm not talking about sex. It's just we don't talk about things. You make all the decisions about our life."

"Like what? I give you most of my paycheck. I wouldn't do that with a child."

Tina sighed. "I know that, but we still don't discuss things. It's like you order and I follow. I don't have any control over anything."

His eyes narrowed. "Is this some crap the Colonel's old lady put in your head, because if it is you're not going to see her again. You hear?"

"No. I wouldn't discuss things like this with her. These are my feelings. Things I was scared to talk to you about."

He frowned, getting more and more upset. "Since when do you have to be scared of me?"

Fear streaked through Tina. She leaned back. "Like right now. You're raising your voice. And soon you'll be smacking me. So let's just drop it. Forget I said anything." Tina slid from his lap to stir the food, her hands trembling slightly. She should have known better than to bring that subject up. But she looked at Arlene, saw how she could take care of herself. She wanted some of that security for herself.

Byron got up, stood by the refrigerator, his hand on his hips. Tina could feel the anger pouring from him from across the room. He pulled a beer out of the fridge.

"So now the next thing I know you'll be wanting a divorce because I don't treat you right."

"I didn't say that, Byron. You're putting words in my mouth. I just told you I love you. Why would I want to leave you? Besides, I wouldn't take our baby away from her father. You know that."

"You damn right you wouldn't. I'd never let you leave with her. You remember that when you decide I'm not good enough for you anymore."

"I never said you weren't good enough. Maybe I'm not good enough for you."

"Where do you come up with this shit?"

"I can't talk to you without you taking it the wrong way. Without you thinking that I think less of you. I never think you're less than a man. You're a hard worker. Some of those guys back home don't know what it is to put in a full day's work unless it's living off women or selling dope. My mama had enough of them coming through our house to last me a lifetime. So why would you think I'd want anything like that for our child or for myself? Why would you think you weren't man enough for me just because I have opinions and want you to listen to me? I'm not a stupid doll that the baby plays with."

Byron sighed. "I don't even understand this argument. But I tell you one thing. I've had a hard day and now isn't the time to deal with it." He glanced at his watch. "I've got to go or I'll be late for that anger management meeting the Colonel's making me attend. I guess it's a good night for it. Don't worry, I won't be smacking you around tonight."

Tina lifted the wooden spoon out of the pot. "But you haven't had your dinner."

"No time," he said as he headed for the door.

Tina closed her eyes. She hadn't meant to start an argument with him or send him out without his supper.

But Tina *was* worried. She didn't know how long they could hold out if she didn't get a job. She knew she was restless, that she had no power in her marriage. She was nothing without Byron. And she didn't like feeling that way. She turned the food off. She may as well let it cool and stick it in the fridge. She'd leave out a plate for Byron knowing full well he wasn't going to eat it because he was mad at her. But if she *didn't* leave anything on the stove, he'd pick a fight with her tomorrow about how hard he worked and can't even get a decent meal when he came home.

Despite all their problems, deep down, he was a good man. And she knew it. She just wished . . .

Tina rubbed her forehead where a headache was beginning. Her hands were still trembling the way they did every time they got into an argument. She never knew if he was going to walk out or hit her. Still she was luckier than most. He never hit her with his fist or anything. Only the flat part of his hand. But that was enough.

And it was humiliating being treated like a child—like she was Makayla. It was true even if Byron wouldn't own up to it.

How could they resolve their problems if he got defensive every time she talked to him? She'd thought about sneaking behind his back to work, but he'd find out somehow and there'd be another huge fight.

Although Byron told Tina not to worry, she worried. She worried a lot.

Arlene had seen Colonel Mayes two days ago and he'd asked her out on another date. Although he was nice, their first evening together had been uneventful. Not nearly as exhilarating as her time with that traitor Neal. She didn't like the idea of using Colonel Mayes, but she was sick and tired of thinking about Neal.

"I'm not pushing you into anything you don't want," Colonel Mayes said. "Just a nice evening out." His avuncular voice was the kind that made you want to curl up and tell him your life's story.

"All right," Arlene acquiesced.

Now they were on their way to dinner again. Arlene dressed a little sexier than usual yet she was thinking of Neal. She was a Lieutenant Colonel after all and she should be able to deal with her husband's betrayal with Neal's sister and move on with her life. Assess the facts, make a solid decision, and move on. She dealt with hard-hitting questions and problems all the time in her job. She'd decided she wasn't ready for a serious relationship. She'd had enough drama.

When the problem hit home, it was easier said than done.

April called her at least once a week to tell her about some new friend she met—especially the boys—or someplace Grandma and Grandpa took her. Arlene knew she didn't tell Neal about the boys for fear he'd hit the roof. From their conversations, her experience was innocent enough. It was more that the girls talked about boys all the time and she didn't want to feel left out. The deep-seated pain lessened each time Arlene talked to April. Arlene couldn't deny the girl had touched a special place in her heart.

Ronald's mother needed to know she had a grandchild. Arlene would have to broach that subject with Neal. She never wanted to see him again. Although he wasn't the one who betrayed her, he'd known. Lying in that hospital, letting her fall for him, and here, letting her get close to April and falling in love with him.

Then she realized she was daydreaming again. Mayes sat quietly across from her as if he were at peace with himself. How could he stand the silence?

"This is a bad idea," Arlene finally said.

"It's just dinner," Mayes responded, patting her lightly on her hand.

"I know, but . . ."

"Colonel Neal Allen."

"Whatever we started is over, but . . ."

He lifted his hand from hers and placed it back on the wheel and smiled. "You'll get over him," he said with an assurance that belied Arlene's tumbling emotions. "In the meantime, I'm here."

"I don't want to use you."

"You can't use me if I'm a willing participant and I'm pursuing this with my eyes open, can you? Besides, when I'm out with you, I know I'm not going to have a boring evening."

"But it's so unfair to you."

"Let me worry about that."

His shoulders looked big enough to carry the world. But so did Neal's.

Arlene had asked several people about that scoundrel. She knew him as a boy, not as a man. "What do you know about Neal?"

He glanced briefly at her before he returned his attention to the road.

"We've worked on the same base before. You know how small the Army can be. Especially for officers. From everything I've heard, he's a fair and good man. When he's in the States, he works very hard on youth programs, trying to get students into the ROTC who otherwise would end up as casualties of the street. He's been very successful at it." He paused a moment and regarded Arlene, then continued. "He's well respected by both his troops and the brass. He takes his work seriously," Mayes said turning into the restaurant yard. "In other words, I have nothing terrible to report about him. I wish I did. Then he wouldn't be my competition."

"He's not."

George switched off the motor. Silence stretched, but the leather seat crackled as he faced Arlene. "It *is* over between you and Neal, isn't it, Arlene?"

Arlene nodded. "Definitely."

The three-to-eleven shift was one of the most taxing eight hours Arlene had ever endured. The sheikh's health was improving, but his temper wasn't. The spoiled, self-centered man was in pain and as cranky as a four-year-old with a splitting earache.

One of his wives was dancing around trying to calm him. He acted as if he was the only patient on the entire floor.

By the time eleven rolled around, Arlene was ready to run screaming out of the building. She stopped long enough to warn her replacement. Hopefully, the adult brat would sleep through the night.

Neal's car was parked on the curb when she arrived home. He was the last person she wanted to see after the night she had.

"I heard you saw Tina a couple days ago," he said as he came up behind her.

"I did."

"How did it go?"

"Pretty well for the most part. I was worried that she'd resent me being thrust on her. But she was very open-minded and willing to learn." Arlene opened the door, then walked the few paces to place her purse on the table. "You could have called me at my office, you know. You didn't have to come here."

"I know. I was in the field today."

He did look like he'd had a long one.

"Have a seat."

Neal sprawled out on the sofa.

"Is Bryon attending his sessions?"

"He hasn't missed one."

"At least that's something."

"Arlene, you can't replace me with Mayes without resolving what's between us first."

"What are you doing? Checking up on me now. Stay out of my business."

"You are my business."

Arlene didn't dignify that with an answer. She stood. "Next time, call me at my office."

Neal stood too. "We have to talk about this."

Arlene went to the door, but before she could open it Neal pressed a hand against it.

"You're a logical woman. You wouldn't have gotten this far if you weren't." He shifted positions. Arlene was pinned between him and the door.

"Let's deal with you and me first. The fact that you think I betrayed you. I didn't know until you started talking . . ."

Arlene looked away from him. He captured her chin in his hand and she glared at him again.

"After the second time we made love, when you mentioned you had no idea who your husband had had an affair with, I didn't know that you were unaware."

"And you think that's good enough? We've been together for two months and you never, not once, brought the subject up. April wasn't with us *all* the time."

"I thought your way of dealing with it was not discussing it."

"Do you really think I'm the kind of woman who would brush something as serious as that under the rug and close my eyes as if it never happened?"

Neal leaned away from her and threw up his hands. "I know now, don't I?"

"You better believe it." Arlene captured the door in her hand and opened it. She glared at him. Her message was loud and clear.

"You've made a habit of throwing me out. This conversation still isn't over. April is innocent in all this."

"April has another grandmother. Nancy is heartbroken from Ronald's death. She never recovered, actually. She needs to know she has a granddaughter."

Neal contemplated her for several long seconds. "Where does she live?"

"In Houston."

"Give me her address and I'll take April to visit her when I go to the States." Then he walked out into the night.

Arlene slammed the door after him. Why did he have to be so damn reasonable about Nancy?

Byron stopped by the pub and drank another beer and ate a hamburger. He knew Tina left a plate out for him. But he wasn't ready to face her. Sometimes he felt like he was losing her. She was growing and slipping away from him. She wasn't the little girl he took away from danger.

Byron shook his head. He'd made sure she'd gotten pregnant quickly. He felt a baby was one sure way of holding on to her. He loved his Makayla. He and Tina both wanted children, but he wanted the marriage cemented.

He'd lost everything he'd ever loved in this godforsaken life. He couldn't lose Tina too.

"Got room for me?" a voice called out.

Byron looked up to see the Colonel standing next to him.

He motioned to a chair. "Help yourself."

As Neal slid into the seat, he asked, "How's Tina?"

"Good. I'm just getting back from the meeting."

"How did it go?"

Byron shrugged.

"I'm glad you're sticking with it."

"What else can I do?" In a nasty mood, he regarded the Colonel and took a swig of his beer. "What're you doing here? Old lady throw you out?"

"Something like that."

Byron chuckled. "Man, you're a colonel. You're a Ranger. You've got women willing to crawl all over you."

Neal didn't respond.

"Maybe she's not for you," Byron offered.

"Maybe Tina's not for you."

Byron took exception to that. "Tina's my life."

"Arlene's the only one for me," Neal said as he ordered a beer for himself. "So what are you doing here all by yourself?"

"Not much. Just going down memory lane."

"How's the trip?"

"Not a pretty sight."

"Tell me about it."

"You don't want to know."

"Try me. It's between you and me. It's got nothing to do with the Army."

"The first time my old lady left me home alone for two weeks I was six. She left a twenty-dollar bill on the table for food." She often sent him to the store with money to buy some supper for himself when she was with her lover. He'd learned young how to handle money.

Byron shook his head and realized his hands were shaking. He balled them into fists.

"Go on," Neal said quietly.

Byron twisted the bottle on the table. "One morning—I must have been about four then—I got up hungry. Mama always kept a box of Cheerios for my breakfast. But when I checked, the box was in the trash. It'd been half full when I went to bed. I ran through the apartment calling for Mama. *Where are you, Mama? I'm scared.* I found her shacked up in bed with some man. When I opened the door to her room, this loser tells me to get out of my own mama's room. I figured out he'd eaten my cereal. Mama didn't eat cereal. Had to be him. So I went back to the living room and sat on the couch. Turned on the tube, and flipped channels until I reached *Sesame Street.*" Byron chucked a dry sound. "Me and *Sesame Street* were real tight back then. In a few minutes, my old lady came out, tying a ragged old robe around her waist. She handed me five dollars and told him to go to McDonald's and get something to eat."

Byron took another swallow from his beer bottle.

"By the time I was six I knew how to buy my own food—how to make the money last cause I didn't know when I'd find a note from Mama saying she'd be back next week." His eyes searched Neal's. "Can you imagine the fear at six, wondering if your old lady was coming home? During the school year, I made out pretty good. But that first time, I was so scared when I went to school that morning. At least I got free breakfast and lunch there, so the only meal I had to worry about was dinner.

"A week passed before Mama came back." He tightened his hand around the bottleneck. "That, as the saying goes, was the story of my life until I turned fifteen—when she left for good. By then, I was working evenings until eleven. It was illegal for a student to work that late but I did it anyway. Had to. Even with Mama there, half the time I paid the rent, so I just kept paying the bills. Besides, by then Tina had moved into the building, and although she was too young for me, I detected a lost soul just like me." Byron chuckled another dry sound. "I fell in love with her the moment I saw her, I think."

Byron took another sip of beer. He loved Tina and he feared losing her just like everything else. He was trying to hold on to her the only way he knew how. And even that wasn't working. He didn't know what he'd do without his Tina.

"She thinks I saved her when I married her and took her away from her mother's home at sixteen, but for real, she saved me."

"Now you have a chance. For something better for Makayla and Tina."

"Yeah," Byron said.

* * *

Midnight had come and passed when Byron slipped into the house. As expected, Tina had left a plate on the stove wrapped in foil. He put it into the fridge. Tina went to bed early. The house was eerily quiet. He made his way to Makayla's room and peeked in on her. He smiled. She always brightened his day. The little tiger slept soundly with her teddy bear propped in the corner of her crib. He wanted to pick up and hold her tight. He wanted to make sure she never knew the kind of fear he and Tina had lived through.

He straightened the covers over her tiny body. God, she was so tiny. Sometimes he could hardly believe she was his. Finally, he tore himself away, then he left and went to his bedroom. Quietly he undressed and slipped into bed beside Tina. She slept as soundly as Makayla. She didn't waken when he gathered her warm, sweet-smelling body into his arms and held her close to him.

He closed his eyes around a sigh. God, how he loved this woman. The only reason he attended those stupid anger management meetings was because he didn't want to have anything bad on his record. The Colonel had the right to report him. And Byron wondered how long he was going to put up with him and Tina disturbing his nights. He knew he was treading shaky ground with the Colonel's old lady. She was a veritable witch. But Tina liked her, so there must have been something good about her.

Bone-tired yet still unable to sleep, Bryon contemplated his career. He liked working in communications. He'd learned a lot, but there was so much more to learn. He'd thought about continuing in that area.

The Colonel believed in him. That meant a whole lot to him and Byron felt awful when he disappointed him. Every time Tina called the Colonel, Byron felt he disappointed him. There was only one other person that ever cared for him. The Stouts—an old couple who lived next door to him back in the hood.

Sometimes when his mama left, they'd have him over to dinner. He'd spend all day there on the weekends. One time, they made him spend the nights. He'd slept in a bed with pretty, clean flowery scented sheets that felt so good next to his skin. She even took him to the thrift store and bought him some clean clothing. That Sunday they went to church. Mrs. Stout taught him things like how to wash his clothes in the laundromat and how to change linen on the bed properly. She always smelled of vanilla and spices. Tina smelled a lot like Mrs. Stout. The older woman had loved to cook and was always baking cookies for Byron.

Often he wished he were her child.

Although he wasn't hers, Byron took her lessons to heart nevertheless. He never went to school again wearing dirty clothes.

When his mama returned one time, Mrs. Stout spoke to her about leaving him alone. His mother thanked her by cussing her out and smacked him upside his head for talking to nosy folks about their business.

Mrs. Stout left it alone, but whenever his mama left, she'd make sure he had food to eat. And she continued to teach him things.

Mrs. Stout died when he turned sixteen. For months she was too sick to shop for herself and he would go to the store and buy her groceries. He'd clean her apartment because she couldn't do it and they were too poor to hire help. Mr. Stout died a year after Byron enlisted in the Army. They had been his only family in a sense, except for Tina.

To this day, he didn't know where his mother was or even if she were still alive. He doubted she cared one wit about him. If she had, she wouldn't have left him in the first place. He didn't know what made a woman leave her own children to go after men who always dumped them.

But that wasn't his worry any longer. Tina was his wife. She'd never leave Makayla for some man.

Byron had to consider their future.

The Colonel was right. What would he do if he left the Army? With no more than a high school education and barely that—from a really bad school, his options were few.

Often he felt he was always behind, and always running trying to keep up. In the civilian world, he'd be competing with college graduates for the few available jobs. Lord knew black men had a tough enough time as it was. Not only were they working with some people who didn't want to hire them in the first place, but now others were pouring into this country left and right looking for new opportunities. Even they got jobs easier than black men. For now, he was better off holding on to this sure thing.

Byron's thoughts continued to roam. His sprits lifted with hope. He began to imagine what it would be like to visit his old school to talk to the students about his experiences as a college graduate. A Nobody from the streets of LA turned into Somebody. His teachers who thought he'd never amount to nothing would sit in the audience when he spoke, along with the teachers who has believed in him, who encouraged him.

He never believed that college could be for him. He tightened his arms around Tina, snuggled her into the crook of his neck. Could this really work out for him and Tina?

Seven

Two days later, Arlene left a message at Neal's office before she went to lunch. She needed to talk to him again about Tina and her macho husband. It seemed when she and Neal got together, anger took over. She was an officer, trained to control her emotions. This time, she'd stick to business and not let him sidetrack her about *them*.

Neal returned the call before she got back from lunch and left a message on her answering machine. He asked her to meet him at the Officer's Club at six for dinner. Immediately, Arlene picked up the phone to call him back. They didn't need a meal to discuss this. They could talk about it over the phone. But she couldn't reach him on his cell phone or his office phone. Every time someone in the office answered, they asked her to hold on. A few seconds later, they always returned with a "he's not available right now". When she tried to leave a message, she was told he wouldn't get it before the next day. She pictured him standing over the soldier's shoulder, issuing orders.

Arlene was steaming by the time she changed clothes and reached the Officer's Club. He was already seated at a table.

He stood as Arlene slid into her seat. "I'm not staying for dinner."

"Well, I'm not talking until after dinner. I haven't had a decent meal all day and I don't want it ruined with another argument."

She snapped open the menu but decided on the buffet.

"I'll have the buffet, too," he said. He was in an awfully jovial mood.

While they stood in the buffet line, Arlene spoke to a couple of people she knew before they returned to the table, plates filled.

"Is Chardonnay all right with you?" he asked her as the waiter waited for him to sample the wine.

"Yes." She needed something to soothe her nerves.

"I talked to Byron's counselor. He's attending his anger management meetings regularly. I'm not just taking his word for it. Although if he says he's going to do something he usually does."

"Except hit his wife. He always promises not to do that again."

Charged silence bounced between them, letting in the background noises of voices and utensils.

"There is one problem I wanted to discuss with you. I feel like an outsider and don't quite know how to help Tina," Arlene told Neal.

Neal frowned. "What is it?"

"Tina gambles because they could use the extra money and Byron opposes her working outside the home."

"I didn't know that."

"He feels that her working is linked to his *manhood*. Every time Tina brings the subject up, he makes her feel that she thinks he's incapable of supporting his family."

"I see." His frown deepened. "That's a touchy subject."

"And probably has a lot to do with his background."

"This isn't something he would change easily, but it's manageable."

"I don't know if it is."

"I know you have your doubts about him. But it takes time for him to work through his past beliefs. And he is making an effort."

"Well, I know I'm repeating myself, but I think since he can't control his tempter, Tina and the baby should be out of that house. If she wanted to return, and I know she would, it should be *after* he has a handle on his anger, not while. She could get hurt in the meantime."

"She isn't going to leave him."

"And he's going to make sure she doesn't by making sure she doesn't have the means to take care of herself."

"Look, you're trying to make it seem as if he's all bad."

"I can't overlook his abusive tendencies. Tina shouldn't have to live with constant fear, worrying about when she'll say something that will set Byron off again. He's like a keg of dynamite. She doesn't deserve that. No one does."

"No, she doesn't, but they're at least working on the problem. Most men in his situation wouldn't seek help at all until it was much worse or if they had no other choice. Give him that much."

"I think his seeking help has more to do with you than his wife."

"He loves her, Arlene." Neal didn't believe that it was acceptable for men to abuse their wives, or in some cases when the opposite happened. Arlene made him feel as if he believed that it was okay. It wasn't. He believed Tina, Byron and Makayla were worth fighting for.

The waiter returned to refill their glasses and discretely left after asking if they wanted anything more.

"Sometimes, Neal, love just isn't enough."

Neal and Arlene glared at each other from across the table. He hoped it was enough to make a difference for Byron and Tina.

"It can be, under the right circumstances. Do you think we can enjoy our dinner?" Neal finally asked.

"By all means. We wouldn't want this wonderful meal to go to waste." She stabbed the fork into her beef, took the knife and tore off a bite.

When she set the knife down, Neal covered her hand with his.

"Calm down, okay? I know you have a point. It's just they started out with everything going against them. Byron practically raised himself. He didn't have a role model like you and I. It'll mean a lot if they can work through this, for both of them."

Arlene sighed, remembering the family situation Tina had discussed with her—her constant fear of rape from her mother's boyfriend. How horrible to have to marry because her mother wasn't being a good parent—wasn't looking after the child's best interest.

"Don't you see that she could be staying with him out of gratitude? Things were horrible for her at home. But you're a man and I expect you to take a man's side."

"That's not fair and you know it."

"The truth isn't always fair, is it? But it's still the truth, nevertheless. Men stick up for each other, especially macho Rangers."

Neal pressed his lips tightly together, drew his forearms on the table and drew even closer toward Arlene. "You know, I've always thought I was a good judge of character. I'm not giving up on either Byron or Tina. I'm going to do what I can to help both of them—whether you like it or not. Where would they be if everybody gave up on them and left them to sink or swim on their own? Nowhere. If you don't want to help out, then don't. Just don't ask me to pull the covers over my head or give up on them."

"I'm trying to get you to pull the blinders off your eyes. And I didn't say I didn't want to help out. You have to give Tina credit for holding on. I'll help her anyway I can. After all, with you sticking up for Byron, Tina needs *somebody* on her side."

"Nobody can make mistakes and try to correct them, can they Arlene? Everyone has to be perfect—as perfect as you. Here's a newsflash for you. Tina isn't perfect either. She needs help with her gambling. Have you thought about that?"

"First, if Byron would let her work, Tina wouldn't have a gambling problem. Second, nobody's perfect. I have my faults. But there are some grievances that are unforgivable and shouldn't be tolerated."

Neal threw down his fork. It clattered on his plate. "Lord forbid that one should seek help when they need it."

"Say that to the women I've seen bloodied and battered in the emergency room. It's not a long stretch from slaps to punches."

Arlene shoved the forkful of steak into her mouth. With anger rolling through her, it could be rubber for all she tasted.

Neal gave up trying to make peace long enough to enjoy the meal. His body was rigid with anger, his jaw clamped tight. The food was all but forgotten as he took a fortifying gulp of wine and asked the waiter for a refill.

As Arlene glared at him from across the table, she guessed Neal had seen about all he wanted of her.

The ringing of Neal's cell phone broke the impasse.

Neal took the phone from his pocket, glanced at the number and answered to April. The first smile of the evening covered his face and it seemed to transform him.

Obviously Arlene hadn't been able to reach him before because he recognized her number. That underhanded dog would do anything to get his way.

"I'm having dinner with Arlene," he responded. He listened, then he handed the phone to Arlene. "April wants to speak to you."

Arlene took the phone and inhaled a deep breath to calm her raging nerves. "April, how is Texas?"

"It's okay, but I miss you and Uncle Neal. I have a very hard time reaching you sometimes."

"You can usually reach his cell number."

"Not always."

Arlene realized that he couldn't use the cell phone when he went on secret missions.

"Are you taking good care of Uncle Neal? He's behaving, isn't he?"

Arlene didn't have a response for that statement. Neal was always doing dangerous things. "He's behaving himself," Arlene finally said.

"Grandpa, Grandma and I went to Carlsbad Caverns last weekend. We took a cave tour and saw the bats fly, but Grandma didn't like bats flying over her head so she stayed at the hotel."

"That sounds like fun."

"We took a lantern trip in one cave. That was even more fun. Some of the kids got scared, but I didn't."

"You're really brave."

"Well, can I speak to Uncle Neal?"

"You take care."

"You too. Love you."

Arlene handed the phone to Neal.

Neal looked uncomfortable with the question April asked him. He was shaking his head and said, "No."

They talked another two minutes before they disconnected. The anger had finally drained out of Arlene. But by then her food was cold.

They made it through the rest of dinner and Neal walked her to the car. He leaned against the driver's door instead of letting her in.

"Now, about us."

"Let's not go there."

"I care for you, Arlene. And I don't like it that you're dating another man."

"Who I date is none of your business."

"What are you angry about, Arlene? The fact that you fell for me as hard as I fell for you?" He advanced on her like the wolf he was. "Or that you enjoyed lovemaking for the first time in your life and it was with me?"

Arlene activated the electronic lock to her car. "I was wondering when you'd throw sex in my face. You're still that awful thirteen-year-old who loved to taunt me."

"I'm way past that and my taunting is a lot more lethal now, especially when you're pushing my buttons the way you have for the last couple of weeks. There's nothing I can do about the past but clear the air. And you don't want that to happen, do you? It's much easier to hang onto the anger and blame me for what happened. I wasn't in your marriage. I didn't cheat on you. I wasn't responsible for its failure. But you were there. Why didn't you do something? You can't tell me that you weren't suspicious that Ronald was cheating."

"You're hitting below the belt, Ranger." She said it like it was blasphemy.

Neal sighed. "Your husband is dead," he said quietly. "He can't hurt you anymore. He can't keep you from having babies if you want them and he can't stop you from loving again. That decision is yours, and yours alone."

Neal pulled her against him, her body plastered against his chest and kissed her. "You wear a sexy dress for Mayes and a business suit for me," he said against her lips. "But that's okay. There isn't an inch of you I haven't seen." He swirled a tongue over her lips. "Or tasted."

His words mesmerized her. Before she could struggle, he lifted his head and his phone vibrated against him.

When it vibrated against her chest, Arlene thought it was her heart tripping. She took several deep breaths while Neal scanned the number and then answered. Seconds later, he hung up, placing the phone back into his breast pocket.

"I have to go," he said. He didn't have to say it. She knew he was going on another mission.

He pulled Arlene into his arms, and with the pent-up emotions raging in him, kissed her with a thoroughness that took her breath away. He ran his hands over her soft body, using up a precious minute holding her close to him.

"I have to go," he repeated. She cradled his face between her hands and kissed him, lingering, savoring every second, then let him go.

"Be safe," she said. He nodded and marched off quickly to his car.

She opened her car door and got in, then leaned her head against the steering wheel. Damn it. She didn't want to care for him.

* * *

A former Soviet Union state in the Caucasus Mountains in the Kara Kum Desert was in turmoil yet again. The country was rich in minerals and oil without the tools to extract either. Yet, they wanted no outside influence. The poor area was run by a dictator.

A U.S. congressional convoy had traveled there on a fact-finding mission to consider ways of beefing up education and examine human rights violations.

A quiet little country, virtually unarmed, was juicy pickings for renegades fleeing U.S. retribution. The government had no money for weapons and could ill protect itself.

The congressional convoy was being held as hostages by Al-Quada loyalists. It seemed the dictator had given them refuge, although he denied it.

Neal and his team were chosen to help with recovery.

The news held front-page position back in the States. The press hounded government spokesmen on what was being done, especially since the U.S. had a policy of not paying for hostage release.

Neal and his team were en route there. They would work with Air Force Special Forces to retrieve the hostages and they wouldn't get news coverage.

Even now they rehearsed their precise tactical moves. The hostage location had been pinpointed using state of the art technology.

Now it was dark—as dark as it can only get in the desert. Wearing desert camouflage fatigues with Kevlar vests and helmets, they each carried about fifty pounds of equipment and ammunition. The Rangers stealthily made their way to the target location. Wearing a headset that allowed him to talk without tying up his hands, Neal and his crew hung low to the ground and perused the area with field glasses.

With their night-vision glasses, they'd detected landmines and now they skirted them.

Most of the compound had settled in for the night. The men toting AK-47s who guarded the area were relaxed and sleepy. Still, every man was alert. Rarely did a mission go as well as the planning. There were always snafus just waiting to happen.

The observation chopper was miles away.

They maneuvered their way toward the building, taking out the patrol without a sound. Then, in teams of two, they made their way inside the building.

As primitive went, this was as primitive as it came. Even the poorest in America lived better. Makeshift chairs and tables dotted the rooms. Primitive cots, if they could be labeled as such—some no more than ragged pallets—lay against the walls, rifles were placed nearby on the floor. Snores from several men bounced off the peeling walls.

Other team members made their way upstairs to where the hostages were being kept. The guards on the door were quickly dispatched. Inside, the frightened hostages were awakened from their sleep at the sound of muffled gunfire.

On the first floor, the men had been contained.

Neal identified himself and the convoy was gathered together with a mixture of fear and relief. They were in a sorry state. Some were injured. The clothing they'd worn was stained with dirt and grime.

"Can you walk, or do you need medical attention before you leave?" Neal asked.

"We can make it," Senator Baisley said. Giving the injured men as much assistance as they could, the group was led down the stairs. Two Rangers checked ahead for enemy soldiers as they descended.

The sleeping Talibans were bundled together for escort to detention and interrogation. But when they reached the door, enemy fire rained down on the building. Amid shouts and screams, the freed men were quickly shoved to the floor as the Rangers took positions. The former guards tried to make a break for it, but some were killed by their own men's firepower. The team stopped the others from breaking away.

Positioning themselves, the Rangers attacked, and within minutes the enemy soldiers were contained.

In another ten minutes, the Air Force Special Forces helo arrived to take everyone away. The injured were attended to and the Rangers were left for cleanup before their own helo arrived to take them and the prisoners to the forward base—a base the Rangers used as their jump-off point because their home base was too far away.

At the forward base, the prisoners would get an escort to a prison camp and the Rangers would fly to Germany.

Little mention of the rescue would occur in the papers. It was one of those "don't ask questions" scenarios. Officially, they were never there.

While in the air, Neal sent in his report.

Several hours later, Neal and his team boarded the plane for Frankfurt. The mission was over and the rescued Americans were on their way to the States.

He settled in his seat, rethinking the mission—the areas that went as smoothly as clockwork versus what had gone wrong.

And he thought of Arlene and her recriminations about abuse. Often people thought of Rangers as killing machines. They were trained to kill, but they were also trained to help people by teaching them new or better ways of providing shelter, how to grow more abundant and varied selections of food, supply special medical care in isolated areas, and in general provide things to make their lives more comfortable. It was far easier to change the hearts and minds of people when you weren't shooting at each other.

People didn't think of the Buffalo Soldiers as far back as the 1800s as special ops, but they were. They were fighters, but they also worked with the rail lines moving west, carried mail and helped with telegraph lines.

"Let's break out the cigars," Private Slade said. "I'm a new daddy. A nine-and-a-half pound football quarterback."

Cheers and whoo-ahs, the Ranger's greeting, filled the air. Neal cheered with them.

A baby. A family waiting for his return from wherever was Neal's most fervent desire.

Finally relaxing, he thought of Arlene and April as the plane taxied down the runway. April had probably called him several times by now, while Arlene probably hadn't given him a second thought.

He hadn't expected her reaction or her continued anger. He understood that Bridget and Ronald weren't available for her to vent her anger, and he was the closest target. Now he regretted some of what he'd said to her at dinner that night which seemed so long ago. He could have been more delicate, although he wasn't accustomed to tiptoeing around when he was really ticked off.

Not only did he and Arlene have their own personal problems, they were also linked with Byron and Tina, and since they disagreed on how to handle them, it only added more contention to an already brewing situation.

When April couldn't reach Neal, she talked to Arlene, asking her to make sure Neal was okay. Arlene assured the child that she would check on him when he returned. Then April talked about her stay with her grandparents. She'd met a boy her age and he was so full of himself. "But I put him in his place," she told Arlene.

Just like your uncle, Arlene thought.

She had become best friends with a girl down the street.

Those conversations with April kept Arlene smiling while she tended to her obnoxious patient. She didn't know how Neal handled her being away. Although they spent only a couple of months together, Arlene missed her more than she realized she would, and at the same time, resented her for being Ronald's child.

She missed Neal too, darn it. And the argument between them left a foul feeling in her stomach. His job was worse than a policeman's. Whenever he went out, there *was* that chance that he wouldn't return. She wouldn't like their argument to stand between them forever.

But the memory of his embrace still warmed her. She was working the seven-to-three shift that week and sometimes in the middle of the night as she slept in her lonely bed she'd think of him and a delicious shudder would heat her body. The memories couldn't replace having him with her, wrapped in his arms, but they were somewhat comforting just the same. She was still working through Bridget and Ronald. And she knew their coupling wasn't Neal's fault.

Arlene was off the next two days. George Mayes called for a date. She declined. So far she couldn't summon up any feelings for him and she knew they would never come. She couldn't use him, even if he were willing.

She was sick of debating—sick of pain. Shelly came back into town and Arlene invited her over for dinner. After they were full, they sat in the living room catching up on news.

"Are you and George still a hot item?" Shelly asked.

"Please. I guess you were right from the beginning. We're history. The vibes weren't there, Shelly. He's a nice man and I couldn't have him hoping for something that wasn't going to happen."

"I could have told you that, but nobody was asking me. So things are hot with Neal I take it? All back on track?"

"I don't want to think about that man."

"Sure about that?"

"Absolutely positive."

"I would dispense advice like 'give the man a chance' and so on . . . but you wouldn't listen to me and Neal can take care of himself."

"I'm sure he can."

"Mind if I . . . ah . . ."

"What's with you?" Arlene asked. "You don't stammer."

"Do you mind if I date George?"

Arlene chuckled. "You and Colonel Mayes? You've got to be kidding?"

"Why can't I be serious? Remember, opposites attract. You can't get more opposite than George and me."

"So how do you plan to approach him about a date?"

"I'll ask him out."

"Nothing wrong with that. Good luck. If anyone could pull this off, you could." Arlene turned serious. "Shelly, if you really like him, I hope the best for you. You deserve someone nice. And Colonel Mayes is a wonderful man."

"I know that. I'm not going to give him time to search out a nice one like you again. And since you aren't taking my advice, let me say, don't wait too long and let Neal get away."

Arlene spent her day off touring. The sights in Germany calmed her somewhat. But when she returned late that afternoon, Neal was sitting on her steps.

Her heart lurched. His steady gaze bore into her in silent expectation. A small scar stood out in stark relief above his left eyebrow. He stood, held his arms out to her and she went into his embrace. Gathering her into his arms, he held her snugly. She buried her face in the corded muscles of his neck and his grip tightened.

His mouth covered hers hungrily. The kiss was deep and frantic with need. Her calm was shattered with the hunger of his kiss.

"We've . . . inside," Arlene barely managed to say.

Neal barely gave her time to fumble with the keys to get the door open. His arms caged her around the middle as they walked in. As soon as the door shut he grabbed her. She shrieked and dropped her purse, keys, brochures, everything on the floor.

He pressed her against the solid door, his body pressing into her, his lips kissing her, his tongue delving into her sweet mouth. He dragged the clothing from her body. Her bare backside pressed against the cold surface. Frantically, she tore at his clothing until he stood, his perfect body bruised, muscles rippling. She kissed the bruises.

"Oh, baby." His deep groan made her hotter, urged her to touch him more. His breathing grew ragged.

He was so solid, he looked so good, he snatched her breath away.

"Do you like that?" she asked.

"Love it."

"Let's see if this is any better." She stroked his chest, his hips, then she cupped him in her hand, stroking him back and forth.

"I've died and gone to heaven."

"Not quite yet."

"Enough." He kissed her body, from her face to her feet. She was a liquid mass when he finished with her. She could barely stand.

And then he grappled in his pants pocket for a prophylactic. He tore off the covering and handed the slippery condom to her. She stroked him as she guided it on. And then she felt herself lifted against the door and he was in her.

Clinging to his strong shoulders, feeling the rippling muscles beneath his skin, she closed her eyes against the explosion of sensations traveling through her at a speed so fast it took her breath away.

They came together in a fulfillment so intense, he fell to his knees. His arms around her, he kissed her stomach. Using the door for support, she stroked his head and shoulders.

This man's body was a war machine. Made to endure the worst of conditions, powerful enemies, and untold elements Arlene didn't even want to contemplate for the fear that ate her insides. But yet, their lovemaking had undone him.

She felt powerful and vulnerable, because he had conquered her too.

Neal planted a kiss on her stomach. The sensation caused a ripple through the core of her body. She was still vulnerable from their lovemaking, yet she wanted more of him. It was many moments before Neal rose and kissed her lips.

"I didn't mean to attack you the moment I saw you," he said.

Arlene caressed his face with her hands and guided his mouth back to hers.

"I missed you, too. How I missed you." Sometimes fear gripped her insides in a vice when she thought of the strength of her emotions for this man. She hadn't felt *this* strongly for her husband. Or maybe it was the complacency after the first blossom of love had worn off that did them in. Whatever, she couldn't think about that now. She needed Neal inside her.

"Let's go to the bedroom," he whispered. He didn't need to repeat himself.

With their clothing littering the foyer, they hustled down the hall and Arlene didn't give a thought to her thirty-seven-year-old body, which wasn't as youthful as it had once been. Judging by their lovemaking, Neal certainly didn't seem to care.

Neal had fallen asleep hours ago. Now it was midnight and he was wide awake. Arlene slept peacefully in his arms. They'd had terrific sex.

Neal was uneasy about this relationship with Arlene. She still hadn't resolved the past. They were making love, but Neal knew that the storm wasn't over yet and he didn't know quite how to reach her. Every time he brought the subject of April and the past up, she refused to talk about it. But they had to talk about it.

Whenever he thought about losing her, a sick feeling clenched his gut. He had every reason to believe they would work it out. But there was that possibility that . . . He didn't even want to think about it.

Eight

The day after Neal returned, Byron attended an anger management meeting. He was getting damned sick of those tired-assed meetings. It was ironic that in the session, the discussion had turned to women working and how it affected a man. Byron wondered if Tina had blabbed to the Colonel about their discussion and maybe he'd put a bug in the counselor's ear. He was red hot that they were talking about him behind his back.

Tina didn't trust him. She was supposed to cover his back, not betray him like that.

Anger rode home with him. Tina had spent the money for the bills on gambling again. Three late-payment statements had come in the mail already.

He slammed into the house.

"Where's the money for the bills, Tina?"

Tina clutched a hand to her collar. "I'll pay them with the next check. I didn't have enough this time."

"I gave you enough for all the bills, food and a little extra. So what happened?"

"I . . ." She looked nervously around the room, backing away from him.

"You keep telling me that I don't let you do anything. That I make all the decisions. I wanted you to feel as if you're a part of this marriage, too. I wanted you to feel secure. The only security I had when my mama left me was that I had a few dollars to pay the rent and buy food."

"I'm sorry, Byron. I didn't know that."

"You've been gambling again, haven't you?"

Tina looked away from Byron, wringing her hands together.

"You been talking about our problems behind my back, too, haven't you?"

"What are you talking about? What problem?"

"About working. Didn't I tell you I could take care of my family? I can if you'd stop wasting our money. You're the problem here."

"I know you can take care of us. I'm sorry, baby."

"Then why did you go tell the Colonel?"

"I didn't. He couldn't have said I did, because I know I didn't. I haven't even seen him."

"Then you talked to that nosy woman of his."

"I haven't seen her since you and I had that argument, Byron. When would I have talked to her?"

"You're lying. About the money and about our problems. Admit it."

Tina looked at him, fear exploding in her eyes, and backed away. "You're going to wake Makayla up," she said in an unsteady voice. "She was colicky all day and I had a hard time getting her to sleep."

Bryon didn't hear a peep from the baby. Tina was lying about that, too. "I don't like you telling my business to that woman. I don't care if the Colonel did choose her as your mentor. Why don't you get her to help you with the gambling? It's tearing our family apart."

"Calm down, will you? Supper's ready. I cooked your favorite meal."

"I don't want any damn supper. I'm talking to you. Do you hear me?"

Tina tried to edge around him to the stove. He grabbed her arm. All kinds of pressure was exploding through Bryon's head. How was he going to make up the money Tina threw away? He'd saved a little bit, but not enough to make up that big a difference.

"Not tonight, please Byron. You said you wouldn't hit me anymore."

"You betrayed me. As hard as I'm trying to make things work, you're trying to tear our family apart."

Tina was trembling in his arms as she shook her head. "No, I didn't. I . . . I wouldn't betray you. Please let me go. I . . . I've got to see about the baby."

He could see the fear pulsing from her and he couldn't help himself. He grabbed both her arms, pulled her so close their eyes were no more than two inches apart.

She screamed. "Please stop! You're hurting me. You said you'd leave before you hit me again."

He took a deep breath, glared at her one last time. Finally, he threw up his hands in defeat and left the house, pulling the door so hard, the walls shook.

Tina ran to the door and bolted it. She was shaking so badly she could barely slide the lock in place. She checked on the baby to make sure she was okay, then checked to make sure Byron hadn't returned. She stood by the phone for several seconds, the clock ticking in rhythm with her heart. Her legs were so weak she sank into a seat. If she left, where was she going to go? She'd never considered leaving him, but what was she going to do?

She was tired of living in fear. She'd been scared all her life. Scared of her mama's boyfriends, now scared of her own husband. She wanted some freedom—freedom from fear. She thought of Makayla securely tucked away in the small bedroom. If it was just her, she could probably make it if she went back to the States. She could work at McDonald's or something until she could get a better paying job. But it was impossible to pay a babysitter on McDonald's wages. She wasn't trained for anything.

God. What was she going to do? She held the cold phone against her forehead until she got tired of the buzzing in her ear.

Finally, she took the portable phone and called the Colonel. Everything was getting worse instead of better. She couldn't handle Byron alone. She loved him, but she was scared of him, too. And it just shouldn't be that way.

Arlene and Neal had just finished dinner at the Officer's Club. Sexual vibes had been bouncing back and forth throughout the meal. Neal couldn't wait to get Arlene home. He hoped she wouldn't think that all he wanted from her was sex, but the best damn sex he'd ever had was damn addictive.

The phone rang. For a moment, he panicked. God, no. Not now! Not tonight. When he recognized the number, he realized it wasn't his unit calling. Byron's number could only mean one thing. He pressed the button. Tina's trembling voice came over the line.

He read the accusation in Arlene's eyes before he even said anything. It galled him that she would have a stronger argument against him than her own. Worse, Byron had hit his wife when he'd promised never to do so again.

"What's happened?" Arlene asked.

"It's Tina. She's frantic."

Arlene wiped her mouth with the napkin. "Let's go," she said.

Neal signaled the waiter for the check, left bills on the table and they were on their way.

The ride to the NCO quarters was made in taut silence.

"Listen, why don't you say it and get it off your chest?" Neal said. "The, you know, *I told you so.*"

"We haven't seen her yet. We don't really know what happened. Believe it or not, my arguments weren't about being right or wrong. I'm concerned about helping a woman who's being terrorized."

"Why can't we help both of them? Then we'll have accomplished something, because they both need help."

"She needs to get more education so she can get a good job. Then she can leave him, because, like it or not, he isn't going to straighten up."

"How do you know that? People can change."

"Change is hard. So hard, in fact, that they usually don't. When Tina leaves him because she can't take it anymore, he'll victimize the next woman. I've seen enough abused women to know."

"Hitting Tina is wrong. But at least she's never been in the hospital."

"Do you want to wait for it to get to that point? And does that justify doing nothing?"

Neal braked in front of a small house. "Let's put our energies into helping them."

He opened the door and they both walked toward the duplex. Neal rang the doorbell.

Tina opened the door.

"Hey," Arlene said, "what did he hit you with?"

"He didn't hit me this time, but he was really mad at me. I'm scared."

"Come on, let's sit down," Neal said, guiding her to the sofa. "Where's the baby?"

"She's sleeping in the bedroom down the hall."

Tina sat on the sofa while Neal held her hand. Arlene had to admit and appreciate that he was very gentle with the younger woman.

"Why don't you tell us what happened," he said.

Tina bit her lip. "He was mad because I went gambling again."

"Tina, I thought we talked about that," Arlene said, disappointed that Tina had wasted money again. When would she learn that she'd get nowhere with gambling?

"But there's never enough money. Then he was mad because they talked about women working in that anger management class."

Guilty dread spread through Arlene. She was partially responsible for Tina's injuries. She had discussed that with Neal.

"I admit I asked the counselor to bring up that topic," Neal said.

"He thought I was telling our business to strangers."

They heard a key in the door. Tina looked worriedly toward it as Byron entered the living room.

"You didn't have to go and call them. I wasn't going to do anything."

Neal stood. "Let's talk." He walked angrily past Byron to the kitchen.

Tina kept looking toward the kitchen. They could only hear muffled voices, not what was actually being said.

In a few minutes, Byron headed toward the back of the house and Neal walked slowly into the living room.

"What's going on?" Tina asked.

"Let's talk about your gambling," Neal said. "I think you should get some help."

"I don't have a problem."

"I think you do."

In a few minutes, Byron came back with a packed duffle bag.

Tina stood. "Where are you going? You . . . You're leaving me?" she said in a weak voice.

"He's going to stay someplace else until he can get his anger under control," Neal told her.

Tears started down Tina's cheeks. "Don't leave me," she wailed. It was a painful scene even for Arlene to witness as Tina clutched her husband close to her. She saw equal pain on Byron's face. Neal was right in that they did love each other. She could see it in their expressions. For once she understood why Neal tried so hard to keep them together.

Tina was crying so hard she was breaking Arlene's heart and she felt the tears welling in her own eyes. She discretely turned away to wipe her eyes.

"I'll stop the gambling, I promise. Then you won't have a reason to hit me. But don't leave me."

Byron held her close. "I'm not leaving you, baby. I'm just leaving for a little while. I'll be back before you know it. You're my lady, and my baby is down the hall. I can't leave you." His voice was hoarse with emotion. "We'll work on our problems while we're separated, okay? I'll be back before you know it."

"I can't manage without you."

"You won't be without me. I'll come to see you and Makayla often. Promise."

"Please don't go."

He gently took her arms from around him. "I'm leaving the car for you so you and the baby can get around, okay? If Makayla doesn't get better, take her to the doctor, okay?"

Tina nodded, but the tears still poured down her face.

"I'm going to take Byron to a friend's place. I'll come back for you," he told Arlene.

Arlene nodded.

Tina seemed completely lost without her husband, as if she'd crumbled into herself.

"If you work your problems out, he'll be back, Tina. You're not good for each other like this. Think of the baby. Can you let her grow up in this kind of atmosphere? You have to do everything you can to make a good home for her."

"What if he doesn't come back?"

"He loves you. Even I can see that."

"I love him, too."

"Look. Neal was right. You need to see a counselor, too. I can't help you the way you need to be helped. By the time Byron returns he'll be able to handle his anger and you'll be more in touch with your needs too. You need help with the gambling. You can work to overcome that while he's away."

By the time Neal returned, Tina had calmed down somewhat.

"Do you think you'll be able to sleep?"

She nodded. "The baby gets up early. I'm usually in bed by now. And I'm tired."

Arlene finally left, a sick feeling in her stomach as she walked beside Neal to the car.

"Okay, you can tell me 'I told you so'. They really do need each other. And you were right," she said, as Neal drove to her place.

"You know what? I don't know what's right, Arlene. It's not right that he's hitting her. It's not right that she's gambling away the household budget. Nothing's right with them."

"But they do love each other."

"Yes, they do. But tell me, is it enough? I love you. Is that enough?"

"Our situation . . . what we have is completely different."

"Is it really? How so?" he said as he parked in front of her house.

"We've had enough to deal with for one night. I don't have the energy to deal with us right now."

"You never have time for us. So if not now, when? Tomorrow? Next week? When?"

Arlene sighed and opened the door.

Neal followed her. "By refusing to discuss us you can avoid dealing with issues that need to be resolved so we can move on."

"So you're my counselor now?"

"No, Arlene. You're in April's life. Whether you like it or not. You're a part of my life, too. You can't disappear from April's life like she never existed."

"Don't you think I know that?"

"Then stop ignoring me. Stop treating me as if I don't exist."

"It's the only way I can handle this mess right now."

"I'm not going to disappear just because some issues make you uncomfortable."

"I've already come to that conclusion. You're like a bad penny that keeps showing up."

He pulled her close, kissed her, and walked away, leaving Arlene in a quandary.

She was frightened of making a commitment again. Was she choosing the same kind of man all over again? It was okay to make a mistake once, but she was a fool if she made the same mistake twice. But in her heart she knew Neal was different. Then, too, how well did you really know another person?

Neal's car had disappeared from sight. Arlene put the key in the lock and went into her house. She needed a night out with Shelly. Thank God she was back.

Arlene picked up the phone. "Shelly, do you remember that girl's night out that was postponed months ago? I'm not counting the dinner."

"Yeah?"

"I need it . . . tonight."

"Right up my alley. See you at 1900 hours."

By the time seven arrived, Arlene had changed out of her uniform and into slacks and a shirt. She picked Shelly up and they drove to a German pub and settled at a secluded table in a corner.

"How long will you be here this time?" Arlene asked. Shelly was an auditor in the Inspector General's office. She traveled almost as frequently as Ronald had.

"At least a couple of weeks. Then I'll be off again."

"What do you want to order?"

"I know it's heavy, but I'm dying to eat German sausages and delicious breads."

"Think you can throw some vegetables in there?"

"Yes, mother, dear. I will eat my veggies."

Arlene pressed her lips together. "So don't eat them. It's your body."

"Let's order a beer. You need to loosen up some. It's good that I'm here. I trust things still aren't going smoothly with Colonel Allen."

"Quite frankly, I don't know and I don't even want to think about it. I want an evening of relaxation. All issues are out that door."

"Girl, I'm really going to have to get you loaded."

"You're right. The Sheikh and his wives are enough to turn my hair gray. They think he's going to die and they're debating which son will succeed. There's an uncle in the picture, too, but if he gets the throne, his son will usurp the Sheikh's descendents."

"Does security have to pull these women apart to keep them from tearing each other's hair out?"

"You know better. They have always lived together. They have learned to tolerate each other. They seem like a regular family."

"I'd like to be a fly on the wall when they're in private. I know I'd rip somebody's hair out."

"Before you pull out somebody's hair, have you asked George for a date yet?"

"I have."

"Tell all."

"Well, I approached him and said, 'Aren't you tired of making dumb mistakes like going out with nice women yet? Aren't you ready for somebody with a little spice?'"

"You didn't."

"I most certainly did. He wasn't wearing his uniform, girlfriend. He was jogging in a muscle shirt and shorts." Shelly fanned herself. "He's got a body to die for. But I already knew that. I could tell just by looking at him."

"How did he respond?"

"He said, 'When you find that spice send her to me.'"

Arlene cracked up.

"And I said, 'She's here. Dinner. Saturday night. Hang on to your brass buttons for a ride on the wild side.'"

"And he said?"

"'Seven sharp. What's your address?'"

"You're kidding?"

"Girl, he's got more spice than I gave him credit for. His eyes roamed over my body like a slow hand. I thought I was going to need to take my blood pressure, but I told him I was driving and I knew where he lived. If an auditor can't find his address, who could?"

Arlene howled. "If only I could be a fly on the wall," she said, wiping the tears from her eyes. "I think the two of you will be good for each other."

As they talked and ate, Arlene felt more relaxed than she had in a long time. But inevitably, the conversation returned to April.

"Bridget must have known that Ronald was lying at some point," Arlene said. "Why would she put up with that? April was eight when she and Ronald died. She was his daughter. He should have wanted to be with her, and if he didn't, why didn't Bridget show him the door?"

Shelly set her beer on the table. "From what you've said, she was accustomed to being neglected. On the surface, Neal and Bridget came from a nice home in a lovely neighborhood."

"But neither of them were given support and the love they needed," Arlene finished.

"Thank God Neal doesn't neglect April."

"No, he doesn't."

"Life can be such a mess."

Arlene called Tina daily to make sure all was well. She seemed to be handling the situation; still, Arlene worried about her. She went days without calling Neal. Finally, when she called his office, she left a message. Instead of returning her call, he came by her house that evening at six. The sun was still bright.

One of the first things Neal learned in the special forces was good planning. Arlene was a soft touch. Although she was being difficult right now, she needed a reason to keep him in her life until she came to terms with Ronald, himself and April. If he called her for a date, she'd decline. If he called about Byron and Tina, she'd talk. She was genuinely concerned about Tina.

"Don't worry so, Arlene. Tina's in Gambler's Anonymous. She and Byron are seeing the same counselor—in separate sessions, of course. Eventually, they'll have sessions together, but not just yet. Hopefully the counselor will be a tremendous asset since she's getting both perspectives."

"I can't help but worry. They're so young. Tina's so vulnerable."

"Their youth is an advantage. They aren't too old to change, or learn new techniques for handling problems." He adjusted his stance. "I took Byron by his house to see Tina today. I don't think it's a good idea for them to be alone just yet. She was a lot better knowing he'll visit her often. It's not as if things are standing in limbo. The wheels are turning to make their situation better."

Arlene nodded. He was right. That was one of the things Arlene loved about him. He truly cared about the people who worked for him. He didn't give a thought to himself or his career when he was helping others. Those traits made the difference between a mediocre leader and a great leader.

And then Arlene froze. Did she love him? She closed her eyes. Yes, she did love this man, very much.

He impaled her with his eyes. The look was a little wild, but controlled at the same time.

The realization that she loved him made her feel as if a lightning bolt had struck her, and she felt vulnerable.

She closed her eyes on the realization. "Okay," she said softly.

He came close to her, threaded his fingers through her short hair, and brought her face close to his. "How do you feel about having me close by most of the time? In a couple of months, things are going to change. I won't be going on missions the way I do now. I'll be more in the planning stage instead of the action."

"Your career decisions don't concern me."

Neal chuckled and shifted positions. Kissing the side of her mouth, he said, "They involve you more than you want to admit."

Arlene wanted to fight the need building in her, but in the end she was tired of fighting.

She linked her arms around his neck, and kissed him on the chin, giving herself up to the pleasure to be found in his strong arms.

She felt his hand glide around her waist, tugging her close to his warmth. It was like coming up against a powerful, unyielding force.

"It's been a while," he said. His touch did all kinds of delicious things to her insides.

Arlene rubbed her breasts against his massive chest. "Then I'll have to make it up to you."

"Your wish is my command." His voice was rough with expectation.

Arlene scanned his taut body. His movements were smooth; he was someone in full command of his body. Heat as hot and sharp as a laser emanated from him. His eyes missed nothing. She tugged at his belt buckle and led him down the hall, and he willingly followed.

His stomach was as hard as stone beneath soft skin. The back of her fingers tingled just with the contact of his body against her hand. Arlene loved touching him—loved feeling all those hard muscles sheathed in velvety skin pressed against her. She was getting exciting at the prospects of the evening ahead.

Arlene was winded from his very presence; nevertheless, she was going to give him something to remember when he was on a mission far, far away from her. Or months down the road when their relationship would be a thing of the past, Lieutenant Colonel Arlene Taft would insure that Colonel Neal Allen would never, ever forget this night.

So help her, she wouldn't either.

The next Saturday was family day for the Rangers. Arlene had been in the Army for fifteen years and was accustomed to viewing buff bodies, but rarely did she see so many men as well-developed as these were at one time. The dress was casual, and most of the men wore jeans. Muscles rippled beneath short-sleeved T-shirts. And they had the self-possessed attitude that went with it. They were a unique fighting force and their body language and carriage was evidence of that fact.

Only one took her breath away, and he was talking to the General right now.

For the first time, Arlene had an opportunity to meet the people who Neal worked with. There was enough food to feed a small third world country, and plenty of games for both children and adults.

Byron carried Makayla, who was dressed like a doll baby and was even more beautiful. One arm was tucked around Tina's shoulders. It was clear that Tina was in seventh heaven to be with him.

Love.

She wished April were here. April would enjoy the games and entertainment with the other children. A couple of them had already asked about her. April. Thoughts of her drew a dagger through her heart, and yet, Arlene loved her, too. She was so giving, so easy to love.

And of course there were plenty of "male competition"

activities. Arlene shook her head. Testosterone was in high gear. And she was enjoying every moment of it.

"Okay, I need a partner for the next game," Neal said.

"What are we playing?"

"The sack race."

Arlene caught a glimpse of the younger women. "You aren't allowed to drag me to the finish line."

"Now would I do that?"

Arlene gave him a steady glare. He threw an arm around her waist and led her to the field.

"You can run, can't you? I've never seen you run before."

Arlene sniffed. "I'm in the Army, aren't I? Of course I can run."

"Your legs are pretty, by the way," he whispered in her ear. His breath fanned the side of her face and Arlene blushed. He didn't need to hear how fine looking he was. He already knew.

The festivities were almost over when Byron caught Arlene alone.

"Did you enjoy yourself, Lieutenant Colonel?" he asked.

"Very much." Arlene worked to keep the frown from her face. It had been obvious that Tina loved him and was happy spending the day with him. Likewise, he'd been very attentive to Tina.

Byron looked to where Tina was talking to another soldier's wife. Both were holding a baby on their laps. "I know you don't like me much, but Tina and Makayla are my whole world. I'm going to stick with those counseling sessions until everything's straight."

"Byron, nothing would make me happier than for things to work out for the two of you. I know you love each other. It's just love isn't always enough. It doesn't solve every problem."

Byron searched out Tina again. "In our case it's enough. It has to be."

Monday afternoon after work, Arlene called her father. It was nine, his time. He was sixty-five today. Perhaps she should have tried his home first. He might have taken the day off. But the receptionist connected her to his number.

"Happy birthday, Dad," Arlene said.

"Arlene?"

"Yes. It's me."

"It's good to hear from you. I got your gift. It was perfect."

"I'm glad you like it." Arlene cleared her throat. "I've been thinking about you a lot lately."

"Same here."

"Do you have plans for the special day?"

"Just dinner out. Nothing special."

"I hope you enjoy it."

An uncomfortable silence stretched.

"I've been thinking that I'll take a trip to Florida to visit you when I come to the States in August," Arlene said, wondering at the strained atmosphere. How were they going to get to where they were before her mother died?

"I won't be here."

Disappointment settled in Arlene's stomach. She hadn't seen her father in two years. She really wanted to see him. "You and Monica will be on vacation?"

"No. I . . . we're moving back to Houston."

"Job transfer?"

"No, I'm retiring in a week. All my friends are in Texas. I want to be around people I know."

"Have you found a house yet?"

"I never sold our house—just rented it out. The people have already moved out. I've had some renovations done."

"Is it okay if I visit you?"

"Of course you can. I'll look forward to seeing you. Have some of our old friends over."

"I'd like that, Dad. I'm looking forward to seeing you again."

"Me too. I've missed you . . . a lot."

Arlene held the phone tightly against her ear. "I've missed you, too," she whispered.

"Give me your phone number. I started to call you a couple of times, then realized I didn't have your number."

"You know you can always reach me through base locator."

"Hadn't thought about that."

"Is everything okay?"

"Just fine. Don't worry about me. Just give me your number."

Arlene rattled the numbers off.

"I'll call you next time."

"Take care, Dad. Have a great birthday."

Slowly, Arlene hung up the phone with a smile on her face. Their relationship wasn't where it needed to be, but at least she and her dad were finally making progress.

Nine

Neal's father, the General, had called him the night before.

"Are you going to visit the Ardennes for the Battle of the Bulge anniversary, son?"

"If I can. I want to take April when I go, Dad," Neal responded.

"There are a lot of memories there. I haven't been back since forty-five."

"I know."

"Your mama's worried about that nanny who takes care of April when you go on missions."

"She's a good woman."

"It's not like it was here, son. We were in the house. We knew she was being well taken care of."

Evidently his father didn't remember that April called him everyday in the hospital complaining to Arlene about the nanny. She hadn't complained once in Germany.

"Everything's under control, dad."

"Well, I was just checking. You know how your mother worry about her now that Bridget's gone. She's our only granddaughter. Doesn't look like you're going to settle down."

"I might one day."

"Is it the soldier April's been talking about?"

"Yes."

"I hope she works out better than the last one."

"She's nothing like Natasha."

In the silence, Neal asked. "Where is Mom?"

"She and April went shopping."

"I hope you told her not to buy out the store. We have to bring all that stuff back."

His dad chuckled. "Shopping is one thing they have in common."

Byron had been on Neal's mind a lot lately. As a general, his father had some pull, even retired. "Dad, this guy's working for me and he's had a pretty hard life. No role models in the home to speak of. But he's a hard worker. He's got a few issues."

"What kind of issues?"

"He's abusive to his wife sometimes. But I have him in counseling."

"He can kiss his chances for promotions good-bye."

"It's private counseling, not through the military."

"That's good. You made the right move on that one."

"Anyway, once we're through this and he has his life back on track, I was wondering if you could get him sent to a base in Texas where he could finish up school. They have a great communications program at the university there. I'm hoping to get him in Officer's Candidate school."

"Once he has his personal life under control, I'll see what I can do."

"And could you keep an eye on them, be sort of a role model for them?"

"Sure son. I've got plenty of time."

"Thanks dad, I appreciate it." They hung up.

His father, a member of the 761st Tank Battalion, commanded a group of black soldiers through six European countries and participated in four major Allied campaigns in WWII. They destroyed or aided in the liberation of more than 30 towns, several concentration camps, four airfields, three ammunition supply dumps, 461-wheeled vehicles, 34 tanks, 113 large guns and thousands of individual and crew-served weapons. They were known as the "Black

Panthers." They also served in the counter attack against the Germans at the conclusion of the Battle of the Bulge. The 761st was the first African-American unit to fight in armored combat.

Though Neal had seen little of his father as a boy, he'd learned discipline and his values from him which had stood him in good stead in his military career. His father had retired a General.

The men of the 761st served their country well—yet Neal knew most of them couldn't vote in their own country. They went home to racism, although they had fought for freedom for men and women in other countries.

After WWII, the KKK resumed their terror on African-Americans in the south.

Even today, racism ran amuck in the black community, and yet black men and women still supported and protected their country. They had since the Revolutionary War and every war thereafter. Not many cultures could attest to that—even those who enjoy more freedom.

His father hadn't been a pilot. He was a commander in the black battalion infantry. They were often forced into the worst fighting positions, often on the front line to protect the white soldiers coming up in the rear.

Although Neal hadn't spent as much time as he'd wanted to with his father, they had spent some time together and his father had secured a good home for his family. When he thought of Byron and Tina, he realized how much worse things could have been for him.

Neal also had Buckley Academy. As part of the football team, he'd learned the true value of discipline and team effort under the leadership of Coach Foster. It had been in his freshman year in high school that Neal had begun to change—to take life more seriously, to become more responsible. It was during that time that he left Arlene alone.

Byron took his responsibilities seriously. Both his work and his family. If Byron had had the opportunity to serve under Coach Clyde Foster at Buckley, by now he'd be a force to reckon with. But he'd get there. Among soldiers Neal could assess that Byron was one who would stand out, who would strive far above the ordinary. Byron had the capabilities to reach beyond his current rank.

Neal and Byron ran around the track and now they were sprawled out on benches, towels wrapped around their necks.

"Let's talk about your counseling sessions," Neal said. "Are they doing you any good?"

"I guess."

"What do you mean, you guess? Either it's working or it isn't."

Byron leaned his elbows on his thighs, his hands dangling between. "I don't like the questions she asks."

"Like what?"

Byron shrugged. "How I feel about women. Things like that. It's almost like a man can't be a man anymore."

Neal scrubbed the towel over his head. "That depends on your definition of manhood."

"That's the same thing she said."

"And?"

"I don't know why I have to go through this," Byron complained.

"Well, if you don't know by now, let me enlighten you. For two reasons. First, you have no business hitting on your wife. She's a grown woman. Treat her that way." When Byron started to say something, Neal held up a hand and stopped him. "Second, I think you have potential. If I didn't think there was hope, I'd have let the military deal with your attitude. You will make a great officer once you get your temper under control. To be an officer, you have to behave like an officer and a gentleman. If you can't handle your personal affairs, how can you handle Army business? And if you got that far without the counseling, this issue would rise again, again, and again. You may be one of many who get passed over for promotions until you're on your way out of a career in the service and back on the streets with nothing to show for your efforts."

"Growing up on the streets, I never thought I would be here, much less an officer in the Army. Hell, I thought I'd be dead by twenty-five," he said. "An officer. Do you really think I can be an officer?"

"Yes, I do. I've observed how you handle the people around you at work, even those who aren't under your command. You're a natural leader. But you must also have control—of your home, as well as business. That's why you're getting private counseling away from the Army, so it won't show up on your records."

Neal wiped the sweat dripping down his face. "I suggest you listen to your counselor and make prudent use of your time. There comes a time when we have to answer the hard questions—whether we want to or not." Neal stood. "I'll see you in the office tomorrow."

Just an hour ago, Lieutenant General Anderson's physician had imparted devastating news to him and his wife. The doctors had given him one good year—more if he were lucky.

Arlene had handed Mrs. Anderson a cup of coffee, but the cup was forgotten in her hand. "What am I going to do?" she asked, dabbing at her eyes with the tissue Arlene handed her. She seemed to remember the coffee and placed it on the coffee table.

"You'll live the time he has left to the fullest."

"He was thinking of retiring in five years. He's up for full General."

"I'm sorry," Arlene told her.

"I don't know how I'm going to handle it."

"You handle it by making it the best year of your lives."

"How does one do that?"

"It isn't easy, knowing. You just have to cherish what you've meant to each other and the time you have left."

"I have to sleep beside him every night and cry silently so he won't hear me. I have to show a smile I don't feel across the breakfast table."

"But he's across the table from you, and he's lying in the bed beside you. Concentrate on that. Don't write him off before he even leaves you."

"No, not that—never that. I can't focus on what the future will be like without him." She pressed her lips firmly together, then she said, "I'm a General's wife. I'm supposed to be strong. Stiff upper lip."

Arlene smiled a gentle smile. "You're also human. It's allowed, you know."

Mrs. Anderson dabbed at her eyes one last time. She straightened her shoulders and stood, then touched Arlene's hand. "Thank you, Lieutenant Colonel."

"If you need me, just call."

The woman nodded and left the room.

Arlene handled dozens of similar cases in the course of her work. She tried to be objective, tried to give the people walking into her office the emotional support they craved, but now she felt drained. She needed to be around people. She'd told the General's wife to straighten up and move on—when she couldn't do the same herself. What right did she have counseling someone else?

She shouldn't feel this emotionally drained over a husband who died two years ago, over his mistress, Bridget, and his child, April. What a mess. The worst part was that Arlene knew she loved that little girl. What was there not to like about April? She was as open as the pages of a book, and willingly gave her love. Arlene should be able to move on and forget the garbage. So why couldn't she do that? Was her heart too frozen to accept April? Why was she acting like a civilian instead of the soldier she was?

* * *

Arlene picked Nancy up from the airport in Frankfurt. The woman came with one suitcase but armfuls of bags. Arlene pulled the car up to the terminal and enlisted the help of the skycap to get the things to the car.

"What's in the bags?" Arlene asked Nancy when they were on their way to her quarters.

"I brought plenty of food. I baked all kinds of desserts and chicken and everything. I know you can't be eating well."

"They have plenty of food here. You should have rested before you came." Even though Arlene loved the woman, whenever she visited, she always brought enough food to feed an army. She must have thought that Arlene hadn't been feeding her son well enough.

They made small talk on the way to her quarters. Once they arrived, Arlene made several trips to the car to unpack. When she brought the last bag in the house, Nancy was standing at the mantle looking at the pictures. Arlene had forgotten she no longer displayed pictures of Ronald. There was one family photo, but that was the only one.

A prominent 8x10 of April and Arlene on their trip to Switzerland was displayed on the mantle. They stood in the snow wearing snowsuits.

"Who's the little girl?"

"She's a friend's daughter. I lived next door to her family four years in Dallas." Arlene wanted to tell her about April, but she thought it best to speak to Neal first.

"She's a lovely child. You look so good with her, like she could be your own daughter."

The muscles in Arlene's stomach clenched. "She is a beautiful child."

Nancy continued to peruse the photos. There weren't many. "Ronald looks so good in that picture," Nancy said. "What happened to all the others?"

"I sent you some and the others I've packed away. They're in the States."

"Oh." For a moment Nancy looked crestfallen and Arlene didn't know how to tell her that she was moving on with her life, if Nancy didn't realize it.

"Well," she said. "I brought some beautiful pictures with me. As soon as I unpack I'll put them up there."

"Why don't you display them on the dresser in your room?" Arlene suggested. She didn't want to build a shrine to a man who betrayed her.

"Don't you care about Ronald anymore?" Nancy asked.

The hurt in Nancy's eyes touched Arlene.

"He was such a good man."

"He was but he's gone now," Arlene said quietly.

"Not forgotten. You were married for a long time."

For the first time, Arlene had second thoughts about asking Nancy to visit. She was, after all, a mother-in-law who still loved her son. Evidently, she wasn't going to take Arlene's moving on too kindly.

"I have the memories, but I have to move on with my life, Nancy. It's been two years."

"I know that, but that doesn't mean the years you spent together meant nothing."

"No, it doesn't."

"Ronald was so good, I don't know how you'll ever replace him. All the good men are taken. Only second picks are left and they aren't much. Better to stay alone."

"You can never replace another person," Arlene said. "I'm not trying to replace him, just doing my best to find space for myself."

"He's irreplaceable."

"Why don't you unpack and I'll fix you a light snack before you rest? Jetlag can make you feel like you're holding up a ton of bricks."

When Nancy headed to the spare bedroom, Arlene headed to the kitchen to put up the tons of food the woman brought with her. Arlene had the feeling the next seven days were going to try her patience.

* * *

An Important Message From The ARABESQUE Publisher

Dear Arabesque Reader,

I have some exciting news to share....

Available now is a four-part special series **AT YOUR SERVICE** written by bestselling Arabesque Authors.

Bold, sweeping and passionate as America itself—these superb romances feature military heroes you are destined to love. They confront their unpredictable futures along-side women of equal courage, who will inspire you!

The **AT YOUR SERVICE** series* can be specially ordered by calling 1-888-345-BOOK, or purchased wherever books are sold.

Enjoy them and let us know your feedback by commenting on our website.

Linda Gill, Publisher
Arabesque Romance Novels

At Your Service

BET BOOKS

Check out our website at www.BET.com

ARABESQUE

* The **AT YOUR SERVICE** novels are a special series that are not included in your regular book club subscription.

THE ARABESQUE ROMANCE CLUB. HERE'S HOW IT WORKS

Accepting the four introductory books for FREE (plus $1.99 to offset the cost of shipping & handling) places you under no obligation to buy anything. You may keep the books and return the shipping statement marked "cancelled". If you do not cancel, about a month later we will send 4 additional Arabesque novels, and you will be billed the preferred subscriber's price of just $4.00 per title. That's $16.00* for all 4 books for a savings of almost 40% off the cover price (Plus $1.99 for shipping and handling). You may cancel at any time, but if you choose to continue, every month we'll send you 4 more books, which you may either purchase at the preferred discount price. . . or return to us and cancel your subscription.

* PRICES SUBJECT TO CHANGE

PLACE
STAMP
HERE

THE ARABESQUE ROMANCE BOOK CLUB
P.O. BOX 5214
CLIFTON NJ 07015-5214

As luck would have it, Neal stopped by that evening without calling first. Nancy was sitting in the living room, crocheting. "I packed the hook in the suitcase. I didn't want problems getting through security," she said. "They might have thought I had a weapon."

"Nancy, I'd like you to meet Colonel Neal Allen. He's April's uncle. Neal, meet Nancy Taft, Ronald's mother." She hadn't told him that she was visiting.

Neal extended a hand. "How are you, Mrs. Taft?"

Nancy gave Neal a narrow stare. "I'm fine. Your little girl is precious."

"Thank you."

"It's a shame that Arlene didn't want children. She and Ronald should have had a few."

"Who said I didn't want children?"

"Ronald said you thought they'd interfere with your work." She tightened her lips accusingly around the words.

"That isn't true."

"Well, my son wanted them. He said you wouldn't and I didn't have the nerve to interfere. I don't like to get mixed up in my child's marriage. And you were so good, I thought you'd eventually see the light. Now I wished I had interfered. Ronald was so good to you, Arlene. Most men wouldn't have put up with that attitude."

"I know you're distraught over Ronald's death, but . . ."

Nancy gathered her crochet things in her fists. "If you two would excuse me, I'll go to my room." She marched off with her head held high. The door closed firmly behind her. In a few seconds she marched back with a frame in her hand. Arlene and Neal still stood perplexed in the middle of the floor. Nancy placed the photo on the mantle. It was Ronald in dress uniform. The American Flag waved behind him. Without looking at either of them, Nancy again marched to the back room.

This was not the woman Arlene had known for more than fifteen years. Where was the woman with the loving heart who wrote to her at least once a month? Where was the woman who had become a firm shoulder to lean on when Arlene had lost her own mother and a year later when her father had married a woman who was young enough to be his daughter?

The closing of the door felt like a bomb reverberating through the house.

"I'm sorry, Neal. I didn't expect her to react this way."

"She's obviously having difficulty dealing with her son's death."

"I know, but . . ."

"We all handle loss in different ways. Lord knows I've had my share to deal with." He held her close, rubbed her back. "Relax okay? How long will she be here?"

"Just a week," Arlene said, but it was likely to be the longest week of her life.

The week finally ended. Arlene and Nancy stood in the airport, almost bitter enemies. Arlene held on to her patience by a thread. She'd taken the older woman on tours—they even toured a castle. They attended musicals in the park, attended wine festivals, took a boat ride on the Rhine and passed by the Black Forest. But Nancy knew Arlene was dating Neal and she didn't like the idea of her son's wife dating another man, even though he was no longer around. To Nancy's way of thinking, if Ronald was still alive for her, then so he should be for Arlene.

Arlene tried again to get her to understand that Ronald was gone and she needed to move on with her life, but Nancy wasn't hearing it. Arlene now realized how fixated she still was on her son.

"Nancy have you thought about grief counseling to help you deal with Ronald's death?"

"I'm not crazy."

"I didn't say you were crazy. Everyone needs help sometimes. It's not considered crazy to seek help with recovery from the loss of a son."

"Did you get grief counseling?" Nancy asked with knowing eyes.

"No."

"Because you don't miss him."

Arlene realized Nancy wasn't willing to take any advice from her. "I'm sorry your stay wasn't good, Nancy. I don't like it that we're at odds for the first time in our lives."

"Well, you have your life to live and I have mine." She lifted her chin. "Thank you for your hospitality."

"I'll be in Texas in August. I'll try to visit."

"If you can spare the time. Good-bye Arlene," Nancy said and walked off.

The way she said it sounded so final, and Arlene felt deflated. Neal had called her several times, but he'd tried to make himself scarce out of respect for Nancy.

That afternoon, April called Arlene.

"I can't reach Uncle Neal. He must be gone again because I tried and tried."

"Is everything all right?" Arlene asked.

"I'm ready to come back. I like not having to go to school, but I miss Uncle Neal and you."

"He'll be there before you know it," Arlene told her.

"That's what he always says. Grandma said we're going to put flowers on Mama's grave when Uncle Neal comes."

"I see. Did . . . did you and your daddy do lots of things together?" Arlene felt like a heel asking April that question.

"Not much. I have pictures of him though, but I didn't see him much. Sometimes I forget what he looks like, then I'd look at his picture. He sent me presents. Sometimes Mama would bring things home and say it was from my dad. Anyway, I got the card and letter you sent me. Thank you. I'm going to write to you tonight. A nice long letter."

"You're welcome. I'll look forward to your letter."

"I have to go. My friend just got here. Her mama's taking us to the movies. I'll call you soon."

Arlene wondered how long those phone cards were going to last. "Have a good time at the theater. Make sure you and your friend stay together at all times. Don't go anywhere alone."

"Okay. I'm not a baby anymore," she said and then she hung up.

Neal visited Arlene that night.

"April's trying to reach you," she said.

"I called her," he responded. "How was Mrs. Taft's stay?"

Arlene sighed. "Trying."

"Did you tell her about April?"

"No. I couldn't. Things were just so tense and I wanted to discuss it with you first. Right now I want to talk about your sister and my husband."

Neal made himself comfortable on the couch. "I don't know very much, but I know that he told her he'd asked you for a divorce."

"He never asked me for a divorce."

"Believe it or not, I came to that conclusion a while ago. He said that at first you complied, but when you discovered Bridget was pregnant, you reneged and threatened to cause problems with his career."

Arlene was outraged. "How could he have said such a thing? That I'm vindictive? If I knew he was philandering, he wouldn't have had to ask. I would have demanded he give *me* a divorce."

"Arlene, I'm telling you because I want to put it behind us."

"I have."

She said it with such finality, Neal's eyebrows arched.

"I have, really."

He continued to look disbelieving.

She sighed. "I don't want to end up like Nancy. I can't

let Ronald's infidelity affect the rest of my life. I really do want to put him in the past and move on."

"That, at least, is something I want to hear."

"I don't want that experience to make me a bitter old woman, you know? I understand Ronald was Nancy's only child. And our disagreement is tinged with a mother's love. She's blind to his faults. But more than ever she needs to know about April—that part of him is still alive. Things were so bitter this week. I didn't know how to tell her. Half the time I was angry at her, and yet, I didn't know how to tell her that her perfect son wasn't so perfect, after all."

Neal rubbed her back.

"I can't believe Ronald told her I didn't want children when I wanted them so much."

"You can still have them."

"My chances aren't as good as they would have been when I was in my twenties."

"They're still good. I want children. Well, at least one. April needs a sister or brother."

"Wait . . . wait. How did we get on this subject?"

"Maybe more of your true feelings are coming out."

Arlene contemplated that for a moment.

"There's a play at the theater tomorrow night. Would you like to see it?" Neal asked.

Arlene's mind was still reeling with Ronald's lies, Nancy's defection, and Neal. But most of all, Ronald wasn't faithful to anyone. Not even his own daughter. They'd both lost. Ronald, because he didn't take the time to nurture the love April so willingly threw at the world, and April, not getting the opportunity to know and love her father. In every sense, Neal was her father. And he deserved the love she lavished on him.

"Arlene?" Neal asked.

"Yes," she said, smiling up at him. "I'd love to go."

"It hasn't been easy for you, I know. And I keep pressuring you. I'm going to let you take your time and deal with all these issues."

"Yes, well, whoever said life was a roller coaster knew what they were talking about."

When Neal left, Arlene reassessed her life. She'd seen it as a fact that with Ronald and Neal she made a habit of choosing the same kind of man. The two men had a lot in common. Both were type A personalities. By its very definition, they were driven and charismatic. Women flocked to their irresistible charm. She was no more immune to Neal's charms.

There would always be firecrackers and champagne between Colonel Neal and herself. The funny thing was, she had grown to trust him. Sometimes she wondered if she were a little too trusting—almost like April.

Perhaps that was why she didn't trust her own judgment sometimes. Because she trusted too easily. She hoped that her trust this time wasn't misplaced. She couldn't give up on life, but caution was still the sensible choice.

It didn't take a genius to note the chemistry that always seemed to erupt between Neal and her.

Ten

Arlene enjoyed the play. When she had weekends off, she and Neal toured Germany together, they listened to music in the parks on Sundays after church, they ate dinner at German pubs, and they attended numerous base functions. They were cementing the relationship in a way Arlene never envisioned, and in the process, he'd completely charmed her.

Neal invited Arlene to a formal event at the Argentinean Embassy. The day marked the Ambassador's sixty-fifth birthday. Neal had trained with the Ambassador's son and they had remained friends through the years.

When Arlene opened the door, the image of him in his formal dress uniform and spit-shined black shoes took her breath away. She had forgone her own dress uniform for a red spaghetti-strap gown that flowed gracefully to her feet.

"Do we really have to go?" he asked her as his eyes scanned her from head to toe. Goose bumps gathered on her arms and he smiled. He tugged her close. "Let's forget about the birthday bash."

Arlene wanted nothing more than to spend the evening in an intimate embrace. "It took me forever to dress. Yes, we have to go," she informed him in stern tones. "But you're gorgeous," she said.

His gaze swept over her once again. "Not nearly as beautiful as you. Woman, you take my breath away."

Arlene steered him out of the house before they skipped the gathering completely.

The drive to the embassy was short.

It was times like these that Neal was grateful the instructors at Buckley Academy in Dallas had taught them ballroom dancing. They used to moan at having to dance the tango, fox trot and waltz, labeling it white folks' dances. He and Nelson Wainwright used to crack up over it. Nelson was a colonel now as well, stationed at the Pentagon. When Neal left for the States, he would stop to visit him. His first visit to the Pentagon since September 11th.

A small orchestra began "La Comparsita," a tango standard. The generals and dignitaries gathered on the dance floor.

"Can you tango?" Neal asked Arlene.

"Can I tango? Do birds fly? Let this sista show you a thing or two."

"All right," Neal said, gathering her hand in his and leading her onto the dance floor.

She could tango. They ate the floor up with the dance. The music changed and they danced the waltz before they left the floor to mingle with some of the officers and their wives. General Sampson introduced Arlene and Neal to several new military attachés. A lot of political wrangling went on under the guise of a party.

At a knock on her door, Arlene put down her romance novel. Only taking enough time to pull a thin robe over her skimpy nightgown, she made her way down the hall. Plucking the glasses off her face, she opened the door.

"I thought you were going home," she said as Neal came in.

"Holding you in my arms is better than a lonely bed any day," he said in a deep hoarse voice.

Arlene's breath caught in her throat. For some reason, tonight there was something different about him, something very male, very foreboding, *very* exciting.

He advanced on her, his aim steady and purposeful. Arlene took a step back and fumbled her glasses on her nose to gain some perspective. The move didn't work.

"Those glasses are sexy."

She'd have to calm down, calm him down a little bit. "You want . . ."

"You," he said without hesitation.

And then she was in his arms—strong rippling muscles encased her against his steel athletic body.

Later they made it to the bedroom, and there he spent the night.

Tina walked up to the slot machines and reached into her purse. Byron had paid the bills himself this time, but he'd given her grocery money. If she used the slot machine, she could double or triple her money. Then she'd have more money.

A friend kept Makayla for her and Byron was working tonight.

As Tina took the fives and tens out of her pocket to exchange into coins, her hands shook. She thought about Lieutenant Colonel Taft and her spiel on money management. Her hands slowed as she stuck the five in the coin machine. But she could make money quicker on the slots. Sure she'd had a bad streak lately. But following bad streaks were always good streaks. She'd just do five dollars. Losing five dollars wouldn't put her in the poorhouse.

Tina started to play. So much adrenaline flowed through her that she felt lightheaded. It had been a long time since she'd felt this lucky. The controls felt as familiar, almost a part of her hands. She played again and again. The five dollars she'd allocated was gone before she knew it, but she'd do better next time. Her mama always said sometimes you had to play the same machine for a while before it let loose some money. She should know. She practically lived off gambling—and men.

Tina looked at the woman beside her. "Hold my place for me, will you?"

The woman nodded, continuing to play her own game. Tina went to the coin machine again and changed ten dollars this time. She peered over her shoulder to make sure nobody had taken her spot. Somebody was headed to her machine. She broke into a jog to beat him there.

"This one's taken," she said, with an edge to her tone and positioned herself in front of the machine. She proceeded to pile quarters in and pulled the lever. She got six dollars back. *There you go,* she thought. Her diligence was finally beginning to pay off. *About time.* Another hour of this and she'd recoup what she'd spent with extra on the side.

The aroma of bacon frying drew Neal out of the bed. He showered and brushed his teeth quickly. Forgoing the T-shirt, he pulled on his pants before he trekked to the kitchen.

Arlene glanced over her shoulder and smiled at him. Then she returned to flipping something in the pan.

Neal came up behind her and wrapped his arms around her waist, tugging her back to him, running his hands over her abdomen.

"Did you sleep well?" she asked.

"Like a baby," he whispered as he flicked a tongue around her earlobe.

"I'm going to burn the food."

"Who needs food when I have a feast in my arms?" he said.

"You'll make my head swell."

"That's my job."

Arlene's hands trembled as she flipped the potatoes. "Ummm," she said. Neal turned her around. She held the spatula away from him so she wouldn't burn him when his lips closed on hers. Men loved morning sex. Good thing she was a morning person and loved it too.

"Turn the stove off," he managed to get out.

"But . . . your breakfast . . ."

He reached around her, flicked off the stove and shoved the pan back. "Breakfast will keep." His promise held lots of wonderful possibilities.

Tina shut the door and leaned against it. What was she going to do? Makayla was still at her friend's place. The fear in Tina's gut increased by the second. She crossed her arms, hugged them tight against her body as if it could relieve the knot in her stomach. She was so damn worn out with living in a state of constant fear. *I'm a horrible person,* She thought. *Byron works so hard. He's a good father—a good husband. And I'm throwing it all away by losing the money he works so hard for.* She never felt so worthless in her life.

Why do I do this to myself? She just didn't understand why she gambled. Afterwards she was always sorry. And she did it again and again even though she lost money.

Byron was going to stop loving her. He was going to get tired of putting up with her gambling and then where would she be?

Would she have to return to her mama's home? She couldn't let Makayla grow up scared the way she did. She didn't know what it felt like *not* to be afraid. That's no kind of life for Makayla.

Tina eased herself into the kitchen chair. She had come to the slot machine with $150.00. She left with $15.00 in her purse, just enough to buy some food for the baby. What was she going to eat for the rest of the week? And what was she going to feed Byron when he came over for dinner?

Oh, God. Byron was going to kill her. Why couldn't she

learn from her mistakes? Why didn't gambling work for her the way it always worked for her mama?

She couldn't handle this alone anymore. Tina surged out of her seat, reached for the phone and called her counselor.

Breakfast had passed. Neal took Arlene out to dinner at one of Germany's most exclusive restaurants. She was beautiful in a green dress. He wore a suit.

He had debated long and hard how to handle this. He'd first thought to let her pick out her own ring. But knowing her, they'd never get around to anything serious if he waited. So he chose one with the option of exchanging it.

They had completed a scrumptious dinner. The waiter brought champagne to the table as Neal had arranged ahead of time.

"Champagne? What's the occasion?" Arlene asked.

Neal watched the waiter discretely leave. He knew there was nothing unusual about the way he was handling this. Men proposed this way millions of times each year. But he was nervous. Sweat beaded on his brow.

"Arlene," he said reaching into his pocket . . . and the phone vibrated in his pocket. He took the phone out and peered at the number in the display.

"Damn it, not now. Not now." He didn't even consider not answering. It was an emergency, even more urgent this time. He signaled for the waiter for the check. He threw some bills on the table and drove to the base.

"I need you to drop me off and take the car home. I don't have time to do both," he murmured.

At the base, he hopped out of the car while Arlene came around the other side. He tugged her into his arms. "I'm sorry it has to be this way, but Arlene, will you marry me?"

"What?" The shock on her face alarmed him, still he

pulled the ring out of his breast pocket. "If you don't like this, you can exchange it," he said as they walked toward the building. Even now the helo had been started.

"Will you?"

"I don't . . . This is such a surprise . . ."

He didn't want to hear no. Not now. "Keep this." He glided the ring on her finger and closed his hand around hers. "Think about it. April and I are a package deal. I know you still have issues with us. We need to talk. We should have ironed everything out before I popped the question." He kissed her ring finger. "Keep this and think about us while I'm away." He kissed her lips one last time, held her body tightly against his.

"I love you, Arlene," he said and then left her. He marched across the tarmac.

"Neal!" she called out.

He turned, backing toward the building.

"I love you," she said and threw him a kiss.

He smiled and saluted.

But Arlene knew that loving him didn't mean they were ready for marriage. Still, not knowing the dangers he'd encounter, she couldn't let him leave without telling him at least what was in her heart.

Full Bird had told Byron to use his counseling time wisely, and he was doing his best, but he was surprised that the counselor was ready for both of them together so soon. Tina sat nervously in a chair beside him. He grasped her hand in his and smiled.

"It's going to be all right. We're getting help. I'm feeling better about things."

Tina wouldn't look at him. What was the matter with her? They were here to get help. Why was she so nervous? He paid the bills this time so the temptation for gambling wouldn't be there for her. Byron puzzled over it for a while before he remembered he'd given Tina some money to buy groceries with.

He gave her a long look. She couldn't have. Tina wouldn't look at him and suddenly he knew there had to be more to this meeting than the fact that they might be ready for sessions together. The counselor had said it would be another two months at least before she put them together. She was dealing with separate issues first.

Byron dropped Tina's hand. "You spent the grocery money on gambling," he said to her and watched the fear increase in her eyes.

"I . . . I'm sorry, Byron. I don't know what came over me."

Byron got up and paced to the window to keep from strangling Tina. He couldn't give her a damn penny without her wasting it on gambling.

The counselor chose that moment to come in. "Sorry I'm late. Hello everyone."

Byron remained silent. Tina dotted a glance between the counselor and Byron.

"Well, I think this is a good time for a session, when you're in the middle of a crisis situation."

"No kidding," Byron retorted.

Several days after Neal left, Arlene received a call from Nancy's sister. Nancy was in the hospital.

"What's wrong with her?" Arlene asked.

"They're running some tests. But I think she's just sick about Ronald. She never got over his death."

Arlene felt guilty. The trip to Germany probably made Nancy worse. The thought that Arlene was moving on with her life without Ronald was probably the straw that finally broke her back.

"I'm so sorry, Pearl. I had planned a trip to the States in a couple of weeks. I'll move the date up. Will she see me? We didn't part on the best of terms."

"Don't worry. She'll be glad to see you. I think she's making herself sick. She just can't get over Ronald's death. He was her son and burying a child is the hardest tragedy a mother can endure."

"I can imagine."

"We'll both be happy to see you. Let me know and I'll pick you up from the airport."

"Don't bother, I'll rent a car."

"You can drive Nancy's."

"I need it for other things. I'm going to land in Dallas and drive to Houston."

"That's the round about way, isn't it?"

"Yes, but it can't be helped. I'll call you as soon as I arrive."

As Arlene put the phone on the hook, she noticed the sparkling diamond on her finger. She was moving on, enjoying her life while Nancy was steeped in depression. She should have done more for the woman. Perhaps taken more time off to spend with her. Guilt gnawed at her for neglecting someone who had been so good to her. She should have been more understanding of Nancy instead of angry with her.

She walked across the room and glanced out the window. The kids next door were playing in the yard. She wished she had children of her own to watch play.

Byron waited several days before he visited Tina. It took that long for him to calm down. He knew he wasn't being fair. He knew he had a lot of personal issues to work on. Every time something came up, he realized just how lucky he was to have the Colonel at his back. He knew seeing Tina alone was breaking the rules, but he wanted to visit her anyway because he had a few things to say to her.

For as long as he'd known Tina he'd shielded her from life as much as he could. Her mama had moved into the apartment building where he lived when Tina was twelve. There was something innocent and intriguing about the shy Tina that pulled at his protective instincts. A whole lot of bad stuff went down in the neighborhood. He didn't want anything bad happening to his Tina. He'd thought of her as his from the moment he laid eyes on her. He wondered if she'd always felt that way about him.

The place they now lived in was nice, not as nice as the officer's quarters, but there were no roaches or rats running around the place. The building was well maintained and clean. He didn't have that worry about bullets flying around Makayla or Tina.

They'd brought furniture, a piece at a time, starting with a Salvation Army sofa and table. The first new piece of furniture had been the queen-size bed. He refused to buy a used mattress. He got hot all over thinking about the way he and Tina had christened that bed.

Months later, they'd saved up enough to buy a living room set. It wasn't terribly expensive, but it was quality stuff. He told Tina he didn't want something cheap that they'd have to replace in a few years. He wanted furniture that would last, which was probably why it took them so long to buy it all. They'd finally furnished the last room seven months ago. Tina kept everything neat, polished, and clean. Growing up he didn't know what it was to live in a place so sparkling.

After he joined the Army, he'd lived better than he ever had before, even in the barracks.

He kept thinking about his conversations with the Colonel—about becoming an officer. As an officer he could move Tina and Makayla into even better quarters. Without conscious thought, he'd already decided that he was staying in the Army. He'd looked into taking college courses for a degree in communications. It wasn't too late to sign up. But he needed to talk to Tina first. After all, they were a couple. The decision should be hers as well as his.

He could have used his key, but he knocked on the door instead. She came to it holding Makayla on her hip.

"How's Daddy's baby?" he asked, reaching for his child. Makayla squealed and kicked her legs with an enchanting smile on her pretty brown face. She almost lunged out of Tina's arms to get to him and he scooped her up, holding her close for a kiss on her soft little cheek. She smelled baby-sweet. He lifted her gently in the air. She squealed with delight, kicking her feet for more. God, how he missed her. How he missed his family.

The kitchen smelled of baking. Tina cooked something delicious. Her mother couldn't cook a pot of beans. He often wondered how Tina learned to cook so well.

"Something smells good," he said to her. She stood wringing her hands and looking scared. This nervousness had to stop. She had no need to fear her own husband. Mrs. Stout had always told him to go to church and take his problems to the Lord. When he'd gone to church services the other week, the minister had said that a woman's world wasn't right when her home wasn't right. A man's security was linked to his job. A woman's was linked to a stable home, especially when she didn't work outside the home. He realized Tina would think the preacher was sexist, but neither of them had ever had stable homes. He didn't want that to be a worry for Tina now. He wanted her to know that no matter what, her home was secure.

He'd been turning a lot of stuff around in his mind this last week. The things the counselor had been dishing out, the stuff they debated in his anger management group sessions, and the subjects the preacher had broached in service. The one thing he could say about that brother was that he knew his stuff. Sometimes preachers turned him off, but he found himself going to church more and more because this one made sense.

He tucked Makayla securely in one arm, threw the other

arm around Tina's shoulder and kissed her forehead. "What're you cooking for supper?"

"Just black-eyed peas, chicken gumbo and rice."

"Guess I chose the right time to come."

"I guess."

"How did you learn to cook all these foods? You aren't from New Orleans."

"My grandma was from there. They moved when she married my grandfather."

"You never talked about your grandma."

"I haven't seen her since I was twelve and Mama and I moved to LA. She died a couple of years later."

"Yeah, I remember now." With Makayla on his lap, Byron settled in a chair at the table. "You and your mama went back there to the funeral. It's a wonder you remembered the recipes after all these years."

Tina seemed to relax a little as he played with the baby. She stirred the pot, throwing surreptitious glances at him. "I always had to cook. Mama didn't cook. Didn't seem to know how to fix much. I don't know how that was possible since Grandma could fix just about anything."

"It's a good thing you learned the family recipes."

"She wrote them all down in this little binder she had. She sent it to me two months before she died. I still have it—still use it."

Byron recalled Tina looking in that dog-eared binder occasionally. "So that's the old book I see you looking in all the time."

"Yeah. It kind of makes me feel close to her. She was so good to me, but she and Mama didn't get along. She begged Mama to leave me with her, but Mama wouldn't. They'd had another of their famous big fights when Mama took off."

"When's the last time you heard from your mama?"

Tina glanced at him out of the corner of her eye. He'd never liked her mother. "Not for a couple of months. I sent her a letter last week."

"Don't be too disappointed. She'll get around to writing to you before too long."

Tina nodded. The beans were ready. She stirred them and put the top back on the pot. Then she stirred the gumbo.

"That gumbo sure smells good. I hope it's almost done."

"If I'd know you were coming by I would have cooked earlier," she said and started to put the biscuits in the oven. By the time they were done, the gumbo would be ready.

"No need. I'm not rushing you. We've got plenty of time. Gives me a chance to play with Makayla before dinner."

Byron was in an odd mood tonight. Tina thought he'd still be mad about the money. He'd taken her to the store to buy groceries after the session, but he was still angry with her. He didn't raise a hand to her, though, and she was thankful for that. Maybe the counseling was making a breakthrough. She wished she were that lucky. As hard as she tried, she still got the urge. Only she didn't have any money to spend. Byron paid the bills and took her to buy groceries. She felt guilty about that because she wasn't bearing her share of the family's responsibilities.

She wished she didn't feel so dependent on him. He said it was his job to take care of his family, but she didn't want to feel like he was caring for her like he did for Makayla. She wasn't a baby.

Tina watched him play with the baby. Makayla was soaking in all the attention. Tina liked for him to play with the baby. She never had a father in her life and she wanted better for Makayla. Still, Tina wondered why Byron had really come over tonight.

She peeked into the oven at the biscuits. They were nearly done. She took platters out of the cabinet, dished the gumbo over the rice, and put the peas into another platter. Then she put the kale in a bowl. By that time the biscuits were ready she'd finished setting the table and sat down with Makayla in her high chair, which was positioned between Byron and her.

She and Byron made small talk throughout dinner. He helped her clean up the dishes after they ate. That really shocked her. Byron didn't do anything in the kitchen.

"Look at my dirty baby," Tina said. Makayla had crumbled cookies all over the place: her hair, her face, the floor and her tray. "Come on, sweetie. I'm going to clean you up."

"Why don't I do that," Byron said. "About time I learned how."

Shocked, Tina looked at him. What was going on with him? Was he trying to learn how to care for Makayla without her so he could leave her and get custody of her baby? A sick feeling came in her stomach and she was beginning to feel nauseous.

"Why don't I help you," Tina managed to get out.

"I've seen you do it a thousand times. We'll be all right," he said with a smile in her direction. "Why don't you relax in front of the TV for a change?"

How was she supposed to relax when he was going to take her baby from her? With nerves eating at her insides, Tina wiped down the high chair, then got the broom and swept the floor.

Down the hallway she heard water sloshing, then giggling from Makayla, the traitor. Nobody but Tina was supposed to have fun with her baby during bath time. That was their special time together when Makayla and she played with the squeegee toys. Makayla loved to hit the water and watch the splash. Tina would make weird noises when the water hit her. Makayla would laugh and repeat the act.

Tina was tempted to go down the hall and watch them, but she stayed in the front of the house.

With the chores done, the place was tidied up and she was left with nothing to do but wait for the bombshell to hit.

"I need some help here, Tina. Where's the towel?"

Byron asked. "Water is pouring off this bundle like a faucet. You're daddy's faucet now, aren't you?"

Tina hopped off the sofa. As she ran down the hall, she imagined her baby dripping wet and cold. She dug in the closet and handed him one of the soft towels she used for the baby. Byron's T-shirt was dripping wet. He needed a towel as badly as Makayla.

"I'll get her clothes," Tina said as Byron wrapped the squirming baby in the towel. She selected a comfortable romper and diaper. Germany's summers were as warm as Pennsylvania or New York City. Byron gathered the clothing in one hand.

"You go back to rest."

"I don't need to rest," Tina told him.

"Go rest anyway. You must have stood for hours preparing dinner."

"Yeah, but I do that all the time."

"I know. We're giving you a break tonight, aren't we Makayla?"

Makayla looked innocent wrapped in her towel, her big pretty eyes following them.

"All right," Tina said and made her way to the living room. Was his helping out really that simple? Did he want to give her a break? Was she worrying for nothing? Her stomach wouldn't completely release its tight clench, but she began to feel a little better.

In a few minutes, he came through carrying a sleepy Makayla. She was pretty in her romper, although he'd put it on backwards. She'd never understand a man's thought processes. As many times as he'd seen her dress Makayla, why did he put the child's clothing on backwards? But Tina remained silent. Makayla looked pleased and comforted. At least the weird-fitting clothes didn't bother her.

They marched to the kitchen. "The bottle's already fixed on the table," Tina said.

When they came through the second time, Makayla had the bottle in hand and she was sucking greedily.

Ten minutes later, Byron was back. He'd changed into a dry T-shirt and he sprawled out on the couch beside her.

"I didn't know getting a baby ready for bed was so much work," he rumbled.

"You get used to it," Tina assured him.

"I guess, but I feel like I've put in a full day. I enjoyed it though."

Tina gathered her nerves around her. "Why the change, Byron? Do you plan to leave me and take Makayla with you? Because if you . . ."

He straightened in the seat. "Just hold on. It's nothing like that."

"Are you sure?"

"Of course I am. I'm not leaving you, or taking the baby away." Gently, he tugged her into his arms. "Look, I've been attending these group sessions. Those guys talk about all kinds of stuff. Things their wives complain about them never doing anything around the house, leaving all the child-rearing to the women and other stuff. How the women complain of being overworked because they have so much responsibility."

"I never complained . . ."

"I know you don't. That's just the way you are." He tightened his arm around Tina's stiff shoulders and pulled her closer. Then they both leaned back in the chair. "Just because you don't complain doesn't mean that you wouldn't like a break now and then. It's only fair. I don't work twenty-four, seven. Why should you have to? We're young, Tina. I've got a lot of learning to do."

"We both do. Thanks for the night off."

"You can expect more of them. I kind of enjoyed spending the time with Makayla. You shouldn't have to do all the work while I get to enjoy the good times."

Tina began to relax for the first time since Byron arrived. He felt her stiff shoulders loosen.

"I want to talk to you about your mama's gambling."

Tina's shoulders stiffened again.

"Just relax, okay? It's just that I protected you from some stuff she got into. Remember that night when you were fifteen, she came home all beaten up?"

Tina thought a moment. Mama had been beaten up more than once, but she did remember the night Byron brought her home. "I remember."

"She'd owed some money to Mickey."

"The loan shark?"

"Yeah. She went gambling trying to make the money she needed to pay him. She lost what little she already had. When she didn't have anything to give him, he beat her."

"Oh, my God. How do you know?"

"She told me, then she asked me not to tell you. She never wanted you to think badly of her."

"Grandma was always telling her how she needed to straighten up and raise me right."

"Tina I'm telling you because Barbara didn't always make money from gambling. She lost more than she won."

"She always told me she won money."

"She told you only the good things—never the bad. I think that's why she let me marry you at sixteen. She knew her boyfriend was no good and you had no business being there."

"I wonder if he's still there."

"Who knows? Doesn't she tell you what's going on when she writes?"

"Just surface things. Nothing deep, or what's really going on."

"Well, when we go back to the States, we'll visit her."

"I know you don't like her."

"She's still your mama. At least she didn't walk out on you the way my mama walked out on me. She never gave me another thought."

"Barbara just couldn't find a good man. She searched and searched. She was one of those women who couldn't live without a man."

"I know."

"I know your mama hurt you, Byron. But you can count on Makayla and me. We're your family and we'll never leave you."

"I don't know about that. Some hard head's gonna come along and sweet talk Makayla right out the door one day."

"As long as he's good to her," Tina murmured. "That's all we can ask for."

"You got that right. No knucklehead's going to take my baby."

"Poor Makayla when she gets to be a teenager. Poor you. She's going to run circles around you."

"Yeah. We've got some tough times when she turns into a teenager."

"I don't know. We'll enjoy those years I think."

"Yeah. Do you ever think you missed anything by marrying so young? You were only sixteen."

"No. I've never thought that. If I didn't love you, I'd probably feel that way. But I do love you and this is where I want to be."

"I'm glad you feel that way. Thinking of family, I brought a phone card." He reached in his pocket and pulled it out. "Why don't you give Barbara a call?"

"Byron, really?"

"Sure. She loved you—in her own way. Everybody doesn't know how to raise a family. Those guys had Barbara's head so screwed up half the time, she didn't know which end was up. I've got to thank her for keeping you safe for me."

Byron chucked when Tina threw her arms around him and kissed him.

"I've got to play the Good Samaritan more often," he said. "But I need to talk to you about something else."

"What is it?" she asked.

"The Colonel's been talking to me a lot lately. He'd been talking more about the opportunities in the Army. How if I got a college degree, I could become an officer."

"Is that what you want?"

"You know if we go back to LA what would we be going back to? I don't have a degree and good jobs are scarce without one."

"I could always work."

"The both of us would have to work just to make one decent salary if we go back there now. I'm thinking that if I stayed in the Army at least long enough to get a degree, then I'd have a better chance if we decide that I should leave the Army."

"That sounds reasonable," Tina said. "I just wish I had some skills."

"Well, I've been thinking about that, too. It might be a good idea if you went to school. Is that what you want?"

"Yes. Yes! Do you really mean that? You've been fighting me about working."

"If you went to school full time, Makayla would be ready for kindergarten by the time you get your degree."

"I thought you wanted more children."

"I do. Do you think it would be too difficult for you to have another baby in a few years? Maybe you could work part-time or something until the baby reaches kindergarten."

"I can't believe this."

"Well, I'm not always right. But I think I want to make a career out of the Army. As an officer, we could have a better life."

"We're beginning to have a better life already," Tina said. "I've missed you so much."

"You don't know how much I've missed you," he said and began to kiss her soft lips.

"We've been doing what we know," Byron said. "We both have a whole lot to learn."

"I'm with you there."

Byron knew their problems weren't over, that they still needed the counseling to get their lives on track. But at least they were making progress.

"Do you have to rush back?" Tina asked, stringing kisses on his neck.

"There's nothing keeping me tonight."

"Ummm. I need some help in the bedroom."

The muscles in Byron's stomach tightened when she blew in his ear and reached for his belt, smoothing her hand against his skin. "You want furniture moved?"

"I need *something* moved."

"Damn, baby. You're driving me crazy."

His hands nudged its way under her skimpy top. He'd been without his wife too long. A lot of it was his stubborn nature. He'd have to work on that, too. He had a lot of things he had to work on, but the best was having his sweet Tina in his arms again.

"I'm the man for the job." He didn't recognize his own husky voice as he hopped off the seat, dragging Tina with him.

Eleven

When someone coined the phrase "hot as hell," they must have been standing in Aden the end of July, a tiny area on the Saudi Arabian coast. The heat scorched Neal's lungs. The men with him didn't fare much better. They knew better than to complain. The best they could do was complete their business and leave as quickly as possible.

Weeks ago, three men from the American Embassy decided to take a little joy ride to the coast and bought a case of illegal liquor. On their way back to the Embassy, their car was searched by Saudi soldiers. After finding the illegal contraband, the three were arrested, and the car which belonged to the American government was confiscated.

In the heat of the day, Neal debarked from the plane in Saudi Arabia with a team of three NCOs and a Jordanian civilian translator. They walked across the tarmac to the waiting car, courtesy of General Rashid.

Evidently the American Ambassador had negotiated with General Hamid for weeks.

The Americans were still incarcerated.

When the embassy finally contacted the protocol department, they discovered that Neal had trained with General Rashid a few years ago while he was stationed in the States. The U.S. often trained allied officers who attended ordinance school. Neal had even entertained the General in his home during his stay in the States.

General Hamid agreed to negotiate with Neal. His friend, Rashid, confided to Neal that when the Ambassador had attended a formal function with his family, the Ambassador's son had mistakenly insulted General Hamid's daughter. To this day, the General hadn't forgiven the slight.

Hamid remembered the insult well when the Ambassador began negotiations with him, and nothing short of a miracle would let that man talk Hamid into anything.

When dealing with many countries and various customs, negotiations often went nowhere for months. One had to be careful not to insult anyone in a higher command whom you might one day have to do political battle with.

The three guys must have friends in high places if the American government went searching for anyone to get them out. It wasn't unusual for Americans to stagnate in foreign jails for years.

Neal never really spoke to General Hamid. General Rashid escorted him to the prison to pick up the three embassy employees. He was told to put them on the first plane leaving Saudi Arabia and the car would be delivered to the embassy. The men weren't even allowed to go back to the embassy to pack their bags. With the three tickets in his pocket, Neal, with the assistance of General Rashid, escorted them to the airport. There were long lines of people waiting, but Neal had arranged for an armed escort to the plane. They walked past the line, between a phalanx of soldiers and proceeded to the waiting plane. Once the men were safely aboard, Neal handed the men their passports.

Then he and General Rashid left the airport and shared dinner at his home. Rashid's wife, Jamila, served a meal fit for any dignitary. Lamb and herb soup with yogurt and swordfish kebobs were just the beginning. After an introduction to some of Rashid's cousins and uncles, Neal and his team were taken to the airport where they caught a plane heading back to Germany.

Neal relaxed in his window seat and peered at the clouds floating by. Not every mission warranted bloodshed and stealth. Often in the quiet times after a mission, he'd think of Arlene. Especially of the sweet kiss they'd shared at the airport. It had astonished him how quickly he'd fallen for her again after meeting her. More than twenty years had passed, for crissakes. Yet, he was every bit as intrigued as he'd been as that lovesick teenager.

Why was he torturing himself this way? Loving Arlene wasn't easy, not with a history behind them.

Neal called Arlene from the base an hour before he was ready to leave. When she picked him up, he looked at her ring finger and felt himself relax. She was wearing the ring, although she kept twisting it on her finger. He was gone long enough for her to get used to the weight on her finger. From his perspective, it looked at home there. He also knew women had different ideas about jewelry. He didn't have a problem if she wanted to exchange the ring for another one.

Other, more pressing matters filled his mind. After an exhausting week, he wanted to hold her in his arms, but he was ripe and desperately needed a shower.

"Could you drop me off at my place? After I shower I'll take you home."

"Sounds fine," she said.

For the first time, he noticed her reserve was firmly in place and he knew this wasn't going to be the relaxing evening he'd envisioned. She wasn't the easygoing, carefree Arlene she usually was. This was the last thing he needed. It looked as if they had issues to resolve, after all. He'd hoped Arlene had used the time he was away to resolve her problems with the past and be ready for a future with him. April would not be with them forever. He glanced at her. Evidently not.

The ride to his house was short. Arlene stayed in the living room while he showered. Then they went to her place. The atmosphere seemed warmer there. Perhaps that was why he liked going there so often, although he'd tried to make his place a comfortable home for April.

* * *

An hour later, Neal gathered Arlene into his arms. His heartbeat began to calm down. The sweat dried on his skin. Damn, he felt like a million bucks. Still, although their lovemaking was as spontaneous and as magnificent as ever, something was missing.

Every time he was away from her, he couldn't wait to get back to get her into his arms. He hoped she didn't think her only appeal was sex for him and a mother for April.

"Have you had dinner?" Arlene asked.

"Food wasn't what I was hungry for." He stroked her arm. "I felt like you were a million miles away."

"Wasn't good enough, was it?"

"Lovemaking is always great with you but I don't want you to feel like you have to 'perform' if you're not in the mood."

"Believe me, I wouldn't."

"Is something bothering you?"

"Not really."

"What exactly, then?"

She stroked his arm. "Nothing, really."

"Does my proposal bother you?"

She was silent so long, he thought she wasn't going to respond. "A little. It's just there are unresolved issues. I'm not sure the timing's right."

"Let's talk about these 'unresolved issues'," Neal said.

"I'm leaving for Texas tomorrow, Neal. I got a call from Ronald's aunt. Nancy is very ill. They don't know what's wrong with her. She's just given up on life. She never recovered from Ronald's death and I can't help feeling that her visit here made her problems worse. I never wanted to do that. I think . . . I think that I should wait until I return before I give you an answer."

Neal understood how loyal Arlene was to the people she loved. "You aren't responsible for her illness. I'm sorry that she's sick. And I understand that you want to visit her.

But what does that have to do with whether you want to marry me or not?"

"She was there for me when I needed her."

"I'm not arguing with you about that, Arlene. You should visit her. I think it's a good thing. But it's no reason to put off your answer. Unless you aren't sure that you want to marry me. Unless you don't love me."

"It's not that. I do love you . . . and April."

He could imagine Nancy putting on such a show that Arlene would call the engagement off. He realized that he couldn't let her leave without giving him an answer. It was true that Nancy loved and missed her son. His sister died with Ronald and he loved Bridget. Nancy's loss would be greater because she gave birth to Ronald. But Ronald was manipulative. Could he have gotten that trait from his mother?

"What is it then?"

Arlene remained silent.

"Could Nancy be using your loyalty as an excuse to separate you from me?"

Arlene patted his hand. "Oh, no. I'm sure she wouldn't do that. She's really sick."

Neal wasn't so sure. Arlene was too trusting. He'd have thought she'd have developed a harder shell after being in the Army so many years. *Did she still have an attachment to Ronald as well as to his mother?* Neal wondered. Was the true reason she couldn't deal with him and April because she still loved Ronald and there wasn't room in her heart for another man?

"The woman is your ex-mother-in-law. Is your loyalty to her getting in the way of your moving on? Do you still love Ronald?"

"No, I don't. I'm sure of that. It's taken me a long time to realize it, but my relationship with Nancy was closer than my relationship to Ronald. Ronald and I would go for long spells without talking, while Nancy called all the time. The last few years he really distanced himself, and now I know it's because he'd formed another relationship with Bridget. Contrary to what men believe, they can't give it all to both women. We were both lacking in affection and everything else. It's just . . . I don't even know how to explain it."

He tightened his arm around her. "I'm not insensitive, Arlene. I understand your connection with Nancy. I just don't think it's healthy to put our relationship aside to appease her. What happens if she gets better because she believes you've left me? Would you leave me to appease her?"

Pulling the covers back, Arlene lifted her head from Neal's shoulder and left the bed. "Of course I wouldn't. I just don't like the way you're pressuring me." She took the robe that had fallen on the floor and covered herself. She felt vulnerable arguing with him about Nancy while standing there in the nude.

Neal came off the bed on the opposite side. "I'm not trying to pressure you. I want you to see the hold she has over you." He didn't bother to cover himself.

"If you don't mind, I have to finish packing. After all, I am leaving tomorrow."

"What about our engagement?"

Skirting the bed to reach him, Arlene pulled the ring off her finger and handed it to him.

Neal didn't reach out to take it. Arlene took his hand and placed the ring in his palm.

"I'm not going to let you force me to make a decision I'm not ready to make. For me marriage is a serious undertaking. I believe in 'Until death do you part'."

"Believe it or not, so do I," Neal rejoined, jerking on his pants. He didn't know how they had gotten to this point. He'd had such hopes. Right now, he didn't know how to handle her. The more he argued, the more she dug her feet in. Most of all, he felt disappointed that she didn't love him the way he loved her. He dragged his arms through his shirt sleeve, slipped his feet into his shoes and made his way to the door.

Arlene's arms were crossed across her chest in an unbending gesture. Neal's plans weren't working out. Obviously he hadn't done an adequate job of planning this mission. At the door he turned back to her.

"Have a good trip, Arlene. And try to think about us for a change."

She nodded, but didn't respond otherwise. It seemed they were at a stalemate.

Anger rode Neal all the way home and then to bed after he downed a shot of quality brandy. He couldn't sleep, so he hopped up and turned on the tube. Just the thought of Arlene in that manipulative woman's grasp had him seeing red. Arlene was so tenderhearted she couldn't see the way that woman was playing her.

He hadn't been able to visit her while Nancy was here. What did Arlene intend to do, plan her entire life around Nancy's whims? True, the woman might be sick, but from what he'd seen the night he'd visited, it was more mental than anything else. The nerve of her coming into Arlene's house and plunking her son's picture in the living room without asking permission!

What bothered him most was the fact that he couldn't reach Arlene. She was so steeped in guilt for the woman, she couldn't see past her maneuvering. If he were a betting man, he'd wager that Nancy would get well quickly once Arlene arrived on her doorstep.

He reached for the box where he'd placed her ring. Their engagement was off and he didn't have a plan for getting their relationship back on target. He didn't have a clue of how to get Arlene to realize she had to live her own life as she saw fit, not as Nancy would have her.

He wondered too if he could have been more understanding. Perhaps if he had, she wouldn't have fought him so hard. But when she kept putting the engagement off, he saw his future with the woman he loved forever going down the drain. He knew she'd second-guess everything once Nancy started pouring on the guilt.

The box closed on a snap, the diamond hidden from view. He put it in the top drawer of his bedside table and flipped off the TV. There was nothing worth watching and he had an early morning tomorrow. His unit would go over everything that had gone right and wrong on their mission. It was a successful mission, but there was a lot they could have done differently.

Arlene had called April's grandparents asking for permission to take April to visit her father's mother. Ronald was such an ass not to have told Nancy about April. He always left her to deal with his mother. It happened when he was alive and now that he was dead, nothing had changed.

Nancy loved children. Ronald was her only child. She would have been overjoyed to know she had a grandchild. Perhaps Arlene should have found a way to tell her while she was in Germany, but the atmosphere had been so hostile she didn't quite know how to broach the subject. Besides, she was sick of Nancy telling her how perfect Ronald had been.

She still couldn't believe that Neal was so adamant about a decision, knowing the stress she was undergoing while dealing with Nancy. Why couldn't he have been more understanding? His old self was showing its face. And now she had another battle to deal with. After their parting, Nancy wasn't likely to be welcoming.

Arlene was really angry with Ronald for leaving all this for her to do. He hadn't carried one picture of his child. Thinking back on it, Arlene realized she didn't find one photo in his wallet or in the possessions she'd gone through after he died. She had to admit she'd tossed his stuff into garbage bags so quickly to send to the Salvation Army, she could have missed anything.

Arlene turned onto Riverside Street. She hadn't been

back there since she left in middle school. She parked in the Allens' driveway. As she exited the car, heat swamped her like a hot blanket.

Inhaling a hot breath, she glanced at the house next door where she had spent four years of her life. A brick ranch house. The shutters were freshly painted. Beautiful flower blossoms exploded in a colorful jumble in the yard. A baby's swing swayed in the tiny breeze on the front porch. *Must be owned by a young couple,* Arlene thought. It was good to know that the house was well-maintained and loved.

She approached the Allens' house cautiously and rang the doorbell.

Energetic footsteps approached the door. Mrs. Allen's footsteps hadn't been energetic, even twenty-some years ago. *Must be April,* Arlene thought.

The door swung open. A shriek, "Arlene!" and April fell into Arlene's arms. Arlene hugged the little girl who seemed to have grown since she last saw her.

"My goodness! Let me look at you. How many inches have you grown? Must have been at least five."

"I haven't grown at all. It's only been two months."

"It seems like forever," Arlene said, and for the first time noticed another little girl hovering in the doorway. "Who's your friend?" Arlene asked.

"Oh, that's Keneta. I told you about her. Keneta, this is my uncle's girlfriend. They're going to get married."

Arlene started. What on earth was going on in that child's mind?

"I'll go get your suitcase for you, Arlene," April said.

"No, I won't be staying."

"Oh. We've got plenty of room. You don't have to go to a hotel."

"I know, sweetheart, but actually I'm here to take you with me. I talked to your grandparents about this last night."

"They didn't tell me. I haven't even packed. Good thing Grandma did the laundry. Otherwise I wouldn't have a thing to wear."

"Are they here?"

"They're resting. Come on. I'll introduce you." April grabbed her hand and pulled her along. In many ways she reminded Arlene of Bridget.

"Don't wake them if they're asleep."

"Everybody wakes them. Don't worry. They're always nodding off. I guess that's what old folks do."

With the introductions, the General slowly made his way out of his recliner. "It's good to see you again. You still look the same," he said. "I'd planned to crank up the old grill to grill steaks for dinner, but I couldn't handle the heat."

"I agree with you there. It's much too hot out there," Arlene said. "I could hardly breathe."

The General chuckled. "You get used to it."

They had lunch before she and April started on the four-hour trek to Houston. Arlene had told Mrs. Taft that she had a surprise for her. She left April in the waiting room with Nancy's sister, Pearl, while she went in to break the news and hopefully dispel the tension.

"Hello, Nancy," Arlene said, handing her a vase of lilies.

"Arlene, I didn't know you were coming."

Arlene was sure Pearl had told her. "I had to come and see how you were. I told you I would visit you in August on my vacation."

Nancy sniffed. "Thought you'd be too busy with your new man."

"Not too busy," Arlene assured her. Arlene's new man was none of Nancy's business and she wasn't going to discuss him with her.

"I'm glad to see you could take out the time for an old friend." Nancy glanced at her left hand and relaxed. Neal's prediction came back to Arlene, but she closed the heated argument from her mind as she leaned down and hugged the frail woman. Nancy had lost weight in the last few weeks.

"I felt so bad about the way we parted in Germany," Arlene said.

"Think nothing of it. You're here now. Aren't you a sight for sore eyes!" the older woman said. Evidently she'd finally warmed up to Arlene.

"What do I hear about you wasting away in here? I thought I'd be able to take you out while I was here."

"I don't know. This old body can't go on much longer. I'm glad you came by here to see me before I go on to my great reward in the sky. I'll be joining Ronald soon. A mama shouldn't outlive her son."

"Oh, listen to you. None of that now. Because I have a surprise for you."

"I hope you didn't spend a lot of money, because it would be a waste." She looked at Arlene's tiny purse. "I don't see nothing. That thing's not big enough to hold anything."

"Brace yourself," Arlene warned her.

For the first time, a hint of light appeared in the older woman's eyes.

Arlene sat beside her on the bed. She'd debated with herself for most of the plane ride, trying to come up with the perfect approach to tell her about her granddaughter. She supposed the truth would have to do. "I recently found out that Ronald has a daughter."

"What? A . . . a daughter? How can that be?"

"I never told you this, but Ronald died with the child's mother in the boating accident. Her uncle is raising her. You met him in Germany." Arlene took a deep breath. "Neal is her uncle."

"The man who was dating you?"

Arlene nodded. "Yes, her name is April."

"She's the pretty thing in the picture with you?"

"Yes," Arlene said. "And I brought her here to visit you."

"You did? A granddaughter? She's here?"

Arlene nodded.

"Oh, my Lord. I look like a scarecrow." She patted her hair. "I'll scare her to death. Oh, you're an angel. Especially after everything that's happened. Just a pure angel."

"I'll bring her in, okay?"

"She's outside? In the hospital?"

"In the waiting room with Pearl. She's very eager to meet you."

She reached for the bed control. "Wait—wait!" she wailed. "Help me straighten up here. And let me comb my hair. I can't scare her away right when I meet her. How old is she?"

"She's ten and full of energy."

"Oh, my word!" Nancy said, reaching for the hospital tray that held her personal items and a mirror. She sprayed some breath mint, ran a comb through her hair, and applied lipstick. She seemed a totally different woman from the one Arlene glimpsed when she first arrived.

"Do I look okay?" she asked Arlene, a frown pulling at her mouth as she patted her hair in place, and straightened her bed jacket.

"You look beautiful." If the situation weren't so bizarre, Arlene would have chuckled out loud. There was no more mention of Nancy going on to her great reward in the sky.

Arlene was on pins and needles when she drove the rental in her father's yard. She hadn't been back to this house in years. Not since her mother died and her father moved away. She thought he'd sold the place.

She parked the car in the yard. She and Nancy had had words because Arlene and April were staying at her father's place instead of Nancy's home. But she might be staying with Nancy if her father's wife had any say in the matter. Arlene always wondered why the woman hated her so. Arlene didn't like the fact that he'd married so soon after her mother's death, but she never said anything to Monica.

"Is this where we're staying?"

"Probably so."

"I'll get my bag."

"Let's wait. We'll go in first, okay?"

Just then her father came out of the house. He'd aged since she last saw him. Truth be told, she was so torn up at the funeral she hadn't been seeing anything clearly.

April hopped out of the car like a whirlwind. Arlene opened the door and slowly climbed out.

"Well, who is this?" her father said.

"I'm April. My grandparents live next door to where you used to live."

He spoke to April, but he kept darting glances at Arlene. She was glad for April's chatter. It gave her a chance to gather her composure.

"How are your grandparents?" he asked.

"They're wonderful."

"Well, there's some good lemonade on the table in the house, and some cookies. Go on in and get yourself some."

He didn't have to tell April twice. She darted into the house and disappeared.

Arlene finally made her way to the wide front porch that still held the old swing her mother had loved.

"Hello, Arlene," her father said, coming toward her and opening his arms. Arlene stepped into them and wrapped her arms around him. He smelled like the cherry tobacco he used in his pipe. He felt so comfortable—like home.

"I've missed you."

"Lord, I've missed you, too."

"It was my fault," he said. "I should have never let it happen."

Arlene's eyes clouded. She had to work to hold the tears back. "We're both at fault," she said. "But I'm glad I'm here. That we're together again."

"Your mama would have wanted that. She would have had a lot to say about the way I've been acting." He kept an arm around Arlene's shoulder as he led her to the swing. He seemed to want to talk.

"How long are you staying?"

"A week. Then we're returning to Dallas."

"We'll get to spend some time together."

"How is Monica? Is my staying here okay with her?"

Her father pressed his lips together, then he said, "Monica and I are separated. We're getting a divorce."

Arlene started. "What!"

"It was bound to happen. I married her on the rebound. I had been with your mother close to forty years. I couldn't stand this empty house any longer. She went to the same church that I attended. When she started coming on to me, I just ate it up, I guess. They say there's nothing like an old fool. It took a while for me to realize she didn't love me and I didn't love her. I just needed some companionship."

"I'm sorry I wasn't here for you, Daddy."

"You had your own life. You couldn't put it aside for me. I just needed time to get over my grief." He leaned back and looked at her. "I should have been there for you when Ronald died. Yet, I just sent you back to Washington, D.C. by yourself to handle everything."

"I managed."

"How are you—managing that is?"

"I'm doing very well. I'm engaged."

"You're kidding?"

"It gets better. You know him. It's Neal Allen. He used to live next door to us in Dallas."

"That rascal. He was the bane of your youth. How did you end up with him?"

"He's changed . . . a lot. You're going to find out sooner or later anyway. I may as well tell you." And then she told him about April.

"I always knew Ronald was no good, that slick devil. Told you not to marry him."

"And I suppose you're going to give me the same warning about Neal."

Her father blew out a long sigh. "No, I'm not. I could

always tell the boy was acting crazy because he was in love with you."

Arlene's eyes widened. "I didn't know that."

"You were too young. I didn't like rascals sniffing after you. Thought he'd turn out okay once he grew into himself."

"Well, he did. He turned into a wonderful man, Dad. Much more so than I would have believed."

That evening, Arlene exchanged heated words with Neal over the phone. She should have known he'd pull a fight about her bringing April to Houston, so she simply hadn't told him until now. Angrily, he demanded to speak to April.

"April? April?" Arlene called out.

"Yes?"

"Your uncle wants to speak to you."

April bounded into the kitchen and took the phone from her. She spoke with Neal for a couple of minutes before April handed the phone to Arlene and rushed back to her television program.

Arlene glanced at the phone, sighed, then held it to her ear.

"Hello?" she said.

"You can't love April and me . . ."

"I never said that I didn't . . ."

". . . but you can use her."

Seconds of silence was interrupted by heavy breathing. "Is that what you really think of me?"

"I only have your actions to gauge by, lady."

Lady was used as a blasphemy.

"I want April back at my parents' home immediately."

"They gave me permission to keep April for a week and she's staying with me."

Arlene slammed the phone down as he cursed, then checked it, hoping she wouldn't have to purchase her father a new phone. Slamming it in his arrogant ear was worth the expense.

After all, Nancy was ill. April was just the medicine she needed to give her the will to live. She had a right to know her granddaughter existed. Selfish, irresponsible Ronald should have informed her years before. No child could ever get too much love.

When Arlene had surgery four years ago, it wasn't Ronald who stood by her side, waiting on her hand and foot until she could do for herself, or who spent the six weeks helping out during recovery. It was Nancy Taft's generosity which helped her weather the surgery and healing process with gentle words of encouragement. Arlene only wished her own nature was half as generous as her mother-in-law's.

The heck with Neal and his permission. Although Arlene was treading a thin line—after all, Neal was April's guardian—the truth was, Arlene didn't have a legal leg to stand on. And they both knew that.

The phone clicked in Neal's ear. His present assignment was completed. Over a year's worth of reconnaissance, secret missions in ungodly places, and harrowing ventures before it ended.

Neal parked his car. He was catching a military flight to Washington, taking care of business for three days there. Then he'd fly out to Dallas. By then Arlene should have April back at his parents' place where she belonged. He'd already told her he'd take her to visit Nancy. He didn't trust Nancy any more than he'd trusted Ronald. He hadn't been able to convince his sister what an ass Ronald was anymore than he could convince Arlene of Nancy's conniving ways.

One thing he knew. He and Arlene were going to settle this stalemate between them once and for all. Either she accepted him without Nancy's permission or they were through. It galled him every time he thought about it.

Two days later, Neal went through the area of the Pentagon where the plane had struck. The workers had refurbished the area before the first anniversary. Offices were restored and workers were in place. He saw a few people he'd known, but because of the trauma, several were unable to return to work.

After work, Wainwright picked Neal up for dinner at the Wiltshire Hotel in D.C. It had one of the most posh restaurants in the area.

The one thing that always bugged Neal about Nelson was that the son-of-a-gun was tall, and it was never more evident than when the two walked together. Nelson's posture said he owned the damn world.

But Neal was still glad to see his old buddy. Though they were two years apart in school, mostly because Neal was a year ahead, they had hit it off right away as players on Coach Foster's football team.

"It's been a long time and you're looking yourself again," Nelson said. "You had me worried there for a while. But that nurse . . . what was her name?"

"Arlene."

"Still remember her after all this time. Well, she seemed to be taking good care of you. I was a little less worried leaving you knowing she was holding down the fort."

"That's Arlene for you."

Nelson stopped for a traffic light. "So I hear you're getting serious about someone in Germany."

"Where did you hear that?"

"Through the grapevine. Heard she's an officer? Is she someone I know?"

Nelson would never use the vernacular 'sista' like most brothers would. He'd known where he was going from the very beginning and he never let language be an impediment. When Neal had asked him once why he didn't use the black lingo when he was kidding around, he said because it became a part of you and he wanted to make sure the wrong word or phrase wouldn't slip out at the wrong time. He was who he was. He was going places. And generals didn't use sista.

Nelson wasn't the only one aiming for general, although Neal did slip into the lingo from time to time.

The light changed and Nelson accelerated in D.C.'s infamous rush-hour traffic. "So tell me about this woman," he said as he changed lanes.

"Would you believe its Arlene?"

"You're kidding." He chuckled. "Falling for the nurse? This isn't one of those kinky kind of attachments is it?"

"Not by a long shot. We hadn't spoken or written until she relocated to Germany. April took to her immediately. And so did I."

"Do I detect a problem here?" Nelson asked.

Neal sighed. "You could say that."

"And?"

"Do you really want your meal ruined by this?"

"Nothing will ruin my meal at this restaurant."

Neal knew that. Nelson only chose high class. "I've heard stories about you, too," Neal said.

"Yeah, well, the mighty fall hard. But you first, and then we'll sink into mine."

As Nelson maneuvered the car in the traffic, Neal revealed the entire sordid story. Before he knew it, they'd reached the imposing hotel.

"So you're on your way to Texas to rein in your lady love."

"If it's possible. It's not the best situation."

"She's a loving, nurturing woman. I gleaned that much from my brief visit."

"It's not easy being reminded of her husband's betrayal for the rest of her life."

"She's a military woman. She'll get over it, she'll accept it and move on, hopefully with you and April."

"Man, you're cold. Women's emotions don't run that way."

"Career officers do. Trust me."

"I know female officers have had a hard battle forging their way in the military. And I know they're strong, but they're still women."

Nelson smiled. "Lucky for us."

Twelve

"I'm going to mail that stuff to Germany for you."

"Thank you for all the gifts," April told Arlene's father. He'd gone crazy spending on her. Just about anything April had liked, he bought, even when April asked him not to. Arlene's father and cousins had taken April to Space Center Houston, Six Flags Astro World, and Moody Gardens, and she'd still spent time with Nancy.

"I'm going to say good-bye to Aunt Mabel." Arlene's father's sister had come over to see them off. Arlene had already said her good-byes.

"Daughter, you look like you've been run over by a truck, skipping from my house to Nancy's. I told you that woman was selfish like her son, but you could only see the good in folks." Joe put Arlene's suitcase in the car trunk and straightened up.

"She's always been nice to me, Dad. The only time we had problems was when she was in Germany."

"That lady is pure poison. Mark my words. Don't trust her too much."

"You don't trust anybody."

He shut the trunk and leaned against it. "I trust Neal. I think he'll be a good husband. I can finally relax knowing you'll be married to a good man. Don't forget that invitation for the wedding."

"I won't. Who else would give me away?"

"Who else?" He was quiet a minute.

"Do you feel better being back in this house?"

He nodded. "I feel peaceful. Just the memories of the life your mother and I shared bring joy to me. And I have friends here. I've renewed old acquaintances. I feel good about that."

"Next time I visit, I just want to enjoy the week with you without all this running around," Arlene said.

"I told you that Nancy would run you ragged. Neal's going to think somebody did something to you."

Arlene laughed. "Daddy, please visit me in Germany."

"I will, baby. Probably at Christmas. That's a family time."

"That will make me ecstatic. Promise you'll come Christmas."

"You can count on it. I'll see to the tickets tomorrow. You're going to get tired of seeing me."

"Never." They hugged and April and Arlene got in the car and made their way to Nancy's house to say their good-byes.

"What would you like for breakfast, Nancy?" Arlene called from the doorway.

"Nothing right now. I'll eat something later. Where's April?"

"Downstairs eating a snack with your neighbor's granddaughter."

"Good. Come here and talk to me. She'll be occupied while we chat." Nancy patted the side of the bed and Arlene sat there. From the firming of Nancy's lips, Arlene knew the subject was going to be unpleasant.

"I can't tell you what joy April has brought me. I feel like a new person. Doesn't April look like Ronald? The spitting image."

Arlene didn't see the resemblance, but she nodded anyway. She resembled Bridget more, but if believing she looked like Ronald made Nancy feel better, what harm did it do?

"I wanted to discuss a few things with you." Nancy

tugged the covers firmly around her. "I don't think a man should raise a girl."

Nancy making trouble for Neal and April was the last thing Arlene had anticipated. She'd taken April without his permission and now Nancy wanted to start trouble.

"He's done a wonderful job raising her," Arlene assured Nancy.

Nancy lifted her chin in her bulldog manner. "I called my lawyer this morning. I'm going to get custody of her."

Rubbing a hand across her forehead, Arlene stood. "Nancy, please don't do that."

"He's always traipsing all over the globe from one place to another. My home is more stable. She had a wonderful time this week and she's already accepted me. I've got plenty of room. She'll love staying here."

"She doesn't even know you. She's known Neal her entire life."

"And who's fault was that?" Nancy snapped. "You were hiding her from me."

"Ronald kept her a dirty little secret from you and me, remember. She's Ronald's daughter. He should have told you about her. April was eight when he died. He had eight years to tell you."

"Well, that was your fault. He probably thought you would have left him had you known. And I bet he was right about that, wasn't he?"

"Yes, he was. But that shouldn't have stopped him. And it isn't the issue."

"Well, what is the point?"

"Once he had April, he barely spent any time with her. Neal's certainly doing a better job than Ronald ever did. And he was her father."

Nancy straightened her shoulders wearing her outrage like a shawl. "How dare you talk about my son that way? Ronald was a good husband and son."

"It's time someone spoke the truth around here. I don't

like to speak ill of the dead, but Ronald was selfish. He lied to you about a lot of things."

"My son wasn't a liar."

"Oh yes he was. He lied that I didn't want children when he was the one who didn't want them. We talked about it a lot, and he was adamant about the fact that we not have them. They might interfere with his career or mine, he would say, although millions of people all over the world have children and careers too. You certainly did. You weren't a stay-at-home mother." As soon as the words spilled out, Arlene regretted them. What good would it do to bring out the past?

Nancy trembled with outrage as she said, "I won't let you stay in my house and talk about my boy that way."

"I'll gladly take April and leave." Arlene took a few calming breaths to compose herself before she continued the conversation in a soothing tone.

"April loves Neal. With the loss of her mother and father, losing Neal will traumatize her. Her home is with him and she's fine with that. She has friends in Germany. She's doing well in school. And she gets an education of the world few children are blessed with. Besides, you're ill and you're nearly seventy. How are you going to take care of an active ten-year-old? April is very active."

Nancy's mouth pressed tightly together. "I'm feeling much better now. I'm getting up today to get back in the swing of things. There's no reason why I can't raise my granddaughter," she said stubbornly.

"There are many reasons why you shouldn't raise her. I'll fight you on this if you take it to court. All the sordid details will come out. Ronald never acknowledged her. In her will, Bridget gave sole custody to Neal. As long as he's taking proper care of her, the courts aren't likely to take her away from him. April is old enough for the judge to ask her where she'd like to live—and to give that special weight in any decision. She won't choose you. She'll choose Neal."

"Well, we'll see about that."

"How do you think April will feel, Nancy, if you try to take her away from her stability? Think of how she'll suffer, having to go through a court system feeling that her security could be taken away any moment. How will it affect her life?"

"But in the end . . ."

"It will shatter her. Think about someone other than yourself for a change."

"How dare you call me selfish!"

"You're acting selfish. Listen, I know you can be a giving and warmhearted woman."

"There are too many things that happen to girls with a man raising her."

"Bad things can happen anywhere. There are usually signs of abuse. And April isn't exhibiting them. April's too outgoing and carefree to have experienced those fears." Arlene took a deep breath. "The fact that Neal's raising her won't be an issue for long. Neal and I are getting married."

Nancy's mouth tightened before she said, "I knew you were carrying on with him when I came to Germany. You betrayed my son."

Arlene sighed, hating this argument, but knowing these things needed to be said. She wouldn't dignify Nancy's statement with a reply. She dated another man two years *after* Ronald died. He dated other women *while* he was married. Even Nancy knew the difference.

"Look. Let's try to keep this relationship so that we will feel safe in sending her to visit you during the summers, just like Neal sends her to spend time with his parents." She was already talking about them as if their marriage was a foregone conclusion. "It isn't the grandparents' place to raise the children, but to share their lives just the same. Don't make it so we don't feel comfortable in letting you share her life. Remember, grandparents have no actual visitation rights—only what the parents grant—and we *will* adopt April."

The stillness in the room crackled between them.

"I promised Neal I'd return to Dallas with April today.

We're already packed. I can stay long enough to fix you something to eat, but we have to leave soon."

Not knowing what more she could say, Arlene glanced at Nancy for another few seconds, then she turned and went downstairs, hoping the girls hadn't overheard their conversation. But when Arlene peeked into the kitchen, they were still eating the breakfast she'd prepared and joking about something. Arlene breathed a sigh of relief.

For the second time in less than a month Nancy and Arlene said their good-byes in a strained atmosphere. Nancy clung to April for long seconds before she let her go.

"You're coming back to see your grandma, aren't you?" she asked.

"Next summer when I visit my other grandparents, I'll visit you, too," April told her, easing herself out of her arms, but smiling all the while.

Arlene led the way to the car, turned and looked at Nancy. Again the older woman had nothing to say to her. Was Nancy always this selfish when she didn't get her way? Funny she never noticed this side of her before. She'd spent a lot of time with her in the past, but she never seemed this way before. Or maybe with the drama Arlene went through with Ronald, Nancy had been a relief.

"Take care of yourself, Nancy," she whispered.

"I'll be fine."

Arlene shook her head.

"Thank you Nancy, for everything you've done for me."

Nancy said nothing. And that hurt. Blood was thicker than water. Nancy wasn't going to relent. And then Arlene and April were gone, navigating the four-hour trip to Dallas. April fell asleep before they made it to I-45, leaving plenty of time for Arlene to view the parched countryside and think.

It was tough loving and trusting again after you'd been betrayed. Sometimes the pain could sap the very life from you, leaving bitterness and disappointment. Arlene was determined not to let Ronald and Nancy destroy her or the love she could share with another man. Life was much too short to waste a second chance at happiness.

Arlene peeked at April. The child had leaned the seat back and she was resting comfortably. Arlene should have insisted she ride in the back seat where it was safer.

Every time Arlene looked at April, she saw Ronald. She also thought that when she was home alone, he was carrying on another life with another woman. That was something Arlene would have to get over. The pain wasn't as piercing as it had been when she first discovered Ronald's betrayal. As a matter of fact, she felt no pain right now. She was looking toward the future.

She trusted Neal. And Neal wasn't Ronald. All men aren't the same.

April had wrapped herself around Arlene's heart. How could she not love her? Arlene chuckled. Lord knew, April told everyone she met that Arlene was her uncle's girlfriend and they were getting married.

Arlene smiled. Neal was a wonderful uncle and guardian. Shelly complained that he should hire a sitter more often to take Arlene out without April, but she understood that he'd wanted the two of them to grow to love each other.

Arlene sighed, and turned on the music to a soul station. Three hours later she took the Dallas turnoff. She loved Neal. She realized when she told Nancy that she was going to marry him, it was the simple truth. She wished she hadn't handed her engagement ring back. She wondered what he'd done with it.

I'll soon find out, she thought before she awakened April. Neal was coming to Dallas today.

When Neal arrived in Dallas, Arlene and April hadn't made it back.

"Arlene called," his mother said. "She and April will be back around three."

Neal glanced at his watch. He had a few hours yet.

"Son, April keeps saying you're going to marry her. I know she was a big help to us when you were in the hospital but I'm worried."

"About what?"

"She was Ronald's wife. Are you sure she wouldn't try to get back at April? Harm her in some way? I know she was a sweet kid, but now . . ."

"Arlene isn't like that, Mama. You don't have anything to worry about. That is *if* she marries me."

"Why wouldn't she want to marry you?"

"Because she knew me way back when."

"Son, April means a lot to your dad and me. She's all we have left of your sister. I'm concerned about her because you'll be away a lot. Arlene will have most of the responsibility for raising her. That leaves room for all kinds of mischief."

"One thing's going to change. I'm getting an administrative position."

"You are?"

"Yes. Mom, don't worry. Arlene is the same sweet person she was when she lived next door to us. I think Bridget would approve."

His mom folded her arms across her chest. "Bridget worshiped her."

"So does April. That must mean something. April's very picky."

His mom chuckled.

After spending some time with his parents, Neal drove to Buckley Academy. As he traveled up the stately drive, he noticed groundkeepers pruning flowers and mowing grass. Each lawnmower was covered with a canopy. The Texas sun was much too hot without it. At least some clouds had descended, lowering the heat a scanty few degrees.

He parked the car around the back near the practice

fields. Coach Foster was practicing and screaming at next year's starting line. Neal watched for ten whole minutes before the coach noticed him.

"You old-son-of-a-gun. Come down here," the coach said.

With a smile, Neal descended the bleachers.

"The General said you'd be home soon. It's good to see you."

The two men shook hands and the coach clapped Neal on the shoulder.

"I heard you were retiring in another year," Neal said.

"I'm thinking about giving it up." He looked out toward the woodlands. "I've been here long enough. Time for me to put up my whistle and travel the globe."

"The place won't be the same without you, coach."

"Always have to make room for the younger ones. Not good to have the oldies in for too long."

"When they're doing a great job, what's the problem?"

"It's good of you to say so."

Neal nodded toward the guys who were still practicing. "Looks like you've got a good starting line."

"We've got a team that's almost as good as yours was. I haven't had a team that good in a long time. Really looking forward to the season. Got a minute or two?"

"Sure," Neal said.

"Let me finish up here." He marched off and blew the whistle. "That's enough for today. Make sure you drink plenty of fluids. Let me introduce you to the best quarterback I ever had. Meet Colonel Neal Allen."

"How are you?" Neal said.

"You're in the Army?" Number 37 asked.

"Yes."

"An Airborne Ranger," Coach said.

"Wow. You must be really tough."

"I like to think so, but what I do requires a lot of thought and planning." He didn't want to give anyone the idea that being a Ranger consisted of all brawn without brains.

"The same skill needed on a football field. You remember that," Coach said. "Good planning is a skill you can use in any area. See you tomorrow, guys."

The team gathered up the equipment and started inside as the coach took him on a tour of the building. It had been renovated in some places, but the intimidating, stately halls were the same as he remembered from his teenage years.

The trophies they'd won during his tenure were still displayed in the cases outside the main office.

"Tell me," Neal said. "Is Mrs. Crutch still here?" Mrs. Crutch was a veritable terror back then. She wore skinny, out-of-style black glasses on her nose and tent-like dark dresses. Behind her back she was called a witch. To her face, the average person was too tongue-tied to say anything. Entering her office was worse than going to the principal's. She had a voice that put fear in anyone who crossed her threshold for punishment.

"She retired a couple of years ago."

"I'm sorry I missed it."

"It was right after your accident. You were still in the hospital. She said a special prayer for you at her retirement party."

"I have to thank her. It worked. She must have been responsible for the angel who cared for me in the hospital."

Coach regarded him with humor in his eyes. "Who would defy her?"

Neal chuckled. "You can say that again."

"Do I get to meet this angel?"

Neal studied the coach, wondering what would happen when he saw Arlene again. The ring was in his pocket. He wasn't giving up. "I think so."

Arlene sat in a wide swing in the Allen's yard. April and she had returned to Dallas and were awaiting Neal's arrival. Evening had fallen, but it wasn't dark yet. Rain had poured a couple of hours ago, lowering the temperature somewhat and the swing had dried enough for her to sit. She welcomed the peace and solitude of the back yard.

It wasn't long before April came out back and sat on a log nearby. She plunked her elbows on her knees and her forehead was creased in concentration.

"How was your stay at your grandmother's?" Arlene asked.

"It was nice. I made a new friend. And I like Aunt Pearl's cooking." She began to pick at the threads on her shorts.

"Is something bothering you?"

"Yeah."

Arlene dragged her feet on the ground to stop the swing. "What's wrong, honey?"

"I know I'm not supposed to listen to grown-up conversations, but I was on my way to the kitchen to get a soda when I heard Aunt Pearl talking to one of her friends. They were playing cards. You went to the drugstore to get some medicine for Grandma Nancy, remember?"

Arlene nodded. "What did you hear?"

"Aunt Pearl said she didn't see how you could love me after what my daddy did. What did he do? Do you hate me?"

The worried look on the child's face tore at Arlene's heart. "Come here."

With tears brimming in her eyes, April left her seat. This instant, she wasn't her usual easygoing self. Why couldn't Pearl keep her big mouth shut? Arlene wondered while she tried to think of what to say to April.

When April reached her, Arlene gathered the child in her arms and kissed her on the cheek, giving her a gigantic hug. "I don't hate you, sweetheart. I love you. And I love your Uncle Neal, too."

April continued to regard her with worried eyes. She sniffed, trying to keep the tears from falling. Then she sat on Arlene's lap. Arlene smoothed her hair back.

"But Aunt Pearl said you can't love me and her friends agreed. They said they wouldn't raise their husband's illegitimate child."

Boiling anger swamped through Arlene. Those gossiping biddies. Arlene couldn't wait to give Pearl a piece of her mind.

"What do they know? Of course I can love you. What if someone said you couldn't love me? Would that statement be true simply because they said it?"

April shook her head. "No, I love you," her courageous voice said.

Arlene's throat clogged with the declaration. Tears gathered in her eyes. April loved so easily. She hoped some careless fool didn't hurt her one day.

"I saw pictures of you and my dad all around Grandma Nancy's house. How come you were in all those pictures with my dad? There were none with me and my mama."

This was something Arlene didn't want to discuss with April. "I was married to your father."

"Then why am I his daughter? Is that what illegitimate, means?"

How did an adult explain the complications of relationships to a ten-year-old?

A charged silence filled the air as Arlene looked up through the thick branches of the tree. The setting sun cast a brilliant twilight tableau. Although April asked tough questions, Arlene felt at home enjoying the sunset with her. For all intents, April was hers. She and Neal would raise her together. They would spend many evenings together, enjoy many events together before April grew up and left, and Arlene vowed to treasure each occasion.

"Look at the sky, April. Isn't it beautiful?"

April looked toward the west. "Oh, yes." She hopped off Arlene to get a better view. "I'm going to miss the sunsets when we go back to Germany."

"Next summer you'll enjoy them again."

"I will, won't I?"

"And there are many things you'll enjoy in Germany. There's something to treasure everyplace you go. And there's something to treasure in everyone. Illegitimate means your mama and dad weren't married to each other. But they loved you. That's what's important."

April nodded. "That's what Uncle Neal says. I wonder if he'll let me call him Daddy. He's like a real dad. He does things with me and he loves me. Do you think he'll let me?"

Arlene was going to cry, damn it. The heck with it, she thought. She couldn't stop the tears, so why try? Arlene cleared her throat. "Why don't you ask him? I think he'll be thrilled."

He certainly deserved the title more than Ronald.

"What about you, Arlene? I wanted us to be a family so bad. But Aunt Pearl said it wasn't going to happen. She said my daddy cheated on you with my mama when he was married to you. Is that true?"

Pearl and her big mouth again. Arlene was stymied. How do you handle the tough adult questions with ten-year-olds? April shouldn't have had to concern herself with adultery. And Arlene felt she'd already stepped over the line by taking her to Nancy's. With the possibility of Nancy taking Neal to court, the move had backfired in her face. Then Pearl and her big mouth made matters worse.

"I think this is something we need to discuss with your uncle."

"What do you need to talk to me about?" Neal asked. He wore shorts and a sleeveless T-shirt and his long legs looked good as he ate up the ground striding toward them.

"Aunt Pearl said my daddy cheated on Arlene with my mama."

Neal threw a narrow glance at Arlene.

"Your mother didn't know about Arlene when she had you. You know she loved you, don't you?"

"I know. But Aunt Pearl . . ."

"Didn't know your mother," Arlene said.

There was only so much they could tell someone so young. Later, when she was older, they would reveal the truth. But not now. April was too young to understand the ramifications of deceit and betrayal.

"You really can love me and Uncle Neal?" she asked, needing the reassurance. "Even though Aunt Pearl and her friends said you couldn't?"

"I *do* love you and Neal," Arlene corrected.

April threw herself in Arlene's arms and wrapped her arms around her neck in a tight embrace before she released her. Then she smiled and threw herself into Neal's arms. "I missed you, Uncle Neal."

"You have no idea how much I missed you, Sprite."

"Not as much as I missed you."

"Wanna bet?"

"Un, Un, Un. I thought you said I couldn't bet."

"Just an expression of speech."

April cocked her head to the side. "Can I call you daddy?"

Neal cleared his throat a couple of times. Obviously, he was too moved to speak. "Nothing would make me happier," he said in a husky voice and tugged April into his arms.

Arlene wiped the tears from her eyes.

Hours later, Arlene sought Neal out. She had sat on that swing thinking for a long time.

"First of all I want you to know that I love you and April."

"If you're going to tell me the but, make it short."

"Just give me a chance to talk, okay?"

He pressed his lips together tightly as if what she would say was a foregone conclusion.

"I had to dig deep inside to ask myself if I had the courage to reach for something bigger, to leave the bitterness of the past behind and capture the future? Is my heart big enough? I know you love me. You love April, and she is your number one responsibility. You can't let her go and I wouldn't want you to. I'm the adult."

Arlene shook her head and said softly, "I have a wonderful man who loves me. Sure, he comes with a package, my husband's child from a failed marriage. But my marriage was over long before Ronald died. We were just going through the motions. So what the hell difference does it make?

"I'm pretty lucky, aren't I? For a long time I wished a dream like you would come along. So I should grab you by the shirttails instead of debating everything to death. The world isn't perfect. I have to deal with situations as they are, not the way I imagined the perfect world would be. I don't want to make a mistake and lose the best thing that has *ever* come into my life. And that certainly includes Ronald."

"I guess that's telling me."

"I guess I needed some hard facts. I had to deal with this just as I deal realistically with patient's relatives when they are seriously ill."

Arlene thought of the Andersons. Their time was limited. She and Neal had an entire life ahead of them.

Neal briefly closed his eyes, then looked heavenward. "I thought I'd never hear those words. Will you marry me, Arlene?" Neal asked, encircling her in his arms.

"Yes! Yes! Yes!" Arlene said, and Neal took the ring out of his pocket and slid it on her finger.

"Now that we're in Dallas, you can choose any ring you want," he said.

Arlene glanced at the diamond sparkling on her finger. "I love this one."

April came charging out the house. "What did she say, Daddy?"

"She said yes."

And then April was in their arms too. The three of them—a family.

Epilogue

That October, Arlene and Neal married. An ecstatic April told everyone that she had chosen Arlene for Neal. April was very much a part of their small wedding.

The baby, a sweet eight-pound bundle of male energy arrived in June. They didn't waste any time getting Arlene pregnant. Often women over thirty-five ran into difficulties, but Neal assured her that they were up to the task.

April was thrilled at having a baby brother.

When they sent pictures to Neal's family, his mother had announced that he looked just like Neal had at that age. Of course Arlene's father announced that the baby was the spitting image of him.

Arlene groaned, remembering the terror Neal had been.

Neal was stationed at the Pentagon in an administrative position and she was back at Walter Reed. Although he liked working in the field better, he felt that the position would put him closer to his goal of becoming a general.

When Terry was a year old, Arlene found herself pregnant again, a girl they named Casey after Arlene's mother. It was an old-fashioned name, but they both liked it.

Neal was recently promoted to brigadier general. One of his major goals had been accomplished and soon the family was waiting for their transfer orders. Arlene wouldn't be surprised if they ended up in Germany again.

The entire family flew to Texas in August. The second they exited the car in front of the Allen's house, the Dallas heat blasted them.

A new car was parked in the yard.

Terry was going through his terrible twos. Neal had lived through his terrible twos for years. Arlene hoped that wouldn't be the case for Terry.

Casey was fast asleep and April carried her all the time like she was one of her doll babies.

They would have to take April to visit Nancy and all the children to visit Joe. Nancy was still being difficult, although she never went through with the threat to gain custody of April. Perhaps her lawyer had talked her out of it.

Neal's mother stood in the door. "Come in, come in. Bring the children out of the heat."

Terry bolted to the door. Grandma picked him up and hugged him, then handed him to Grandpa.

"Look at you. You're a little man now," Neal's father said. "You'll be in the Army soon."

April got there next. They hugged her and took the sleeping baby from her and hemmed and hawed over her.

After grabbing the diaper bag, Neal threw his arm around Arlene's shoulder and they made their way to the house.

"I think she looks like you, Arlene," his mom said.

"Thank goodness," Neal said. "I thought she was going to be a linebacker the way she eats."

Arlene elbowed him.

"Come on in and rest yourselves."

They heard Terry talking to another child in the other room.

"You've got company," Neal said.

"Come on in and meet them," the General said.

They walked into the living room.

"Oh, my goodness," Arlene said. Laughing like loons, she and Tina embraced. Then Bryon hugged her. The two of them had grown closer over the course of the counseling. She'd grown to realize that Byron was serious about changing.

"How did you know we were coming?" Arlene wanted to know.

"The Allens told us."

"They spend a lot of time with us." The General handed the baby to his wife. "It's nice to have kids around again."

They weren't exactly children.

Arlene sat on the couch beside Tina. "So tell me, what's going on?"

"Byron and I are in college. I'll finish next year. Since Byron is working, he'll finish two years after."

"That's wonderful!" Arlene told her.

"We have more good news," Tina said.

"What is it?" Neal asked.

Tina blushed. "We're going to have a baby."

"I'm so happy for you." Arlene hugged her again.

Another round of backslapping and hugs occurred around the room.

Arlene settled back and watched everyone. She never realized she could be so happy. Her heart overflowed.

Neal sat beside her, pulling her into his arms. "What's wrong, honey?"

She sniffed, took the handkerchief he offered her. "It's silly."

"Yeah?" A frown pulled at his lips. She'd gotten everybody's attention. She was a soldier and she felt like a fool for crying.

"I'm just so happy."

Everyone laughed. Neal's mother looked fondly at her. "That's okay, honey. You're due for some happiness."

Neal pulled her close and kissed her.

April rolled her eyes. "They're always doing that. How gross. You're too old."

"You sure you're not pregnant?" the General asked.

The tears dried up. "No," Arlene said. "I'm sure of that. You've had your last grandchild."

"We're blessed," Mrs. Allen said. "Truly blessed."

Arlene couldn't agree with her more.

When she thought of all they'd gone through, including Tina and Byron, she realized how much courage it took for the young couple to change.

She squeezed her husband's hand. It had all started with him—with the courage he'd extended when he tried to save so many people, and inadvertently had placed himself in her path. She'd grown to understand that this was a natural part of him. He put himself on the line every day trying to help others. He'd taken a chance with Byron. His good deeds could have backfired in his face, but he pushed forward anyway. The fact that he was willing to face the repercussions put him above the ordinary man.

All of them had undergone transformations, and were better for it—even Arlene.

Suddenly, cheerful yells burst out.

"What's going on in there?" Neal asked.

Then they spotted Pippy playing with April. The dog was barking and hopping excitedly around the kids.

Arlene smiled. Long before Ronald died, she had given up on having children. And now she had three. Children were a special gift—all of them.

For a sneak peek at
the first book in the
At Your Service series

Top-Secret Rendezvous
by Linda Hudson-Smith

from BET Books/Arabesque

Just turn the page . . .

One

"Hi, beautiful, what are you drinking this afternoon?" Smiling at the rare beauty daintily perched on a high, cane-back barstool at the Hotel Meridian's poolside bar, Zurich Kingdom lowered his hulking frame down onto the stool next to hers. "I'd love to buy you a refill when you're ready for one."

Hailey Hamilton took her good old time in sizing up the newcomer. Her amber eyes shamelessly roved his physical attributes with a definite spark of interest. As her gaze came to rest on his sun-bronzed face, she decided that she loved the warmhearted smile still pasted on his sweet, juicy-looking lips. As his smile broadened, she got a good glimpse of toothpaste-white teeth, all of which appeared free of cosmetic dentistry. His twinkling sienna-brown eyes appeared sincere, but she didn't know if she should be flattered or annoyed at the reference to his opinion of her looks. It had slipped off his tongue a little too easily for her liking.

"Would you like me to supply my measurements for you?" he asked.

"That won't be necessary, since I've got twenty-twenty vision. But you can tell me your name if you like." She playfully purred from deep within her throat. "I bet it's a strong one."

"Zurich Kingdom." He grinned. "How's that for strength?"

"It's packed with power and it personifies your physical

make-up—tall, strong, Marine-like build—yet you seem so tender and sincere. There are a lot of manly powers packed into your six-foot-plus physique. I would be surprised if your ancestry didn't include royalty. I can imagine you running an entire *kingdom* single-handedly or commanding an entire army of men and women. Zurich brings to mind the majestic ambiance of the Swiss Alps. That thought definitely conjures powerful imagery. I can see you raising the flag of victory after your strength and fortitude has allowed you to scale your way to the very top. However, your approach needs a little polishing." Smiling smugly, Hailey was pleased to share her own brand of bull.

"Please don't stop, lady, now that you have me falling in love with myself. No, I'm only kidding, but enough about me for now. What's your name?"

"Beautiful! But I thought you already knew that since you said it when you first sat down." Her amber eyes flickered with devilment.

He nodded, smiling broadly. "Okay, okay, you got me there. Sorry for being a little overly flirtatious and forward, but I certainly wasn't lying. You *are* a very beautiful woman." He quickly arose from the stool and walked away. He only took a few steps before he turned around and came back to claim his seat. "Hi, I'm Zurich Kingdom. Mind if I join you for a drink?"

She tossed him a dazzling smile. "Hailey—with an 'i'—Hamilton won't mind if you do."

"Now that name certainly speaks to mystifying allure. I like it way more than *Beautiful*. How is it that your name is spelled like that? Isn't it different from the normal spelling?"

"I think some people spell it the same as I do."

"I don't know why, but I'm fascinated with the spelling. Is there a story behind it?"

"The story on the origin of my name is a long one."

"Am I already running out of time in your engaging company?"

"We've got a little time yet, Zurich."

"Good!"

Zurich summoned the cocktail waitress. Upon her arrival, he found out what Hailey was drinking and asked that the waitress keep both of their glasses refilled. It surprised him to learn that Hailey was only drinking lemonade, the same sort of refreshment that he enjoyed. A glass of wine or two was the only alcoholic beverage he ever indulged in, and even that was infrequently.

"Ready to tell me your name-related story, Hailey with an 'i'?"

"I guess I can tell you the story without going into all the boring details, which my parents, Martin and Marie, love to do. They lived in the small town of Palatka, several miles from the hospital in Gainesville, Florida. A horrible hailstorm had hit the morning my mother went into labor. As the conditions worsened, my father pulled off the road to help me into the world. I was born in the backseat of his car. From what I'm told, I was also conceived there. That's a longer story; another weather-related one. To finish up, my father decided to name me Hail. When it was typed into the official records, two additional letters were accidentally inserted. But I think someone felt sorry for me and decided to show some mercy, thus, Hailey."

"After hearing the story, I'm even more intrigued than before."

"Daddy wanted to change it when he first saw it, but Mom loved it. She wasn't too keen on Hail from the beginning, but there are times when she and Dad shorten it to just that."

"A beautiful story befitting a beautiful lady. In what twentieth-century year did that miracle of miracles occur?"

"In 1975. So, what's your story? What are you doing here on South Padre Island?"

"Vacationing. But I never thought I'd find literal paradise in my favorite Texas coastal city. Silky auburn hair, sparkling amber eyes, an indescribable figure packaged in a hot tangerine-orange bikini, soft-looking burnished-brown skin; all highlighted by a winning smile and a bubbling personality add up to my definition of a living, breathing paradise. Earlier I was in Dallas to honor my old football coach, Clyde Foster, during a special weekend event at my alma mater, Buckley Academy. I always make the Meridian Hotel Resort my playpen when I'm here in my great birthplace of Texas. That is, after a couple of days at my mom's modest ranch."

His loquacious description of her didn't earn him so much as a blush. Referring to her as *paradise* had awarded him the same number of points as his earlier reference to her as *beautiful*—zilch. "I've heard a lot about your alma mater. Buckley Academy is the most prestigious prep school in the country."

"So I've been told. I attended Buckley from 1981 to 1985. I also played football for the Buckley Eagles. It was sort of a reunion for all the students, especially the football team, though we were really there to honor our coach. Three of my friends, Neal Allen, Haughton Storm, and Nelson Wainwright were on the team with me. We're still the very best of friends. All of us live in different parts of the country, and travel extensively, but we always manage to stay in touch. It was good to see them again."

"I'm glad your reunion was a success. Mind if I refer to something you said earlier?" After his replying shrug she asked, "You used the word *playpen* in reference to the resort. Now that's an interesting choice of words. Do you consider yourself a playboy, a player, or just a mischievous baby boy needing a safety net in the form of a playpen for security?"

"None of the above. But that was kind of cute if it wasn't meant as an insult."

"No offense intended, Zurich."

"No umbrage taken. To answer your question, I'm no player. I came here to relax and thoroughly enjoy myself. I want to have lots of fun without any emotional entanglements. Whatever I get into in the next couple of weeks will definitely end when I leave here. I have the kind of job that keeps me moving. I'm single and I want to keep it that way, that is, until my professional obligation is stable. I wish I knew how not to come off so direct, but I don't."

"A man after my own heart. It seems like we have a lot in common; I'm here for the very same reasons you are. I like all the cards to be placed right out there on the table where I can see them. I'm leery of people who keep less-than-desirable traits hidden and then spring them on you after you've given them your complete trust and loyalty, usually based on their false representation of self. I like to refer to that kind of person as the poker-playing hustler. I don't play cardshark-like games with others' emotions and I don't allow anyone to play me, period. What profession are you in, Zurich Kingdom?"

Zurich's eyes narrowed. "That's highly sensitive information, classified as top secret."

Zurich was surprised and pleased by her mature attitude. But in no way did he think she was the kind of woman who was going to take pleasure in having a physical tryst with someone for a couple of weeks only to have it end abruptly. In his thirty-five years he'd run into every type of woman imaginable. After numerous failures to read the signals right, he had finally learned how to easily differentiate between the women who were in the game strictly for pleasure, the ones in it for money and prestige, and the ones who weren't interested in either. The kind of woman who loved without reservation, without expecting anything in return, was a rare find indeed. That's the same sort of love Zurich wanted to offer to his wife when his career finally allowed him the freedom to marry.

It was his opinion that Hailey belonged to the latter group. He'd be willing to bet the ranch on his hunch. He might be eight years her senior but she seemed to have as much savvy as he had in how the game of life was played.

"Wow, we really do have a lot in common. I have the same type of job as you do. Maybe we're both members of the FBI, the CIA, the Secret Service, or some other covert organization. This vacation is suddenly starting to look up. I never thought I'd meet a very interesting man here at the resort, let alone one as fine as you. What's so amazing to me is that you like to play by the very same rules as I do: no hang-ups, hassles, or heartbreak."

He didn't know whether she was kidding. Her expression gave nothing away, and there hadn't been a hint of sarcasm in her gentle tone. Zurich didn't know what to make of her, but he couldn't recall a single female whom he'd ever been more impressed with or totally intrigued by. Hailey Hamilton had already scored an exorbitant number of points with him, effortlessly. Zurich was truly hoping that they could spend more time together.

As he studied her alluring profile, he cursed his profession under his breath. That was something he couldn't ever remembering doing, since he was extremely proud of his chosen field. In fact, it was all he knew, the only job he'd ever had. There were countless married folk in his line of work, but he wasn't the type of man who could divide his loyalties. Plain and simple, Zurich was married to his job and he loved it as much as he could ever love a woman.

"Hailey, are you saying that you and I can hang out and have a good time without having any hang-ups or hassles when the vacation is over?"

"That all depends on your definition of hanging out."

"Dinner, a movie or two, dancing, and enjoying the sunsets. And, if I'm really lucky, perhaps we can even share in a few sunrises."

"Sounds like you're making a bid for exclusive dibs on my time. Are you?"

"As much of it as you're willing to share with me."

"That seems like a great way to spend the next two weeks. However, if at any point I decide that I'm not having such a grand time, I'm back on my own. Okay?"

"As long as it cuts both ways."

"Absolutely. I believe wholeheartedly in equal opportunity and treatment. As for the sunrises, don't count on Lady Luck. The odds aren't in your favor."

He grinned. "Don't be so sure about that. I don't have any aces up my sleeve, but I think you'll be genuinely pleased with me as a date. I'm a man who knows how to treat a lovely lady. By the way, sunrises can be enjoyed from a variety of locales. So if you're thinking I'll be trying to get you up to my room, you're probably right, but not for any X-rated activity. I only make love to a woman when there's mutual consent. Lovemaking can't possibly be the beautiful, intimate experience it was intended to be if both parties aren't willing participants."

"My instincts tell me that I'll be completely safe with you. If they somehow fail me, be forewarned. My feet are registered as lethal weapons." She winked at him as she got up.

He laughed heartily. "I thought we had more time. Where are you off to all of a sudden?"

"Up to my room to get a few winks of beauty rest before our first dinner date. I'll meet you in the main restaurant at seven. You can have the hotel operator put a call through to my room should you need to cancel. I'm registered under my intriguing name. No aliases or secret code names were used this time around. I save those babies for when I'm on a special undercover assignment." *If only he knew the truth, he'd probably run.* She laughed inwardly.

"Lady, I do like your style. You're utterly fascinating! The only call you'll be getting from me is the one I'll make if you fail to show up at the appointed time and place."

"In that case, see you at seven sharp, Zurich. It's been such a pleasure."

"You can say that again." He stood and then leaned down and kissed her cheek. "So long for now, Hailey Hamilton. This is one evening I'm more than looking forward to."

"The feeling is mutual, Zurich Kingdom."

Totally intrigued, Zurich stood stock still as he watched Hailey disappear into the hotel. The woman had certainly left him with a lot to think about. He didn't know if meeting her was luck or a curse, since their relationship wouldn't last beyond the next two weeks. A blessing was a more accurate description of his first-time meeting with one Hailey Hamilton. It had felt like the angels were smiling down on him the entire time they were together. Grinning, Zurich prayed that the angels would continue to smile on him for the duration of his vacation.

Hailey awakened to a loud knock on the door. Wondering who could possibly be on the other side, she looked at the clock. She'd been asleep a lot longer than she'd intended. The steaming-hot shower had relaxed her completely. As three short raps sounded on the door, she thought of Zurich. No, she mused, he wouldn't come to her room, not without calling first.

Quickly jumping out of the king-size bed, Hailey slipped on a loose-fitting cover-up, dashed across the room, and asked who was there. Upon learning that it was a hotel service employee, she became a little leery. She hadn't ordered anything from room service. Further inquiry let her know that the gentleman had a package to deliver.

Curious as to who'd sent her a package and why, Hailey flipped the locks and opened the door. Her eyes grew bright with surprise when the deliveryman handed her a large, white wicker basket wrapped beautifully in lavender cellophane and tied with a huge purple bow and curly streamers. Since the basket was done in her favorite color, she suspected her parents. It had to be from them. They were the only people who knew where she was. Smiling, she thanked the young man and closed the door.

The sensuous smell of Tresor perfume wafted across her nose. Body lotion, shower gel, and a host of other fine toiletry items in that same heady scent filled the basket. The lavender heart-shaped candle touched her deeply. Looking at the accompanying card, she saw that the gift wasn't from her parents. Zurich was the one who'd sent it to her. That made her smile.

As she thought about his statement, *I'm a man who knows how to treat a lovely lady*, she laughed. He certainly hadn't been lying about that. This was such a nice way to start a first date, as well as the gift being such a lovely gesture. After all the cards had been laid out on the table in front of them, she'd felt relieved. His plans fit perfectly into hers—no hassles, hang-ups, or heartbreaks. Once the vacation time was up, she and Zurich would go their separate ways. Her next mission was far away from home; she had to be fit for duty, both mentally and physically.

Hailey didn't know if Zurich was serious about his job, but she certainly was about hers. She was so close to her ultimate goal, so near to fulfilling her lifelong dream. If all went as she hoped, a promotion was imminent. Six more weeks of intense technical training would be no problem for her. She never once regretted all the blood, sweat, and tears that's she'd already poured into her job. Hailey was extremely proud of her career.

Hailey decided she wanted to look extra special for Zurich. What to wear out to dinner wasn't a problem for her. Everything she'd brought along with her was versatile. Hailey had chosen articles of clothing fashioned in fabrics of linen, silk, spandex, or pure cotton in soft but bright colors, solids, subtle prints, and basic blacks. She could go casual, classy, or dressy by simply adding or subtracting an accentuating piece or two. A couple pairs of denim jeans, linen blazers, lightweight shells, and sleeveless tops completed her fashionable wardrobe.

Since the basket was cellophane-wrapped in her favorite shade, she decided to wear her lavender silk dress with the bandeau top, which was classy and sexy with or without the matching jacket. If Zurich had chosen the color scheme for the basket, then he just might appreciate her wearing the same hue to show her appreciation of his choice.

Hailey plugged in her portable steamer after filling it with tap water. While waiting for the small appliance to heat up, she sat down on the side of the bed and put on fresh silk undergarments. She then seated herself in front of the mirrored dressing table and applied a fresh layer of foundation to her face. Earlier, before her nap, she had given herself an herbal facial.

After steaming her silk dress, she slipped into it. Her jewelry, a pair of diamond dewdrop earrings and matching pendant, came next. The two-carat diamond tennis bracelet she had a hard time fastening was a gift from her parents when she'd recently earned her college degree. Cute lavender-and-white medium-heeled sandals were her choice in footgear. While dabbing the Tresor on her pulse points, Hailey made a mental note to leave for the date early in order to purchase a thank-you card for Zurich from the hotel gift shop. She suddenly realized that she hadn't given the delivery guy a tip. Hailey recalled what he looked like, so she could easily remedy her mistake the next time she saw him around the hotel.

There were numerous first-rate hotels on South Padre Island, but the Meridian was Hailey's choice because it was smaller and more intimate than the larger resorts; it was also easier to recognize the staff and get to know them. There would be no touring or other outside activities on this trip since she planned to stay inside the self-contained entertainment complex and get caught up on her rest and relaxation, just another of her reasons for choosing the Meridian. Her next work assignment would take her far away from the comforts of home—and her next opportunity to take a vacation wouldn't come anytime soon.

A last minute glance into the mirror left Hailey satisfied with her stunning appearance. Smiling smugly at her image, she reopened the bottle of Tresor and dabbed a bit of the engaging scent onto the base of her throat, just in case Zurich desired to shower one of her more sensitive pulse points with his affection. He seemed like the romantic type, and she couldn't wait to find out if she was right. She needed a little romance in her life; romance without the worry of commitment was the best kind. But she definitely had her boundaries preset.

The thank-you card she chose for Zurich was lightly humorous, but with a sincere message of gratitude. She had purposely looked for a card in the same lavender color he'd chosen to have her gift wrapped in. Hailey felt really lucky when she'd found the cute one done in lavender and white. Two boxes of chocolate-covered raisins, one of her favorite treats, and a roll of wintergreen Lifesavers completed her gift-shop purchases. Hailey had less than two minutes to make it to the restaurant, but it was just a few steps away and around the corner from where she was. She wouldn't have to run, but she'd have to step lively.

Zurich's sensuous smile caused her pulse to quicken. All this man wore was a crisp white shirt, dark pants, and a designer blazer that defined his broad shoulders, yet he looked the part of a highly successful businessman. Zurich also seemed extremely relaxed.

His hand came up to her face and tenderly stroked her cheek. It was an innocent enough gesture, and certainly brief, but it made Hailey sizzle. The pleasurable experience lit up her eyes like sparklers.

"You look radiant, Hailey. And I just love a woman

who's punctual. Did you bring a good appetite along with you?"

She smiled sweetly. "A ravenous one." She handed him the special card. "This is for you, Zurich. I hope you like it as much as I loved the gift you had delivered. Thank you so much."

Zurich was taken by the way Hailey showed her appreciation for the gift. He raised an eyebrow. "My thanks to you, as well. Mind if I open it once we're seated?"

"Not at all, Zurich."

He took her hand. "Let's go inside and get our table. I reserved one by the window. We should have a great view of the Gulf. It won't matter once it gets dark, but we still have an hour or so of daylight left."

Zurich gave his name to the willowy, blond hostess, and she instantly directed them to the cozy, elegantly set window table. The restaurant was practically empty, but Zurich knew it would quickly fill up with patrons. With that in mind, he hadn't objected when Hailey had chosen a time for their date that was about thirty minutes earlier than the most popular dining rush hour. Le Meridian was one of his favorite places to dine when he visited the island.

Hailey gave Zurich a dazzling smile as she sat down. "Did you arrange for this little surprise?" She picked up the placard with her name on it. "Miss Hailey Hamilton," she read aloud, "AKA Beautiful."

He seated himself directly across from her. "I'll only 'fess up if you're impressed."

"Intrigued is more precise. It's also a very sweet gesture. As I looked around at the other tables, I didn't see any other placards, so that's why I asked. When did you request this little extra nicety?"

"Right after our first date was set up. Glad you're not offended by it."

"Quite the contrary. Why would you think I'd be insulted?"

He grinned. "Earlier, you weren't too thrilled at being referred to as beautiful, so I thought I'd like to show you that I wasn't using the term flippantly. As I said earlier, you *are* beautiful, Hailey, and I am being sincere."

"Thank you, Zurich." Hailey looked up at the waiter as he appeared at the table. "Looks like it's time to order dinner." Hailey positively loved Zurich's unique way of expressing himself, as well as his seemingly romantic nature. She could hardly wait to see what else he had up his expensively tailored coat sleeve. He seemed as sweet as he was handsome.

"What do you have a taste for in the way of appetizers, Hailey?"

She picked up the menu. "Maybe I should first take a quick peek at what they have to offer. It'll only take me a minute or two. This is my first time eating here."

"Take your time, Miss Hamilton. I have no desire to rush us through our evening." Zurich looked up at the waiter. "We'd like a couple of more minutes to look over the menu, please. In the meantime, I'd like to request a carafe of chilled sparkling cider."

The waiter nodded at Zurich and then quickly moved away from the table.

As his eyes zeroed in on his lovely companion, Zurich's breath caught. Bathed in the soft glow of the candlelight, Hailey's near-flawless complexion had an angelic appearance. Her full, ripe lips were the next of her delicate features that caught his eye. Zurich imagined that a lot of women would love to have a sensuous mouth like hers. He could almost taste its sweetness.

Hailey made eye contact with Zurich. The softness exposed in the depths of his eyes made her heart tingle. "I'd like a shrimp cocktail for my appetizer, Zurich. What about you?"

"I love their stuffed mushrooms and fried mozzarella

cheese. I even order the same from room service every time I stay here. This is my favorite restaurant in the hotel."

"How often do you come here?"

"Every time I visit my mom; at least twice a year. I love visiting this island. It's so quiet and peaceful here." He removed a couple of colorful brochures from the inside pocket of his jacket. "I picked these up from the hotel lobby so we can decide on a few fun things to do. I used to venture outside of the complex for my entertainment pleasures, but on my last few visits I've just stayed around here. I'm sure there have been a lot of changes on the island since then, and I'd love to re-explore this paradise with you." He handed the brochures to her.

She laid the pamphlets next to her place setting when the waiter reappeared with Zurich's beverage order. The young man removed the carafe of cider from the tray. After pouring the liquid into the crystal goblets, he set them in front of the couple.

"Are you ready to order, sir?" the waiter asked, dining check and pen in hand.

"Appetizers first." Zurich wasted no time filling in the waiter on their pre-dinner choices. Zurich then decided they should go ahead and order their entrees at the same time.

Once the waiter took the meal orders, he hurried from the table.

Hailey picked up one of the brochures and glanced it over. "I had actually made up my mind not to leave the hotel complex. I planned on catching up on my reading and relaxation. A lazy, daily stint of lying out by the pool was also on my slate of things to do. I want to get my tan on, too," she joked, laughing.

He smiled at her. "Your coloring is already perfect. But I'd love to rub the suntan oil on your body for you. Interested in my hands-on services?"

"Maybe, maybe not. However, I do have a hard time reaching my back. I just might let you handle that area for me, but only if you can control your hands and keep them from roving into the 'no trespassing' zones." Her smile was a tad smug, but the laughter within was joyful.

The waiter's arrival kept Zurich from responding verbally, but the responsive thoughts in his mind had him laughing inwardly. Controlling his hands was the easy part. It was his inability to exercise restraint over the lower part of his anatomy that had him worried. Just the thought of massaging oil into Hailey's sexy body already had him physically aroused.

Hailey hadn't expected the pink, plump shrimp to be so large. After squeezing lemon on her appetizer and then dipping one into the cocktail sauce, she bit into the seafood delicacy. Her taste buds instantly went wild. The red sauce had a tangy, gingery flavor to it, different from anything she'd ever tasted. She could barely refrain from moaning with pleasure, but her amber eyes had the tendency to give away even her simplest thoughts.

Zurich was mesmerized by the expression of utter satisfaction he saw in Hailey's eyes. "You look like you're having a divine culinary experience over there. Is it really that good?"

"Hmm, you'll have to see for yourself." Taking another shrimp from the glass rim, she dipped it in the sauce. With a slight arm stretch across the table, she held up the shellfish to Zurich's mouth. Hailey's heart rhythms accelerated when his tongue made slight contact with her fingers. Wondering if the look on his face matched the one he'd seen on hers, she laughed. "What do you think, Zurich?"

"I think I need to place another order. From the heavenly look I saw on your face, I get the feeling you may not want to share another one of those delectable shrimp with me."

Repeating the same steps as before, she offered Zurich another one of her appetizers. The totally unselfish gesture caused him to eye her with mild curiosity. This time, he allowed his tongue to linger a little longer on her fingers. His attempt to effect a tender moment between them didn't go unnoticed, nor was it unappreciated by Hailey; her smile told him at least that much. The sensuous connection had been made, and each of them was feeling it.

"Thank you. That was very generous. There are people who don't like to share."

"I guess you could say that, but since you're the one paying the bill, I can afford to be generous." Although she was joking with him, she kept a straight face.

"Oh, it's like that, huh? How is it that I'm paying when you're the one who asked me out to dinner? Or was I mistaken in my assumption, Hailey?"

"I know I don't have amnesia, but you're remembering something that I'm not."

"I distinctly recall someone saying they were going to their room to rest before our first dinner date. Does *I'll meet you in the main restaurant at seven* ring a bell?"

Hailey couldn't have lied even if she wanted to. There was no denying what he'd remembered. Her own words rung in her ears with such familiarity. "Well, in that case, it looks like this dinner is my treat. But I don't mind if you order another appetizer. What's a few dollars when you're having a wonderful time?"

His eyes fell softly on her face. "It's nice to know you're enjoying yourself, Hailey. And I wouldn't think of having you pay the check. I realized you were joking when you made the statement about me paying. The laughter in your eyes allowed me to ignore the poker-bluffing look on your face."

"Oh, so you think you can read me that easily, Mr. Kingdom?"

"No, but I'd like to learn how." His expression turned pensive. "I know you and I have already set the ground rules, but what happens if one of us falls in love?"

She raised an eyebrow. "One of us? Why can't it be a mutual thing?"

He shrugged. "It can be. It happens all the time. I didn't

come here looking to fall in love, but I didn't know I was going to find you here, either. We said a lot of things earlier about what we are and aren't looking for during our vacation time and what we're going to and not going to do. I'm now wondering if perhaps we made a mistake by doing that. What's your take on it?"

"We made those comments because we both knew that we weren't in a position to look back when it's time to go our separate ways. I think we're the type of people who have to keep it real. I know that every comment I made earlier about my life was an honest one. What about you, Zurich?"

Zurich gave Hailey's comments a minute of thought. "It has often been said that I'm too honest. But in my opinion, honesty is the only way to fly. The story will always be the same when you're telling the truth. Lying is the most confusing to the one doing it. You're right about keeping it real. It's easier that way. To answer your question, I was honest with you."

Zurich definitely knew how to keep it real. But what he didn't know was if it was going to be so easy to leave Hailey Hamilton behind without looking back. Their imminent separation might indeed be a hard one to pull off, especially without bringing about some sort of a change in him. For the better or the worse? He just didn't know. But this woman was truly different.

"*I wish I knew how not to be so direct, but I don't*. Do you remember who said that?"

He cracked up. "Sounds just like me. Well, here comes the waiter. We'll have to get deeper into this conversation after we eat. Okay with you?"

She nodded. "Fine, but what about ordering another appetizer?"

"It was good, but I really had enough. The main course is here now, so I'll be just fine. Thanks, Hailey."

Zurich quickly picked up the envelope he'd received from Hailey. He then opened it and read it. The simple words of thanks put a smile on his face. "This was really nice of you. I appreciate the way you show your appreciation. You're very thoughtful."

"I'm glad you like the card. It was the least I could do to show how much your gift meant to me." She stretched her arm across the table and put her wrist under his nose. "How do you like the perfume on me?"

His heart raced as he traced her wrist with feathery kisses. "It smells divine on you. It looks like I picked out the perfect scent for you. You two were definitely made for each other."

Seated across from one another in one of the popular lounges inside the hotel, where a live band played top-forty tunes, Hailey and Zurich had yet to experience an awkward moment as they enjoyed getting further acquainted. It was a little difficult to communicate above the loud music, but they somehow managed to converse despite the noise level.

His lips grazed her ear as he spoke into it. "Do you want another ginger ale, Hailey?"

"That would be nice. While we're waiting for the waitress, I'm going to slip into the ladies' room." She stood and reached for her purse.

Smiling, he got to his feet until she walked away.

After coming out of the stall, Hailey washed her hands. She then stood in front of the mirror as she freshened her lipstick and dusted her nose with corn silk. A slight smile appeared on her full lips as she thought of the good-looking man waiting back at the table for her. Zurich came off as a very genuine person, and she had to admit that she already liked him a lot.

Too bad they only had two weeks to click with each other. She could really get into Zurich, but when duty called she had to be ready and all set to go. Even if they did make a love connection, they'd still have to go their separate ways. Each of them had laid down the ground rules from the start: two weeks of fun in the sun and then it would be all over for them. The fact that Zurich thought they might've made a mistake in laying down the rules surprised her. Sighing with dismay, Hailey picked up her purse and left the ladies' lounge.

For a sneak peek at
the third book in the
At Your Service series

The Glory of Love
by Kim Louise

from BET Books/Arabesque

Just turn the page . . .

Prologue

Franklin "Amadeus" Jones had gone completely mad.

Carl Baer stared at his lifelong friend with a rancid mixture of pity and revulsion.

"What do you think, Carly?"

Carly! He hated being called that. But he'd put up with it for the twenty-five years that they'd been friends. Carl swallowed, forcing a bitter rise of bile back into his stomach. Yes, he admitted; he'd put up with a lot.

Carl's nerves flickered with unease. "I think it's time to get him back before the toxident wears off."

Amadeus cackled, then strutted around like a peacock, as though the world were in his hip pocket, as though they all weren't living on borrowed time.

There were three other men in the motel room. Amadeus's muscle looming quietly in the shadows. They had helped to incapacitate and carry the soldier. After they got him on the bed, they bound him so that Carl could *do his thing*. The injection had taken only seconds to administer, and the man on the bed started talking soon after.

Amadeus had hurled a barrage of questions at the soldier. Pulling out his innermost feelings had been like extracting a tooth, and Amadeus played the masochistic dentist role to the hilt—drilling, picking.

Needling.

He acquired more information from the soldier than he could ever use.

"Look at him, Carly. A warrior. A killing machine. They

don't come any better than Chief Storm, here. He'll be perfect. Don't you think?"

Amadeus hadn't lost *all* of his faculties. He was right about that, at least. A Nubian king. The hard detachment of a warrior. Bulky. The guy tied down on the bed looked as though he could rip a man in two with his bare hands and had probably done so on several occasions.

"He will be formidable," Carl admitted. It was one of those times that he couldn't stop staring at his friend. Pillsbury Dough Boy complexion and bright yellow hair. He was the only individual with albinism Carl had ever known personally.

Drool glistened at the corners of Amadeus's mouth. "What about the sample?"

Carl pulled a long, thin syringe from a case. The surgical steel glinted angrily in the harsh overhead lighting. As a scientist, what he was about to do had thrilled him once. And God help him, aspects of it still did. But the implications of his actions felt like hands choking him sometimes, made him physically ill.

Amadeus turned to him before he had time to mask his wave of repugnance. The pale man drew closer. Just a soft whisper above skeletal, his body gave new meaning to the word gaunt. He always dressed more like Beethoven than his namesake, and Carl could smell the scent of mental decay rising like rotting flesh from Amadeus's pores.

He closed in. That thin mouth and those tiny teeth grinning. Desperation sparked inside Carl and he slapped Amadeus quickly across the face. Knowing his own strength, he was sure the blow sounded much worse than it felt.

To no avail. The grin was still there. Still moving toward him. Carl closed his eyes for his punishment, but what he received was a cold kiss on the cheek from lips that weren't quite there.

He shuddered.

He'd always been afraid of Amadeus, especially the light

flickering just behind his eyes that made him look like a wolf on the verge of being rabid. He hadn't wanted this friendship. But they were *both* freaks. They'd been outcasts since birth, and had found each other.

Like the man lying on the bed, their fate was sealed.

One

He would need surgery soon. Commander Haughton Storm lay low in the dry night air, obscured by brambles and thin, lifeless bushes. Just when he thought he'd be going home, his squad had gotten an order for recon in Gabon.

The pain slicing across his lower back stemmed from an old football injury. In the past, if he'd ignored it, the pain would give up and go away. This time he'd had it for a week and it only gotten worse. Soon he might be forced use a hot pack or buy, God help him, Icy Hot.

He squinted his eyes against the darkness. The heat of the tropics began to cool. Storm's search-and-rescue unit had been stalking for hours. The inch-by-inch crawl toward their target would have sent ordinary military forces packing for home, but his team of highly trained Navy SEALs was the best at what they did. As SEAL operators, they consumed a regular diet of search and rescue, demolition, and recon. The kind of dirty work he lived for.

He listened, and slid forward another inch. His recent-issue fatigues could barely be seen beneath the leaves and twigs he'd covered himself with. Any potential sweat or shine from his face was obscured by the black hue of burnt paper he'd covered his face with.

Another inch and they would be in range.

A twinge of pain vied for his attention. It had been years since he'd had any serious lumbar problems. Years. The slow, dull pain felt more like a warning, a premonition of bad things to come. On mission after mission, he'd learned to trust what his body told him. By the pounding, his body was preparing him for something out of the ordinary. He summoned his training and turned his mind from the ache. Just like a switch, he shut the pain off.

En route to the target, four of Storm's seven men swept the perimeter in preparation for their seizure of the building. They would ensure there were no outside threats.

Almost there now. He and his men inched closer and reached for their assault rifles, which they'd kept tucked beneath them. War in slow motion, he thought as each man drew up his weapon and took aim.

First, they would take out all personnel they could see, both inside and outside the building. Then, in a swift rush forward, they would advance.

Storm gave a barely perceptible nod. A thunderstorm of shots bombarded the still night air. Guards fell like targets on a shooting track. And those who didn't, ran into the hills after seeing the bodies of their comrades shatter and explode in the barrage.

A short whistle, a sweeping hand, and they attacked. Scouts, patrolling the perimeter, covered them as Storm and three of his squad took snake formation and entered the building single file.

Storm moved in first. Their mission was to search and secure the building where an American scientist was being held, and bring him home.

Checking corridors. Checking rooms. Searching. Looking. Hands on weapon. Mind on mission. Haughton Storm had never lost a man during a mission and had had very few wounded. His gut told him to make this quick or that fact might change.

His operators called out from above and below. "First floor, secure!" "Third floor, secure!" Check hallways. Check doors. Gunfire! He was being shot at. Storm got off a round, ducked behind a door, and slapped in another magazine. One operator was on his left. He signaled him to go around to the other side of the hallway and into the holding room.

The picture they reviewed in the mission briefing had not done justice to the man they'd been sent to rescue. The photo was bad, but this guy looked worse. Storm could tell he was African-American. The problem was he looked as though a vampire had come along and drained all the blood from his body.

His second in command took out the last guard in the room.

Storm ran toward the pale man. "Are you injured?" he shouted.

The man shook his head and his eyes widened and seemed to dance a bit. Storm registered that the man had one gray eye and one ice-green eye.

"Then down on the ground! Now!" As per his training, he treated all rescued personnel as hostile.

The man did as he was told.

"Put your hands behind your back!" Storm had drawn his nine-millimeter handgun and had it pointed toward the man's head. He patted the man down on all sides. "Are you armed, or concealing anything that can be used as a weapon?"

"No," the man said, with what sounded like a smile in his voice. Storm was immediately distrustful. While one of his operators trained his weapon on the man's head, Storm put him in handcuffs and yanked him up.

"Let's move!"

Again, his men maneuvered into snake formation. This time, the hostage was in the middle. With eyes like eagles, each one of his men checked side to side, above, and below. Their movements were precise like the internal workings of the finest watch. The enemy could be anywhere.

When they reached the lower level, three men from his squad fanned out to sweep the area for their departure. They took the hostage with them.

There was a rhythm to mission deployment, something a few soldiers tuned into like a sixth sense. Sensing like a hawk or panther exactly when to move, when to strike, when to retaliate. Many of his men said he had it—the rhythm. He wasn't sure what he had, but he knew it was like a pulse in the earth pounding in his brain. A tremor only he could feel sometimes. It told him when to strike, when to stay put, when to lie low, and when to take risks. And that tremor was telling him now that his squad was in danger. Maybe something in the orders they'd received was off, but the game had changed within the space of the last few minutes. And suddenly the whole thing smelled like rotten flesh.

Storm made a series of gestures with his hand. Closed fist. Open. Open. Point north. Three fingers, two circles. Closed fist.

They had to get out of there now.

The message traveled quickly, and the men of Cobra One fanned out one by one and pulled back from the edge of the enemy camp.

Storm's skin prickled. Closed fist.

Footfalls in the jungle. They were in trouble.

Shots fired. They hit the deck, each man rolling and scampering behind the shelter of the dilapidated building. The familiar surge of adrenaline charged through Storm's body as he barked orders through his headset. As customary, his team was in perfect sync. They followed his commands as if they had read his mind before he could think his thoughts.

Back out.

T-formation.

If he could get the men back to the perimeter, they could return to the extraction point and be lifted out by helicopter.

"Alpha Six this is Cobra One!"

"Alpha Six, over."

"Need extraction! ETA ten minutes!"

"Copy that."

Over a dozen enemy soldiers scrambled from the shadows, guns drawn.

Storm tagged a guard, who buckled with the impact and went down.

Gunfire filled the jungle night. Explosions lit up the sky like an erratic strobe. As his men fought for their lives and their country, Storm defended himself and swore that whoever was responsible for setting this trap would pay.

"I'm hit!" a voice said, slicing through the thunder of gunfire.

"Sharky!" Storm shouted, recognizing the call of his second-in-command.

A sniper pinned Storm down in a thicket. If Storm didn't take him out soon, he'd never get out of there to help Sharky.

Storm jerked himself against a tree for cover. His pulse pounded loud and hard. Jungle shadows provided some cover for him. His eyes swept the perimeter quickly. Bullets whizzed by on both sides of him. The enemy was behind them, stationary, not following—yet. He had to get to Sharky before that was no longer the case.

The footfalls and suppressing fire from his unit told him they were regrouping, but not fast enough. Without his men to cover him, he would have to run unprotected to where Sharky lay, at the foot of a thick bush, unmoving.

He could see one leg. The rest of his comrade's body was motionless. A bolt of pain struck Storm in the middle of the chest, and he sprinted toward the man's location.

For years he'd trained against letting the sight of injuries, wounds, or blood affect him. Every SEAL had. But for a millisecond, he lost his training as a sliver of remorse slid though him. Then it was gone and he knew that the man, shot in the side but still reaching for his gun, needed and deserved every bit of military training Storm could summon to get them out of the ambush.

"Just get me on my feet and put my gun in my hand,"

Sharky said, stark determination making him seem much older than his thirty-two years.

"You got it, soldier," Storm replied.

More shouts and bootfalls as the SEAL Team Cobra One aborted their reconnaissance mission. Storm hefted Sharky up and handed him his weapon. With a nod from the injured man, they scrambled toward the extraction point, arm in arm, rifles drawn and blazing.

"SEALs, we are *lea-ving!*" Storm shouted when his unit had regrouped.

The enemy was following close now.

"Alpha Six this is Cobra One, over."

"Alpha Six, go ahead."

"Zone is hot. Repeat, zone is hot, over."

"Roger that, Cobra One. What's your ETA?"

Storm tightened his hold on Sharky.

"Two minutes, and we got injuries, over!"

"Two minutes, Chief. We'll prep for medical, over."

"Copy that. Cobra Out."

"Alpha Six, out."

Storm's breathing matched the pace of his run with Sharky through the heat and brush. He sensed the anxiety of his team. "Cobra team sound off."

"Sandman, on your six, Sir!"

"Hardgrove, side by side, Sir!"

"Mills, on the move, Commander!"

"Fox, still in the pocket, Chief!"

"Tuxedo, kickin' up dust, Sir!"

"Faison, bringing up the rear!"

Good. His team was intact. He'd be damned if he'd lose any men to an ambush, which is what this was.

As the sound of gunfire grew behind him, he realized that what they'd experienced was a brush-off. If the guards had wanted a confrontation, he and his men would have had to do a lot more fighting than simply retreat.

Why did this feel like a test?

When they arrived at the extraction point, the chopper flew in, cannons blazing. All seven of his men were by his side, and ready to lift out.

"Go! Go! Go! Go!" Seconds into the helo, and Storm issued the command to leave.

The helicopter lifted up and away sharply, guns still blazing.

"What happened back there?" one of the pilots shouted.

"Ambush. Somebody set us up." After making sure the hostage was secure, Storm knelt beside his teammate. He and Sharky went all the way back to Hell Week in BUDs training. They had endured every horrendous test thrown at them. He was the closest thing Storm had to a brother.

Sharky was getting worked on pretty good by Raymond "Doc" Collins, the best med tech Storm had ever worked with. If he couldn't save Sharky, no one could.

Doc looked up. "Punctured lung. I'm going to intubate and patch to keep his lung from collapsing. He's bleeding like a stuck pig, but I'll get it stopped and he should be okay."

Relief slowed Storm's raging pulse.

Sharky trembled on the floor of the helicopter. His eyes widened. It was the first time Storm had ever seen anything close to fear in his eyes in all the years they'd served together.

"Suck it up, soldier!" he barked. "That's an order!"

He touched Sharky on the shoulder. "You're gonna make it," he said.

"I gotta . . . gotta make it," Sharky replied, heaving with each word. "Or else there'll be no one who can keep . . . keep your . . . sorry carcass in line."

Storm grinned and nodded. Sharky was going to be fine.

Relieved, he sat back, reflecting. At the beginning of each

mission, Storm would take a mental snapshot of his platoon. Every time, he etched their faces into his memory.

Failure is not an option to a Navy SEAL. Each mission is carefully planned and rehearsed to be successful without casualties or injuries. If either occurs, the commander has made an unacceptable mistake.

His head rocked back and forth against the cold metal of the chopper. Vibration from the propellers strummed inside the vehicle like the heartbeat of a giant bird.

He shifted, as his back sent out another twinge for good measure. The hostage hadn't said a word. Not "thank-you." Not "much obliged." Not "kiss my behind." He only sat in silence with a strange grin that gave Storm a jolt of unease.

He knew his men. Their body language was clear. Seven men, twitching and snorting like nervous bulls. The inside of the helicopter was uncharacteristically quiet, and their gazes moved to and away from the man. Something about the man they'd rescued put them all on edge.

Storm closed his eyes and wondered why his green-faced warriors, a platoon of the most highly skilled soldiers in the U.S. military forces, were spooked by a tiny little man.

For a sneak peek at
the fourth book in the
At Your Service series

Flying High
by Gwynne Forster

from BET Books/Arabesque

Just turn the page . . .

One

Nelson Wainwright, Colonel, United States Marine Corps, glanced at the overcast sky, dropped his briefcase, and switched on the television. He hated getting wet when he was fully dressed; in fact, he disliked untidiness and considered a wrinkled uniform the its epitome. He turned on the television to check the weather, and read the news beneath the picture: Sixty-eight and cloudy. Rain likely. Cooler than usual for May.

"What will a man endure to achieve his aims?" the motivational speaker said, as Nelson reached to switch off the television. The question mocked him, enticed him to linger and listen. "How much will he sacrifice? What will he give? What will he gain? And what can he lose?"

Ordinarily, Nelson did not allow media gurus or other self-styled motivators to impress him, but those words hounded him as he drove from Alexandria, Virginia to his office in the Pentagon. He had spent eighteen of his forty-one years in the Marine Corps, and as recompense for working so hard and shaking hands with death more times than he wanted to remember, he intended to retire with four silver stars on his collar. He'd love to retire with five stars, but nothing less than four-star general would satisfy him.

Nelson knew two reasons why, even with good fortune, hard work, and shrewdness, he had a less-than-even chance of retiring as a full general. His superiors did not know that an injury to his neck pained him sufficiently to make him unfit for duty, nor did they know of his failure to report a corporal whom he'd discovered sleeping while on guard duty in Afghanistan. He didn't doubt that if his superiors knew of the unremitting pain he suffered, they would force his immediate retirement. And if he managed to camouflage that, he could be dismissed, or at least disciplined, for not having reported that marine's misconduct. Either meant he would finish military life as a colonel.

He parked in the space reserved for officers of his rank, and as light rain drops spattered his shoulders, he dashed inside the Pentagon. But as he entered his office, an eerie feeling settled over him, and very pores of his skin jumped to alert as if he were back in Afghanistan anticipating a missile. He rushed to answer the telephone even as dread washed through his system.

"'Morning. Wainwright speaking."

"Good morning, Sir," a female said. "This is Lieutenant McCafferty in the Commandant's Office, and I'm sorry I have to give you this sad news."

Nelson leaned forward, mentally bracing himself, and listened as she told him that his brother had perished in an automobile accident that morning.

"You're listed as next of kin, Sir, and as guardian for Commander Wainwright's child, Richard Wainwright. Let us know what we can do for you. This office will send you an order for two weeks leave beginning now."

He sat there for an hour dealing with his emotions and collecting his thoughts. Joel, his younger brother and only known relative other than little Ricky, had been looking forward to a great future in the Navy, and now . . . Well, what was done was done. The navy would take care of Joel; he had to look after four-year-old Ricky.

As the days passed, Ricky didn't respond favorably to the succession of foster mothers with whom he placed the boy, and he couldn't help noticing negative changes in the child's behavior, from bright and cheerful to sullen and quiet.

"That does it," he said to himself when, on one of his daily visits, Ricky clung to his leg in a fit of tears and wouldn't let go. He picked the child up, paid the foster mother for the remainder of the month and took Ricky home with him.

He wasn't a religious man, but he gave sincere thanks when Lena Alexander, whom his secretary recommended, walked into his house. She greeted him, looked down at Ricky, who loitered behind, dragging a beach towel, and her face lit up with a smile as she bent to the child and opened her arms. "My name is Lena, and I love little boys. What's your name?"

When Ricky smiled at her and told her his name was Ricky Wainwright, Nelson relaxed. Seconds later, Lena was giving Ricky a hug, and the child was telling her about his imaginary friends. The next morning, he moved her personal belongings to his home and settled her in a guest room.

It had been years since he had shared his living quarters, not since the four months during which he lived with Carole James, the woman who had brought another man—his closest friend—to the bed they shared, and had cared so little for him that she let him catch her cheating. The woman who would have been his wife within six weeks. In the more than five years that followed, he had enjoyed the quiet, though not the loneliness, and hearing Ricky's joyful noises and Lena's humming as she worked and her laughter with Ricky buoyed his spirits. Home was suddenly a pleasant place, especially at dinner when he had company for the delightful meals Lena prepared.

"What's the matter with your neck, Colonel?" Lena asked him at breakfast several days after joining his household. "Looks to me like you always favoring your neck. Better get it looked after. Trouble don't stand still in this world; either gets better or worse. You know what I'm saying?"

He did, indeed. Didn't the pain in his neck get worse daily? "I'm dealing with it, Lena. Don't let it bother you."

"Ain't bothering me none, Colonel. You the one that's uncomfortable. I declare, I wish somebody'd tell me why men so scared of a doctor. In the almost thirty years that I worked as an LPN—you know, licensed practical nurse—I never yet saw a male patient who didn't wait till he was half dead before he went to the doctor. You better do something before you get a problem with your spine."

He didn't have to answer her because she left the breakfast room humming what he suspected was her favorite hymn. "What's the name of that tune, Lena?" he asked when she came back with a carafe of hot coffee.

"If you don't know that song, you in trouble. Even the devil knows 'Amazing Grace.'"

He held his breath, watching while she filled his cup to the brim. When it didn't spill over, he bent over and sipped enough so that he could raise the cup to his lips without spilling the coffee.

"That surprises me, Lena. I would have thought the devil was more creative than to . . ."

He stopped. Her expression amounted to wonderment at his low level of intelligence. "Colonel Wainwright, I never said he sang the song; I said he knew it."

She walked with him to the door, holding Ricky who enjoyed telling him good-bye and getting a hug "You go see a doctor today, Colonel."

"See a doctor, Colonel," Ricky parroted.

"Ricky, you have to call him Uncle Nelson," she heard Lena say as he headed for his car.

"You sit down here and build your castle or read your book while I tend to a little business," Lena said to Ricky one morning about a month later as soon as Nelson left home. Ricky talked to the pictures in his books and pretended to read.

She dialed the hospital. "Let me speak to Dr. Powers, please."

"Dr. Powers speaking. How may I help you?"

"Audrey, honey, this is Aunt Lena. I love my boss. He's a wonderful man, so good with his little nephew. I wish—"

"Aunt Lena, I am not interested in your matchmaking. I'm glad the guy is a good father, and I'm glad you like your job. Now—"

"Hear me out, Audrey. Something is wrong with this man's neck. If he's not holding it and rubbing it, he's got something wrapped around it, and I can't get him to see a doctor. It's free for officers at Walter Reed Hospital, but I can't get him to go. Last night, he stopped eating his dinner, got up and put something around it. I hate to see him suffer like this. Come over one night, or maybe this Sunday when you're off, and have a look at it. He's such a good man."

"If it bothers him enough, Aunt Lena, he'll do something about it. I'd rather not meddle in that."

"Well . . . I, I just don't know what to do. It's not like he was hiding from the law." Lena hung up. She would find a way to get him to a doctor, he could bet on that.

"You didn't commit no crime, did you, Colonel?" she asked Nelson one night at dinner. When he stopped eating and stared at her, she pretending not to notice. "I mean, you not hiding out or something. You know what I mean, don't you."

He half-laughed and pointed his fork at her. "No, Lena, I don't know what you mean, and stop needling me." Then he laughed outright. "It just occurred to me that you're a blessing to my ego. I get so damned much deference in the Pentagon that I've started to believe I deserve it, but I can count on you to bring me down front and keep my feet to the fire, so to speak."

She turned her back in order to get the piece of celery that had lodged in the gap between her front teeth, then turned back to him. "I didn't mean to get familiar, but—"

He laughed. "I don't believe you said that."

"Well, truth is I care about what happens to you, and I've had plenty experience with people who've been injured, so I know that neck of yours is a serious problem."

"That's right. Sometime I forget you're a nurse. Lena, I'm not entirely foolish. A missile hit the helicopter that I was piloting in Afghanistan, and when the copter crashed, I got some injuries, and this whiplash was one of them. My other injuries healed; this one is taking a little longer. That's all."

"Hmmm. You had that before I came here, and I've been working for you over three months. That's more than long enough for a whiplash to heal. Why don't you go over to Walter Reed and let them take care of it?"

"I can't do that, Lena. If my superiors find out that my neck is still giving me trouble, they may force me to retire. It's bad enough that I'm still on desk duty."

"Oh, dear. I see what the problem is. And if you go to a private doctor, it'll be reported. Well, I'll pray for you. I sure will."

He seemed relieved to get that subject out of the way, but he didn't know that she wasn't used to accepting defeat. She put Ricky to bed, and while Nelson read the child's favorite story to him, she figured it was a good time to call her niece.

"Audrey, could you do me a favor?" she asked, after they greeted each other. "I want to go on my church's outing Saturday, day after tomorrow. They're going to Crystal Caverns down in Strasburg, Virginia, and I always wanted to go. Year before last when they went, I couldn't get away from work. Could you look after Ricky"—she didn't dare mention Nelson—"for me Saturday? Just give him lunch and read him some stories. He's no trouble, and sweet as he can be."

She listened to the silence until she thought she would scream. Finally Audrey said, "What time do you think you'll get back there?"

"Around seven."

"All right. I'll do it this once, but you know I don't cook."

"Sandwiches will do just fine." She hadn't planned to take the excursion, but she phoned the organizer and got her seat. Maybe she could kill two birds with one stone. Nelson Wainwright was a catch for any woman.

Audrey Powers did not relish the thought of baby-sitting, not even for half an hour. But her aunt had been so supportive during her struggles first to get through college and then to complete her medical training that she could hardly think of anything she wouldn't do for Lena. She stuffed half a dozen Chupa Chyps into her handbag, and stepped out of her house at barely sunup. Owing to the sparse traffic, the drive from her house in Bethesda to Alexandria, circling Washington on the Beltway, took her only twenty minutes early that Saturday morning. She parked in front of the beige-colored brick town house at 76 Acorn Drive. Lena greeted her at the door. "You're just in time. My taxi will be here in fifteen minutes." She turned around and pointed to the little boy. "This is Ricky. Ricky, Audrey is going to stay with you today."

Audrey looked down at the child who stared at her with an almost plaintive expression, and her heart seemed to constrict as she knelt beside him. "Hello, Ricky."

"Do you like little boys? Miss Lena loves little boys." His expression had changed to one of challenge.

"I love boys, especially little ones, and since I don't have a little boy, I can love you, can't I?"

He nodded, but kept looking at her. Suddenly, he smiled. "You can play with my bear and my blanket."

Realizing that that meant acceptance, she hugged and thanked him.

"Nelson will be down for breakfast around eight-thirty," Lena said as the horn blast signaled the arrival of her taxi.

"He'll be . . . Well if he's here, why am I . . ."

Lena closed the door.

Audrey took Ricky's hand and followed him to the refrigerator. When she opened it, he pointed to the milk. "Chocolate milk, please."

She poured the milk, thinking that she couldn't wait to give her aunt a piece of her mind. "I've been had," she said, when she didn't see any cooked food in the refrigerator. "I'm thirty years old, and I let my aunt hoodwink me."

He held the glass up to her. "Sugar, pease."

"I don't believe anybody puts sugar in your milk, but since nobody gave me any instructions, have a field day."

She put a teaspoon of sugar in the milk, stirred it and watched his eyes sparkle with delight. Now what? Her search for cereal or anything else a child would eat for breakfast proved futile.

"What do you eat for breakfast, Ricky?"

"Cake."

"Don't even think it. Try to bamboozle me, will you." She found some bread, toasted it, and, aware that he had a passion for things sweet, slathered the toast with butter and raspberry jam, poured a glass of orange juice, and sat Ricky down for breakfast.

"How old are you, Ricky?"

He held up four fingers. "Five."

She wondered if that was another of his games aimed at addling her, and it occurred to her that she might have to spend ten or twelve hours dealing with Ricky's little shenanigans. While he ate, she looked around for a coffee pot and the makings of a good cup of coffee. She didn't remember having gone so long after awakening without her caffeine fix. As soon as the smell of coffee permeated the kitchen, Ricky held out his glass.

"Can I please have some coffee, Audie?"

She would look back one day and know that that was the moment when he'd sneaked into her heart. "You little devil," she said as laughter spilled out of her. A lightheartedness, a joy, seemed to envelop her, and she lifted him from his chair and hugged him.

"No, you can't have any coffee, and you know it."

His lips grazed her cheek in a quick, almost tentative, kiss, delighting and surprising her. "Now be a good boy and finish your milk."

"Okay. I'm four."

She was about to thank him for telling the truth when the sound of heavy steps loping down the stairs reminded her that they were not alone, and her belly tightened in anticipation.

Nelson stepped out of the shower, and as he dried his body it occurred to him that a man of his height had to spend twice as much time on ablutions as a did a shorter man of slight build. But he wasn't complaining; he liked his six-feet-five-inch frame. He slipped on a red, short-sleeved T-shirt and a pair of fatigues and followed the aroma of coffee, his spirits high as he anticipated getting in a solid day's work at home.

He was used to Ricky now, and thought nothing unusual as he strode down the hallway enjoying the sound of boy's chatter. He stepped into the kitchen.

"'Morning, you two. What's for break . . . What the? Who are you, and where's Lena?"

"Unca Nelson, Audie gave me toast. I love toast, Unca Nelson."

She looked up at him, her lips parted in what was surely surprise, and immediately her lashes covered her remarkable dark and luminous eyes. *Who was she?* Jolts of electricity whistled through his veins, firing him the way gasoline dumped on a fire triggers powerful flames. He thought he would explode.

"I said . . . who are you?" Her grudging smile sent darts zinging all over his body. Poleaxing him. He groped for the chair beside Ricky where Lena usually sat, and slowly lowered himself into it.

"What are you doing here? If I may ask."

"I'm Audrey Powers," she said. "My aunt Lena had to go on a church outing today, and asked me to fill in for her. I can't believe she didn't get your approval."

Dignified. Well-spoken. Yes, and lovely. "Lena get my approval for something she wants to do? She tries, and if she doesn't succeed, she deals with matters in her own way. Thanks for helping out. I have a lot of things to do around here today, and it's good that you're here to look after Ricky. Any chance I could get some breakfast?"

Her reticence didn't escape him. "Cooking isn't something I'm good at, Colonel. I noticed some grits in the pantry. If you can handle grits, scrambled eggs, and toast . . ."

She let it hang, and he knew it was that or nothing, so he didn't mention the sausage or bacon that had to be somewhere in that refrigerator.

"I'd appreciate it, and if you wouldn't mind sharing your coffee . . ."

As if seeing him for the first time, or maybe questioning his temerity, her eyes narrowed in a squint, and suddenly he could feel the tension crackling between them. *Good Lord, I don't need this. I don't know a thing about this woman.*

She got up from the table, exposing her five-feet-eight inches of svelte feminine beauty, rounded hips and full bosom emphasized by a neat waist. He gulped air as she glided toward the kitchen counter, got a mug of coffee, and handed it to him.

"If you want a second cup, the carafe is over there beside the sink."

Her message didn't escape him; she wasn't there to pamper him, but to take care of Ricky. "Thanks. I'm not much good before I get my coffee."

"Somehow I find that hard to believe, Colonel. I'd bet you do what you have to do, no matter the circumstances."

His left eyebrow shot up. "I try to do that, but how did you know?" He gripped his neck with his left hand as the familiar pain shot through him, took a deep breath, and forced himself to relax. Thank God Lena wasn't there to start her lecture. "When it comes to duty, a man ought to set personal consideration aside. And call me Nelson. Do you mind if I call you Audrey?"

"No, I don't."

"I like Audie, Unca Nelson."

"After conning me into putting sugar into your chocolate milk, I guess you do." She looked at Nelson. "He told me he eats cake for breakfast."

He couldn't help laughing. "Ricky is skilled in getting what he wants. He doesn't get sugar in his milk, and I hope you didn't give him any cake."

"He got the sugar, but I knew better than to give him cake."

"I like cake, Audie. Miss Lena makes cake, and it's good, too."

Her gaze lingered on Ricky, and it was clear to him that Ricky had won her affection. "I'm sorry, Ricky, but I have never made a cake in my life. Excuse me, Nelson, while I get your breakfast."

"It's okay. Miss Lena will make the cake," Ricky called after him.

If only his neck would stop paining him. He had to finish installing the bookcases in his den and get some work done on the paneling in his basement.

He finished his breakfast, started upstairs to his den, and glanced around to see Ricky following him with his "blanket," the navy-blue beach towel trailing behind him.

"Rick, old boy, you're going to have to give up that blanket. Wainwright men do not romance blankets." He looked up to find Audrey's gaze on him. "They romance women." Now, why the devil had he said that? He whirled around and dashed up the stairs feeling as if he'd lost control of his life. And he always made it a point to control himself, and, to the extent possible, his life and everything that affected him personally.

"She's not going to detour me," he told himself, "I wouldn't care if she was the Venus de Milo incarnate. And I'm going to give Lena a good talking-to when she gets back here."

Damn! He jerked back his thumb, dropped the hammer and went to the bathroom to run cold water on the injury. If he had been paying attention, if the picture of Audrey Powers sitting at his kitchen table smiling at Ricky hadn't blotted all else out of his mind . . .

I don't care who she is or what she looks like, I'm not getting involved with her. He laughed. Getting involved was a two-sided thing, and she hadn't given any indication that she was interested. He corrected that. She'd reacted to him as man, that was sure, but the woman displayed her dignity the way the sun displays its rays. And she kept her feelings to herself. He'd give a lot to know who she was, but he was not going to let her know that. She was here for one day, and he'd make sure that was all.

Audrey cleaned the kitchen, something she seldom had to do at home, and tried to figure out what to do with Ricky. Finally she asked him, "Where's your room, Ricky?" Perhaps she could read to him or he could play with his toys.

The child beamed with glee, grabbed her hand, and

started with her to the stairs. "Up the stairs, Audie. I have a big room."

She started up with him, and stopped. She did not want to encounter Nelson Wainwright right then, for she hadn't reclaimed the contentment that she'd worked so hard and so long to achieve, the feeling that she belonged to herself, that her soul was her own. One look at Nelson Wainwright, big, strong, and all man with his dreamy eyes trained on her, and she had nearly sprung out of her chair. Like a clap of thunder, he jarred her from her head to her toes, an eviscerating blow to her belly. She thanked God she'd been sitting down.

"Can you play my flute?" Ricky asked her as they walked into his room, a child's dream world.

Her gaze fell on a full-size harp, and her heart kicked over. She had studied the harp and once played it well, but hadn't touched it since her father died. He'd loved to hear her play it and would sit and listen for as long as she played.

"I'm sorry, Ricky, but I've never played the flute."

"Unca Nelson can play it. Can you read me Winnie-the-Pooh?"

She told him she could and he handed her the book, surprising her when he climbed into her lap and rested his head on her breast while she read to him. The prospect of motherhood didn't occupy much of her thought, because her one experience with love and loving had erupted in her face. And since she wanted nothing more to do with men, certainly not to expose herself to an intimate relationship, she blocked thoughts of motherhood and children. But she couldn't deny that Ricky stirred in her heart a longing for the joy of a child at her breast.

When the story ended, Ricky scampered off her lap, ran across the room, and put a compact disk on his player. Then he ran back and looked up at her, waiting for her response as Ella Fitzgerald's "A Tiskit A Tasket" filled the room. To let him know that she appreciated his gesture, she sang it along with Ella, while he clapped his hands and jumped up and down laughing and trying to sing along with her.

"Hey, what's going on in here?"

She settled her gaze on the door and the man who stood there wearing a quizzical smile and a soft, surgical collar around his neck.

Ricky ran to his uncle and tugged at his hand. "Audie read my book for me and I'm playing my CD for her."

He picked the boy up and hugged him. "Don't wear her out, now."

"How old is Ricky?" Audrey asked Nelson.

"He'll be five next week." His left hand went to the back of his neck. "He's made tremendous progress since Lena's been with him. I had him in foster care for a couple of months after my brother died, and that experience set him back considerably. I brought him here to live with me, and I could see an improvement within a week."

She watched as he held his neck without seeming to give the act conscious thought. It was not a good sign. "I'm sure he feels the difference. Some foster parents give a child love and understanding as well as care; others don't, often through no fault of their own. Tell me, do you play the harp?" She pointed to the instrument there in Ricky's room.

He lowered his head. "Wish I could. That one belonged to my brother, Ricky's father. He played it very well indeed. I put it here in case Ricky takes an interest in it."

Speaking of his brother obviously saddened him, and she found that she wanted to know more, but she didn't dare invade his privacy with a personal question.

"I'm hungry, Audie. Can I have some ice cream?"

"May I have some ice cream?" Nelson said, correcting the child. "No, you may not. You get ice cream after you've eaten all of your lunch. You know that."

With innocence spread over his face, he turned to her. "Don't give me much lunch."

She stifled a laugh and got up, surprised by the realization that she had spent half a day enjoying the company of a four-year-old. Still holding Ricky in his arms, Nelson didn't move from the doorway as she attempted to leave the room. Her nerves skittered as she neared him, and when she couldn't help glancing up at him, he looked down directly into her eyes and caught his breath. She managed to pass him, but only the Lord knew how she did it.

Something in him, something hard, and strong, blood-sizzlingly masculine clutched at her. An aura like nothing she'd experienced before jumped out at her and claimed her. And all he'd done was stand there. How she got downstairs she would never know; he blurred her vision and sabotaged her thoughts. Worse, her heart threatened to bolt from her chest. She leaned against the kitchen counter. Nelson Wainwright was just another man, and she had no intention of making a fool of herself over him. A long sigh escaped her. One piece of her father's wisdom claimed that the road to hell was paved with good intentions.

"Girl, you need to get out more," she chided herself. "Stuck in that hospital all the time, you forget what it's like out here."

Within a few minutes, she called up to him. "Lunch is ready, Nelson, such as it is."

He took a long time getting downstairs, and she couldn't help wondering why. "Thank you for taking care of this, Audrey," he said. "I get the feeling this is aeons away from what you normally do."

He stared at the food before him. "I take it you don't cook much. These look good, though," he said of the tunafish salad and cheese sandwiches.

"I cook not at all."

Ricky clapped his hands and laughed. "No potatoes and no veggies, Unca Nelson. I like this. I want Audie to stay with us all the time."

Nelson seemed to wince as his hand went once more to

his neck, and this time there was no mistaking his pain. Without considering her action, she rose from the table, stepped behind him and examined his neck.

"What the . . . what are you doing?" he demanded as her fingers began the gentle massage that she knew would bring him relief. "I said . . . Look here. You're out of line."

"No, I'm not," she said without pausing in her ministrations. "I'm a physician, Nelson, and physical therapy and sports medicine are my specialties. This will make you feel better."

"You're a *what?*"

"A physician. I can't help noticing your problem, and it's clear to me that the pain is killing you."

"Look here! You can't—"

"Don't you feel better already? Fifteen minutes of this and you'll feel like a different man. Just relax and give yourself over to me."

"What kind of—"

"Shhh. Just relax."

"Does it hurt, Uncle Nelson?" Ricky's voice rose with anxiety, and she hastened to assure him that she was helping, not hurting his uncle.

"I'm making him feel better, Ricky. Go on and eat your sandwich. Isn't the pain easing already, Nelson?"

Her fingers, gentle yet firm, kneaded his flesh. "Relax," she'd said, but how could he, tense as he was with the pain that was his constant companion. He thought of pushing back his chair and leaving the table, but if he did that, he could hurt her. How could Lena betray him so blatantly?

"Relax. Drop your shoulders," she whispered.

No one dictated his life, as Lena was trying to do, and he wouldn't have it. He attempted to move, but with deft fingers Audrey soothed him, easing the pain, giving him the first relief he'd had in nearly a year, reducing the throbbing to a dull ache. Her hands massaged him with soft circular movements, squeezing and caressing. He lowered his head and luxuriated in the relief that her gentle strokes gave him. Then, with his eyes closed, he saw her fingers skimming his entire naked body, caressing and adoring him, preparing him for the assault of her luscious mouth.

Good Lord! His eyelids flew open, and he gasped in astonishment. He'd been within seconds of a full erection. Better put an end to that bit of heaven, and fast. He put both hands to the back of his neck and gripped her fingers.

"Thanks. You're right, I feel better, but can I finish my . . . my sandwich now?"

She went back to her chair, but she didn't sit down. "You're not angry, are you? I know it made you feel better. The problem is that the relief is very temporary. Massage is not a cure."

He didn't pretend, nor did he attempt to depreciate the comfort she gave him; Audrey Powers obviously knew her business, and anyway, he didn't want to seem ungrateful. "How could I be angry? I feel better right now than in a year."

She sat down, her eyes wide and a look of incredulity on her face. "You've been suffering like this for a year? How could you stand it?

He let the shrug of his shoulders communicate his feelings. "You do what you have to do. Simple as that."

She leaned toward him. "But it isn't necessary for you to suffer like this."

"It is, Audrey, believe me. The Marine Corps is a unit of men in perfect physical and mental condition. We are the crown of the Service, the cream of the crop. If you can't hack it, you get a letter of thanks, and that's it. I can handle it, and I will."

"But can't you go to Walter Reed, or the Navy Medical Center?"

"Sure, if I want an honorable discharge. I'm not ready for that."

"But . . . You mean your superiors don't know about this?"

He stared at her, and if he seemed threatening, he didn't care. "No, and nobody's going to tell them."

Not many men stood up to him, but he could see from her demeanor that if he pushed her, she would shove right back. Apparently having thought better of an alternative response, she nodded and said, "I see. What a pity."

Even at the tender age of four, Ricky appeared to sense Audrey's concern, for he attempted to pacify her.

"I'm eating all of my sandwich, Audrey."

She smiled and stroked Ricky's cheek, though he could see that her thoughts hadn't shifted from him to the child.

"Am I going to get my ice cream, Audie?"

It amazed him that Ricky had so quickly handed over his care to Audrey. Maybe he just liked women; if so, he wouldn't blame him, and he certainly understood Ricky's preference for this one. She'd gotten to him the minute his gaze landed on her. Not that it would make a difference in his life. He meant to give Lena a stiff lecture about her underhanded little trick, and he didn't expect to see Audrey Powers again.

"If your uncle Nelson says you may have ice cream, I'll get you a nice big scoop," he heard her say to Ricky.

With a smile obviously aimed to captivate Audrey, Ricky said, "Miss Lena always gives me two nice big scoops."

Laughter rumbled in his chest, and he felt good. He couldn't remember when he'd had such a light . . . He pushed the word back, but it returned, and he admitted to himself that he felt happy. He looked from Ricky to Audrey, and tremors shot through him at her unguarded expression. It was there only for a second, but he didn't mistake it; she wanted him. It had been there when they met. He'd had enough experience to know that an attraction as strong as what he felt for her couldn't be one-sided.

Questions about her zinged through his mind. Why

would a medical doctor baby-sit even for one day? Where was her office? She wasn't wearing a ring, not even a diamond, so why was a woman with her phenomenal looks single? He voiced none of them. He didn't like revealing himself, and therefore he didn't request it of others. He pushed back his chair.

"Thanks for my lunch, and especially for that great massage. I'd better get back to work while I'm still pain-free."

He looked at Ricky and marveled that the child didn't jump from the chair and trail after him as he usually did. Ricky ignored him.

"After you give me my ice cream, Audie, you can play with my robot."

He went upstairs, almost reluctant to leave them. As he worked, their chatter and laughter buoyed him, but after a time a quiet prevailed. He walked over to Ricky's room to find them both asleep, Ricky in her lap with his head on her breast and she with both arms around him. The longer he stared at them, the lonelier he felt. Disgusted with himself, he put on a leather Eisenhower jacket, went out in his back garden, and busied himself building a fire in the brick oven. He couldn't say exactly why he did that, but he was certain of his need to change the scene and recover the part of himself that, within a split second, Audrey Powers had stolen. He sat there in the cool and rising wind until after dark warming himself by the fire and reminding himself of Carole James, the one woman, the betrayer, he'd allowed himself to love. Thoughts of her brought the taste of bile to his mouth.

"I'll die a bachelor," he said aloud, shoveled some dirt on the coals, and went inside.

Audrey prowled around Ricky's room, fighting the vexation at her aunt that was rapidly escalating into anger. It was time Ricky had dinner, she didn't know what to give him, and his hot-shot uncle was no where to be found.

"I wanna eat, Audie. I'm hungry."

She looked at her watch for the nth time. Seven-fifteen. Of course he was hungry; so was she. She heard the back door close, grabbed Ricky's robot, and rushed to the top of the stairs.

"Who's there?"

"Sorry, Audrey. It didn't occur to me that I might frighten you. Lena isn't back?"

"No, she isn't, and Ricky's hungry. Maybe you'd better phone a restaurant and have something delivered."

He reached the top of the stairs where she stood holding Ricky's hand, or maybe Ricky was holding her hand. The cloud covering her face and the set of her mouth told him to tread carefully. He didn't enjoy tangling with women in the best of circumstances, and this one was angry. Moreover, she had a right to be.

His hands went up, palms out. "I'm sorry about this. I was out back, thinking Lena—"

"She isn't here, and—"

He wasn't accustomed to being interrupted, but he thought it best not to tell her that. "As I was about to say, if you'll tell me what you'd like to eat, I'll order dinner. I know a great seafood restaurant that will deliver full-course meals within forty minutes.

"I'll take shrimp and whatever goes with it."

A deep breath escaped him. Thank God for a woman who didn't feel she had to wash his face with his errors. "Great, so will Ricky. Be back shortly." He went into his room and ordered dinners for the four of them. He had a few things to tell Lena, but that didn't mean she should be deprived of a good meal.

His hunch told him the less Audrey was required to do, the better her mood would be, so he set the table in the breakfast room and opened a bottle of chilled chardonnay.

"Would you like a glass of wine while we wait for dinner?" he asked Audrey.

Suddenly, she laughed. "I may be furious with my aunt, Nelson, but I won't bite off your head."

"Thanks for the assurance. You had such a dark look on your face that I wasn't sure I should say a word to you. This wine is usually pretty good."

"Thanks, I'll have half a glass. I don't drink when I have to drive. Say, that's the doorbell, isn't it? Mind if I answer it?"

"Uh, no. If it's Lena, give her a chance to explain before you blow her away."

She rushed to the door with Ricky and his "blanket" trailing behind her. "Oh. It's the food," she called to Nelson, looked up and saw that he was beside her. He paid the deliveryman and took the food.

"Come on, you two, let's eat."

They sat down, and the doorbell rang again. She moved as if to get up, but he raised his hand. "I'll get it. You should have cooled off by now."

"I never cool off till I get my due," he heard her say as he headed for the door.

"How you doing, Colonel? I know Audrey's mad by now, but I got back quick as I could."

"Audrey? What about me? I'm the one you've got to reckon with."

"Now, now, Colonel. Give me a chance to get in. I bet your neck feels better."

The audacity of the woman! "Dinner's on the table. I'll speak with you later."

"Miss Lena, guess what? I had toast this morning, and I didn't have to eat any veggies for lunch. Audie gave me san . . . sandwiches"

"I bet she did. Audrey, honey, I'm so sorry."

"No problem," Nelson said. "Audrey's mad at you, but you two can deal with that later. Right now she's going to smile if it kills her. We're going to enjoy our food."

They listened to Lena's tales of the famous Crystal

Caverns and her picturesque account of the scenery during the drive. He knew she meant to placate both him and Audrey, but he didn't think she achieved either.

"I'd better be going," Audrey said when they finished eating. "Be sure and take care of your neck, Nelson. My judgment is that if you don't, you will have serious trouble down the road."

It struck him as silly; he didn't want her to leave. "Uh, thanks. I . . . It was good to met you, Audrey."

"I want Audie to stay," Ricky said. "I don't want her to leave, Unca Nelson. Please don't let her leave."

Audrey knelt beside the child and placed an arm around him. "I have to go, Ricky. I hate to leave you, but I have to go home."

"No!" Ricky ran and stood with his back against the door. "No, you can't go."

He looked down at his nephew and wondered whether Audrey had sprinkled some kind of dust over him and the boy. Then, he reached to lift Ricky into his arms, but the child evaded him.

"I don't want Audie to leave." Ricky sat down on the floor and began to cry. "Unca Nelson, don't let her leave. I don't want her to go."

Lena bent to take the child into her arms. "Ricky, darling," she said. "It's time for bed. Kiss Audrey good-bye and off we go to bed."

He twisted away from her. "No. I want Audie to stay."

"I'll come back to see you, Ricky. I promise."

He stared at her. "Don't tell him that, because you don't mean it."

She squinted at him, and a frown clouded her face. "I wouldn't dare lie to a child. If you don't want me to come see him, say so."

"I'm sorry." He picked up the recalcitrant boy, hugging and comforting him. "It's all right, Ricky. She said she will come to see you, and she will. Now give her a big kiss and let her go home. She's tired."

Ricky reached out to kiss Audrey. "I'm sorry you have to go, Audie. Bye."

Ricky didn't usually hold on to him so tightly, and it struck him with considerable force that the effect of so many losses in the child's young life lay close to the surface of Ricky's emotions. He wondered if Audrey reminded Ricky of his mother. She didn't bring to his own mind any other woman he'd ever met, and he doubted he would forget her soon, if ever. He remembered her promise to visit Ricky, turned, and, still holding the child, loped with him up the stairs to his room. Who was this woman who had changed both their lives? He put the boy to bed and stood looking down at him as he dozed off to sleep. *You will forget her long before I will.* For the first time in seven hours, pain streaked through his neck.

Dear Reader,

I hope you enjoyed Arlene and Neal's story. This novel marks a special milestone for me, as it is my tenth novel with Arabesque.

Readers like you help me to continue working with the craft I love. Thank you so much for your support and for so many kind and uplifting letters.

I love hearing from readers. Please visit my Web page, www.erols.com/cpoarch, or write me at:

P.O. Box 291
Springfield, VA 22150

With Warm Regards,
Candice Poarch

ACKNOWLEDGMENTS

My sincere thanks go to readers, booksellers and librarians for their continued support.

Fervent thanks to Sam Glasker, Therome Spivy, Ferdinand Thomas and my sister, Evangeline Jones, who often accompanies me to book signings. Special thanks to my husband, John, for his continued support in my writing. I couldn't do it without him. As always, profound thanks go to my critique partner, Sandy Rangel, and my editors, Chandra Sparks Taylor and Karen Thomas.

ABOUT THE AUTHOR

Reared in Stony Creek, Virginia, best-selling author Candice Poarch portrays a sense of community and mutual support in her novels. She firmly believes that everyday life in small town America has its own rich rewards.

Candice currently lives in Springfield, Virginia with her husband and three children. A former computer systems manager, she has made writing her full-time career. Candice is a graduate of Virginia State University and holds a Bachelor of Science degree in physics.